OWN

BLOOD BROTHERS
BOOK THREE

HEATHER LONG

OWN

The closer I get to the truth, the further away it feels. Every step I take is met with resistance—not just from the monsters still chasing me, but from the very men who have sworn to protect me. Especially Bones.

Cold. Controlled. Ruthless.

He watches me like I'm the problem he's been ordered to solve, not the woman desperate to find her missing sister. And maybe I am the problem—because I won't stop. Not for him. Not for anyone.

But when a lead surfaces, one so risky even I can't believe I'm willing to chase it, he doesn't shut me down.

He should. Especially when the others are so violently opposed.

Instead, he offers help. Conditions attached. Motives unclear.

For once, Bones and I are on the same page, even if that page is stained with blood. Maybe he wants me to fail. Maybe he wants me gone. Or maybe, somewhere under all that armor, he understands what it means to lose someone and not be able to let go.

Either way, I'm taking the chance. Because this might be my last shot at finding Amorette before she disappears forever.

And if I have to break every rule—and every heart—to get to her, then so be it.

This book is for the glorious mess-makers, the rule-breakers, and the beautiful disasters who refuse to tone it down. Keep causing problems. It's clearly your superpower.

SERIES SO FAR

Burn
Lure
Own
Oath

FOREWORD

Dear Reader,

Welcome to the third of five books in the Blood Brothers series. This is a series that should be read in order so if you have not read Burn and Lure, please pause and begin there. If you are curious about where the Blood Brothers story came from, I shared some background on that in the foreword of Burn.

Previously in Blood Brothers: Rescued from human traffickers, stunning model Grace expects freedom and wants desperately to find her twin sister—but what she gets is a team of dangerously skilled men who saved her... and don't plan to let her go.

Lure opens with Alphabet and Goblin locating Grace in the barn near the temp base they've set up in Mexico. Interrupting the attack, Alphabet has Goblin guard Grace while he takes out the attacker. Then he gets the hell out of Dodge with their gear, Goblin, and Grace as they race across the desert to meet up with the guys. When Grace wakes up, Alphabet pulls off to let her clean up and change out of her bloodied clothes. She also learns that Alphabet has a prosthetic on his right leg from below the knee when she sees a knife sticking out of his foot.

On the way to rendezvous with the team, they set up an ambush to help the team eliminate their pursuers. Grace helps by counting it down for him and she has to acknowledge that she helped kill people. Back in the U.S., they return to their home in Montana as Grace struggles with the situation and her feelings, also her nightmares.

Debriefing together, they put together a timeline and a list of names to investigate. The guys also work to try and distract Grace from her internal struggles. When the team deploys again, they leave Grace with Alphabet and Goblin at the house. She struggles to sleep, and stays up with him. Though she does wake in his bed one day along with Goblin and the rest helped.

Their hunt for answers leads them to France and Maurizio Gallo, the billionaire who kept trying to "buy" her time. With a target in their sights, the team along with Grace and Goblin set out for France. They split up to travel separately, Grace flying with Voodoo. Once in Paris, they reunite with the team, then split up again to head south while others get supplies.

Once at their safe house, they plan to take Gallo and question him. Bones considers the angles based on what answers they have received. Needing to get more information from Grace, he takes her for a walk. They've been trying to communicate more with both listening to the other. As they return to the safe house, they come upon an assault. Bones forces Grace to go with him, *away* from the danger. She doesn't want to leave the guys and just as they get into a car, she sees Goblin racing toward them.

That brings us to now.

Please be aware this book contains content with dark

themes and intense situations intended for mature audiences only, including but not limited to: sexual assault, dubious consent, physical violence, emotional and mental abuse, as well as kidnapping, stalking, manipulation, and other potentially triggering topics.

And now, as always, the housekeeping notes:

For those of you who have never read a why choose, or reverse harem before, first let me thank you for picking this up and giving it a shot. Second, the heroine will not make a choice in this book or any other between the guys in her life. It may take her a while to reach that conclusion, but it's the journey that drives it. There are many ways to frame this kind of relationship, currently why choose fits it very well.

I'll see you on the flip side.

xoxo

Heather

P.S. The dog doesn't die.

CHAPTER

ONE

GRACE

"Goblin," I said, his name fell from my lips like a gasp of horror twisted with a prayer. The sweet puppy was racing toward us from the front of the house. The engine growled as Bones dropped his hand to the stick shift. And it was a stick shift. Dammit.

"Backseat," Bones ordered and I didn't argue, I just freed my seatbelt and climbed over. "On the floor and get ready to open the door."

He waited only long enough for me to slide into the back before the car did a hard reverse. I bumped into the front seat even as I braced against the backseat. As much as I'd like to see where we were versus Goblin, I didn't say a word and just waited.

The car spun to the side.

"Now," Bones ordered.

I shoved the backdoor open. "Goblin!" The beautiful dog raced toward me. There was no mistaking the blood on his fur as he leapt onto the backseat. The heavy scent of copper made me want to gag, as did the wet sound of him slicking over the seat.

1

A bullet sparked off the door and I stretched over to yank the door closed before covering him even as Bones hit the accelerator and spun the car. Thankfully, the force of his curve helped the door to slam shut.

The explosive sound of his gun firing was violently loud, sharp, and almost deafening. It seemed to bounce off everything around us, like the car amplified the sound of the weapon. My ears rang with a high-pitched whining static that threatened to drill through my brain.

Goblin made a low sound or maybe it wasn't low, I couldn't *hear* him so much as feel the sound vibrate through him. If my ears hurt this bad, then he had to be in hell. The air seemed to compress, then pop almost painfully before everything muffled again. If there were other sounds —I couldn't hear them at all.

The car slammed forward again, the acceleration shoving me against the seats and I braced one hand and one foot to keep from squashing Goblin. The good boy had his claws digging in to keep himself in place too.

Bones said something—maybe. It was muffled and distant. I might as well have been underwater for how many syllables I could make out. The car shifted gears, then lanes, and slid around corners, all the while the acceleration varied.

Goblin slurped my face and I lifted my head in time for Bones to downshift abruptly before we took a hairpin turn that plastered me to the outer door.

"Fuck!" The word exploded out of me as I wrapped a hand through one of the seatbelts and clung to it as much as Goblin was to the seat.

In front of us, Bones shouted something. Or at least I caught the sight of his lips moving, but the words were still muffled as hell. When he raised his gun, I ducked.

Hopefully, he'd been saying duck.

Though maybe he'd yelled fuck too.

At least when he fired this time, my ears were already too clogged to flinch. Goblin wiggled against the seat as Bones downshifted again. We were climbing, the engine seemed to whine beneath my feet as if the car were giving its all.

Heart pounding, I stole a look toward the side mirror on the passenger side. I could lean to look at it without raising my head. Where were we?

Town. We were somewhere in the mixture of old and new worlds that made up the town. We were whipping through narrow backstreets, crossing bone jarring cobblestones, then skidding out onto wider open boulevards.

I was surprised we didn't have police chasing us. Maybe we did, I couldn't hear anything over the rush of static and wind. Then I saw a motorcycle in the side mirror.

No.

Two motorcycles. They were racing after us, all in black, leaning over their bikes as they accelerated and closed the distance. This shit looked so exciting in movies.

It was nowhere near as fun in real life. Fear pumped through my blood as I hung on. When Bones hit the brakes abruptly, I slammed against the back of the passenger seat. Teeth gritted, I managed to *not* hit my head, but I had a good view of the motorcycle racing up on us.

I shoved the door open abruptly and winced as the bike and rider slammed into the open door.

"Shit!" The one word came through like a clarion call from the front. The man hanging on the door had lost the gun in his hand but he lifted his head and turned to look at me.

The dark helmet and visor hid his facial expression and ice water flooded my veins. Goblin bared all of his teeth.

"Down!"

The order came from behind me and I ducked, covering my head and Goblin's with one of my arms as I curled over him.

Three rapid-fire shots exploded over my head. There was a shatter of glass and a horrific meaty *thunk* then a clatter before the car jerked forward again.

The door thudded to the frame, not quite catching because it swung open as Bones navigated around another corner. I tightened my grip on Goblin and the seatbelt. The last thing I wanted to do was fly out of the car.

Something like the wee-woo sound of the local police or maybe an ambulance penetrated the roar in my ears. My hearing returning? Good. The warning of that rising siren? Not so much.

We slid around another hairpin curve, and it was definitely a slide with the rear of the car leading us around. I managed to steal a look at Bones. His expression was a fierce mask of concentration. A feral energy radiated off him as he seemed to glare ahead of us.

When the car slowed, I tried to suck in a deep breath. My ribs ached. My head hurt. My teeth felt like I'd been clenching them too hard. With a sudden lurch forward, the vehicle bucked like a wild bull released from a chute.

Just as abruptly, Bones slammed on the brakes and we were reversing backwards at nearly the same speed we'd been going forwards only to come to another sudden and violent stop as the second of the two motorbikes crashed into the back of the car.

There was no mistaking the crunch of metal, the crush of glass and the vivid image of a helmeted head striking the rear window. A spidery pattern of cracked window radiated out from where the helmet struck.

Unlike with the man who struck the open door, the rider didn't lift his head. Horror slow-crawled through me as we pitched forward again and the body didn't move. Or at least the helmet didn't. One of his hands was partially *through* the glass and my stomach rolled.

I tried to breathe through my mouth as the body bounced and shifted with the movement of the car. Were they still alive in that helmet and just unconscious? Were they staring sightlessly forward?

Between the rusty smell of blood, the musky stink of my own flop sweat, the cloying stink of burnt rubber, and the acrid smell of charcoal and sulfur—probably from the gun Bones had been firing—mingled with something that might have been gasoline, it took everything I had to not vomit.

Another hard turn, then a hard jolt of brakes as the car sputtered before the engine came back to life and he gunned it down what appeared to be an alleyway. I watched it all fly past kind of distantly as I flexed my fingers around the straps of Goblin's harness. Metal sheared as he took a corner too tightly and there was a crunch and a thunk.

The body on the back window was abruptly gone. All that remained was a glove still partially through the cracked glass. My stomach rolled and I squeezed my eyes shut.

Please don't have a hand in there. Please don't have a hand in there. I rocked from side to side with the vehicle as we navigated these ancient routes. They had to be ancient really, narrow and bouncy with the cobblestones.

The sunlight cut abruptly and we were under cover

inside a parking garage. It took me a moment to let my eyes adjust. He wound us down. Oh, the parking garage must be inside a hill. That made sense.

The guttural cough and choke of the engine replaced the hiss of static in my ears. Oh my hearing was definitely coming back. Goblin panted. I stopped pressing down against him so tightly and he slurped my face.

Finally, we came to a stop and Bones twisted in the front seat to whip off his sunglasses and look at me. "Show me."

The order pulled me around and I raised my eyebrows. My sunglasses had disappeared somewhere in the wild bumper car ride we'd taken. When he touched two fingers to my jaw, it was the lightest of brushes and I tipped my head obediently. When he ran a thumb along my throat to my collarbone, it stung and I grimaced.

"Just a cut."

I'd gotten cut?

"It's not bad," he said and his voice was so deep, and had a bit of a growl like the engine had. "But I want to clean that out. We need to leave this car here."

I glanced at the cracked back window, then the door that still hadn't closed all the way, before looking at the front where it was also sporting a couple of bullet holes. "Are you okay?"

"Good enough," he said. "Let's go, I want to stash you and Goblin away from the car while I get us alternate transport."

Oh, that totally made sense. I carefully unwound my arm from the seatbelt. The strap had dug grooves into my skin and I winced. Definitely some burn from the nylon. Bones slid out then opened the rear passenger door behind the driver's seat.

He snapped his fingers and Goblin pivoted and jumped out. He wasn't limping.

That was a good sign, right?

I followed him, but I was a lot shakier and if Bones hadn't gripped my arm, I was pretty sure I would have dropped on the spot. My legs were spaghetti.

"You're a very good driver," I told him, then patted his chest as I firmed my legs beneath me.

He quirked a brow at me. "Is that so?"

"Yes," I confirmed. Taking a couple of shakier steps forward before I glanced back at the vehicle. It was more than a little crunched. The rear bumper was gone, as were the hubcaps on this side. Nearly every single window sported some damage.

There was something dark splattered over the back of the car, blood probably. But I wasn't going to focus on that. The glove sticking out seemed to taunt me.

Yeah, I wasn't going to think about that either.

They started it.

"Very good driver." Because that car had taken a battering and while I was pretty sure my bruises had bruises. We were all in one piece.

The corner of his mouth kicked up. He secured his gun and then moved to the trunk where he yanked out a couple of bags. "Follow me."

"Yes, sir," I said. It probably came out a little bitchy, but I was tired. So I just followed him and Goblin trotted with us. As soon as he "stashed me" or whatever, I wanted to go over the dog and make sure he wasn't hurt.

We left the car on one side of the parking garage and he made his way over to the other. There was a stairwell in the corner, then a little cubby of space tucked between it and the wall. It would be putting me in a corner, but no one would see me.

It was cool down here and I shivered a little. He set one of the bags down, then thrust the other at me. "There's water in here and clean clothes. Change if you can."

I nodded.

Then he handed me a taser.

Oh, it was my taser.

Well, the one I thought of as mine. It was the one Voodoo had given me. *How had they gotten the taser through security?*

You know what, Grace? Not important right now.

"Remember how to use this?"

"Yes."

"Good girl," he said, then he crouched down to look at Goblin. "Stay with Grace. Guard."

He spared me a look.

"If you tell me to stay with Goblin and guard, I promise to not growl."

The corner of his mouth kicked up again. "Just get changed and stay put. You have your phone?"

I patted over my pockets. Then pulled it out. Yes, and it had a charge. Not much of a signal though. "Should I message the guys?"

"Not yet." He just gave me a long look. "Don't message anyone. If you get a message from me, it means move. Get out of here. The street is two flights of stairs up. Go straight up and out. Take your bag and Goblin with you. Head south toward the beaches. Strip down as you go, so if you can put a suit on when you change, you'll be ready to hide by the water."

"Okay."

"I'll find you."

I blew out a breath.

"Okay."

"Tell me the plan." He still crouched, his gaze steady on me.

Deep breath. "Stay here, clean up and change. If I get any message from you at all, take only my bag, and head upstairs two flights. Go outside. Go south toward the water. Strip so I look like I'm just out for a day in the sun with Goblin. You'll find me."

He nodded once. "Keep that taser with you, and Grace... if *anyone* comes near you, trust Goblin's reaction."

"I can do that."

I glanced down at Goblin then back at Bones. "Please don't get lost or hurt or disappear. Cause I'm not sure how we would find you."

Another flash of a smile. "Like I said, I'll find you."

Then he was gone and it was just me and Goblin. I swallowed, then shook off the feeling of loss. He would be back or he would find me.

Believe it.

"Okay, boy," I said to Goblin. "Let's get cleaned up. Are you hurt?"

TWO

GRACE

The fact it was still daytime out there and Bones had practically vanished on silent feet left me more than a little shaky. One of these things was not like the other. A squeal of a tire on the concrete had me freezing briefly, bottle of water in hand. I had no idea who put these bottles in the bags, but it was right at the top and I needed to clean my hands and Goblin.

As brief as the screech of that tire was, the fact it repeated and then faded away along with any sound of an engine almost made me weep. My heart hammered too hard. The ba-dum, ba-dum, ba-dum echoed loudly in my ears. Too loud. Like I stood next to one of those huge marching band drums and they kept hitting it.

With trembling hands, I splashed a little too much water over the cotton top I'd pulled out and then I went to work wiping Goblin down. Crouched next to him, I focused on cleaning away as much of the blood as possible.

If he was upset by any of this, it really didn't show. His tongue lolled out as he panted, though he sat patiently while I wiped him down. I tried to work fast, but efficiently.

It wouldn't do us any good if someone spotted the blood on him or on me.

Wiping him down also let me check him for injuries. He had none. The blood was definitely not his.

Was it AB's?

My stomach bottomed out. Would Goblin have left him if Alphabet was hurt? One theory after another began to swirl in my head until sweat dotted my forehead and began to trickle down my neck.

Stop.

The order didn't do much until Goblin slurped my face, I jolted back to myself.

"Right," I whispered. "I need to change."

He closed his mouth and canted his head as though assessing me.

"I know," I admitted in a hurried whisper. "I should have already changed." Panicking and freezing were just not options right now. Ignoring where we were, I stripped off the bloodied top and bra, then shucked off the shorts. It left me in shoes and panties.

The chill air whispered over my skin and dried the sweat. I ignored the cold water on a fresh bit of cotton t-shirt and used it to wipe myself down. It wasn't going to be floral and sweet, but I could at least stop smelling so gross.

My nails were in shitty shape. I studied the cracked and jagged edges. As soon as I found a nail file, I'd smooth those out. Probably not the thing to hyperfocus on. Was this what shock felt like? The bag contained at least three changes of clothes, that many pairs of panties, one extra bra, and a bikini.

When did they get me a bikini?

If they had it, why hadn't they...

Right, I just balled up that whole line of inquiry and

tossed it away. Not important. The bikini was a straightforward string type with a pair of triangles for my tits and one for my crotch and maybe half of one for my ass.

Whatever, it would do.

I shimmied out of the panties and into the bikini, halting briefly at least a half-dozen times whenever an unexpected sound echoed through the parking structure. The location and the materials seemed to make everything louder down here. The shadows weren't helping, even if the chillier air did.

Once I was in the bikini, I pulled on a button down shirt but left it open before I dragged on some shorts. If I paired it with sandals, that would be perfect. I'd rather be able to run, so I stuffed my feet into fashionable sneakers.

I checked the time on my phone and gawked. All of that had taken me less than ten minutes, even if it felt like an eternity. Goblin licked my cheek and I stroked a hand over his head.

"I'm okay," I promised him. "Let me finish packing this back up, then we can share some water." There was a plastic laundry bag in the duffel—the kind that hotels used —so I stuffed the bloodied and damp clothes into that, yanked it closed then stuffed that in with the clean stuff and zipped it up.

I spilled some water into my palm and Goblin slurped it up. I went slow, giving him several sips until he relaxed. I downed the last of it. My throat felt almost cracked and raw, worse than I expected.

Checking the time again, I stored the empty bottle in my bag. Other than the splashes on the ground, I didn't want to leave any sign of us. Giving into the need, I hugged Goblin and he tucked his chin onto my shoulder.

Stroking my hands over him, I petted him thoroughly

one more time. I needed to know he hadn't gotten hurt for real. Though, he could be bruised. Fuck knew, I was. The harness was a little twisted so I leaned back to unclip and reclip it. One of the straps had been turned over.

It didn't quite lay correctly, so I ran my fingers over it to flatten it out and felt something harder slid into the nylon strap of the harness itself. With care, I pulled the thumb drive out and stared at it.

"I really wish you could tell me what this is," I told him as I studied it. "Should I put it back? Or put it in my pocket?"

Was it just info on Goblin? Like microchipping only on a thumb drive? That might make sense if he was separated from Alphabet. Or was it something else? Had AB given him that to carry out of the house?

Worry was a permanent burn in my gut. I had so many questions and not enough answers. I finally stuffed the thumb drive into my pocket.

"We'll ask Boney Boy when he gets back." He could make the call. Chances were, he'd know exactly what it was. Finally, I pushed up to stand and stretch my legs. At least they weren't trembling so much.

Goblin moved when I did and he adjusted to sit closer to my legs, positioning himself between me and the opening that led back out into the garage. This narrow little slip behind the stairwell was hardly a fortress, yet being out of direct sight settled me on a really primitive level.

Having Goblin right there, ears perked forward and his gaze focused but body relaxed also did wonders for the shakiness in my soul. Tilting my head back, I closed my eyes and focused on calming my breathing.

Deep, slow inhales. Long, easy exhales. One after another until the deep, thunderous rhythm of my pulse finally settled. Goblin let out a low, almost inaudible *woof*. Eyes snapping open, I gripped the taser and shifted my attention to the opening.

Tires hushed over the concrete, not squealing so much as whistling a little? I strained to catch the sound of the engine, but there was nothing. Maybe a hum? But did engines hum?

The soft thump of a car door closing made me jump. I slapped my free hand over my mouth to stifle the near scream of surprise. Thankfully, it was my freehand and I neither clocked myself in the mouth with the taser nor stunned myself.

That would have been painful *and* embarrassing. When Goblin's tail began to wag a few seconds ahead of a very noticeable scuff of shoe, relief spilled through me.

"Don't shoot," Bones said in a dry, almost droll tone. "I come in peace."

An inelegant snort escaped me as he followed his voice around the corner. Like earlier, he'd pushed his sunglasses up and he swept me from head to toe with a look.

"Cleaned up, changed, and ready to go." Hopefully I sounded more confident than I felt. I was half-torn between thanking him for coming back and complaining that he'd taken forever.

He really hadn't, but my seesawing emotions were just not prepared to be reasonable at the moment. With that in mind, I clamped my lips together.

"You didn't doctor that," he said, gesturing toward my neck. I frowned. When he touched two fingers to my chin, I froze in place and then tilted my head when he nudged my face upward. "It's still angry."

"Oh, the cut." I'd forgotten about it. "It doesn't really hurt that much. It doesn't hurt at all at the moment."

"It's not bleeding. Did you clean it out?" The heat burning in his fingertips threatened to leave marks on my skin. No sooner did he withdraw them, though, than I almost shivered from the absence.

"I washed up as much as I could. I had water, no soap. But I tried to get rid of any blood. So I think we're fine for now. When we get wherever, we can look at it again."

The weight of his gaze said he was assessing me steadily, but he finally nodded. "We can." Then he reached for the second duffel before he took mine. "Let's get you two out of here."

He didn't have to tell me twice. As soon as he led the way, I was right behind him. The parking garage felt so much bigger, and a little brighter, with his presence. Or maybe the sun had just shifted because there were shafts of light illuminating the gloom.

Probably just the whole rotation of the Earth and its axis and all that.

Bones hadn't parked right next to our hiding spot. I scanned the area as we crossed to the other side from where he'd dropped us off. The car he returned in was *brand new* and shiny. The Peugeot e-308 looked glossy as hell and sat, backed into its spot, nose facing out and looking really sharp.

It looked freshly polished and it was a weird color. Almost turquoise on the right side where the sunlight seemed to touch it, but red on the driver's side where it was tucked into the shadows.

Electric car.

That was why I didn't hear an engine. They were damn near silent.

"Where did you get this?" I exhaled the question as he dropped the bags into the trunk.

He paused at the backdoor, where he tapped his leg before opening it. Goblin glanced at me and then trotted over to climb into the backseat. "I bought it."

"You..." I gawked. Genuinely, gawked. My mouth fell open and I stared at him. Then I pulled out my phone to check the time.

Thirty-three minutes.

Thirty-three minutes from when he left me to returning. *And* he bought a new car.

A dozen questions cascaded through my mind, but only one sputtered out, "How?"

The last time I bought I car, I had to sign away my soul in triplicate times three. The sheer volume of paperwork had been *absurd*. You didn't sign that much to buy a damn house.

Then again, a house didn't go 0 to 150 in 3.5 seconds, but who was counting?

He circled the car and took my arm lightly before walking me to the passenger door. When he opened it, I tried to shake off the shock holding me captive.

"With money," he said after I was in the seat. Then he pulled the seatbelt over me and strapped me in. He touched my chin again, then scanned my eyes. "Did you hit your head at all during the chase?"

I frowned. "Probably, but it was against the seat. So, padded."

"Headache?" He still searched my face.

"What are you looking for?"

"A concussion. You've taken too many hits to the head. But you're focusing."

I was. "Yeah, I'm fine." I told him. "Sorry, I'm a little scattered." I thrust a hand through my hair. I'd pulled it down, and it fell in a jumble. I should probably have tried to comb it, but I hadn't felt like it. "And there's no bumps that I'm feeling..." I checked.

He nodded, seemingly satisfied, then closed the door before he circled the car and climbed back into the driver's seat. Without a word, he started the car and it was every bit as silent as I expected. The interior was plush and it *smelled* like a new car.

I really wanted to know how he pulled this off but... it wasn't that important and I wanted to know about the guys more. I also wanted to go back for them or at least know when we would be going back.

As he pulled out of the garage, I took the sunglasses he passed me. I slid them on and scanned the town as he took a slow turn. It was like the chase had never happened.

There was surreal and then there was this. He'd told me to trust him, and I was.

Still...

"What do we do now?"

THREE

ALPHABET

I gave it a beat as they headed out, Bones leaving with Gracie wasn't my favorite. Especially with the research we still needed to do. Gallo would break far sooner than he realized. He'd already provided us with a great deal of data. Accessing his data servers from offsite was a hell of a lot easier with his biometrics.

Goblin huffed out a sigh as the door closed behind them. I got Bones wanting to talk to Grace. He didn't trust her. Not fully, but he also didn't *know* her. The challenge there was he didn't *want* to know her. That was an issue they needed to resolve for themselves.

In choosing to go with him, Grace made a good call. At least, I hoped she had. The friction between the two needed resolution. Cap wouldn't trust her until he got to know her. His dismissive attitude and coldness would keep her at arms length and she already struggled on so many fronts.

He made for an easy target for her anger, disappointment, worry, and hurt. If I saw it, then I knew he'd seen it too. "Good first step," I murmured. They needed to find detente.

It hadn't been ten minutes when the alert sounded that the gate was opening. That was swifter than expected. I tabbed swiftly to the security cameras. The gate was closed. No vehicle. No people.

The yellow light flickered on the pad. That meant the gate was open or opening. The camera said one thing, the screen said another.

We had company. I sent the alert down to Voodoo and Lunchbox before I patted the laptop in apology. Terminating all external connections, I locked it down. It had a deadman's switch in its programming. Any attempt to decrypt the password and it would auto erase several times until the data was utterly unusable.

One single opportunity to enter the correct passcode or the machine was toast. So either I opened it or it didn't boot up. "Komen," I told Goblin as I rose, and yanked the thumb drive from the computer. I stowed it into the pocket of his harness. Afterwards, I closed my laptop with one hand and carried it with me. Too much glass right here and I wanted a better position to welcome our guests.

Lunchbox was already at the top of the steps as I rounded the corner. Voodoo appeared right behind him. "How many?" Voodoo asked as he checked his weapon.

"At least one full five-man team, and a backup." I passed them my phone. I'd tied security through it. "They have the gate cams looped. Swipe right, you'll see the street cam."

"Got it." Voodoo eyed it. "Two vehicles. Four motorbikes. Five man team on point and another in reserve. They have a couple keeping watch on the gates."

He cut his gaze up to me then Lunchbox. We had options. The bigger question was how did we want to do this? We'd known an attack would come, it was only a matter of time. Grace not being in the house *helped*. I wasn't a fan of her being where I couldn't see her during this, but she also wasn't right in the middle either.

"Bones is going to be pissed," Lunchbox said, though his wry tone shrugged off any actual emotional weight for the sentiment.

"Luck of the draw," Voodoo said as he passed my phone back to me. "Third team just arrived, probably for the scoop."

"I'm starting to think these guys don't want to take no for an answer." Lunchbox pressed a hand to his chest. "It's almost touching."

"Well, Lieutenant," I said as I scanned the screens one last time before tucking it away. "Sixty seconds. What's our play?"

"Well, they're knocking, and it would be downright rude to keep them waiting." Voodoo pursed his lips before he glanced at Goblin.

"Rude can be fun under the right circumstances." The observation from Lunchbox made me grin.

"So can taking them up on it." Which was where I leaned at the moment. Frankly, Gallo had information we could use. Getting it out of him wasn't even that challenging, save for the fact he didn't seem to really understand what he actually knew. Irritating, rich dick.

A little pop of breaking glass had Voodoo moving as a canister landed on the foyer's tile floor. He picked it up and lobbed it right back out the broken window. The gas exploded out there, along with a lot of cursing.

"We'll think about taking them up on their offer," Voodoo said over his shoulder. "But they need to woo us first."

"Woo?" Lunchbox snorted, but he raised his gun at a

flash of movement from the rear of the house. I drew back a step with Goblin pressed right to my leg and out of sight. He fired three shots rapidly. Two in the chest and one in the head of the man trying to get through the glass door.

I shifted around the corner and fired at the next pair coming up. One in the knee, the other in the head, then back to the downed guy and shot him through the throat.

The spray of blood was going to be messy as hell.

Oh well, so sad.

Moving on.

"Woo," I picked up the conversation. "Persuade. Seriously, we are not cheap dates. They definitely need to work for it."

"Somehow," Lunchbox said in a grimmer tone as the hiss of something burning around the front door carried. "I don't think they're that into *us*."

No, I didn't think he was wrong. They wanted Grace.

"Too fucking bad for them." Voodoo deadpanned. "Let's make a hole or we're going to be here longer."

Agreed.

After that, we didn't need more words. There was a blast from upstairs. Their teams were hitting from all angles.

Smart.

By unspoken agreement, Lunchbox headed to the second floor while Voodoo and I took position in the hall that let us cover the front and back. "Cover," I said as the hinges and lock blasted off the front door in rapid succession and it tumbled inwards from the shattered frame.

Goblin snarled next to me as the black garbed team stormed the door in two-by-two formation, alternating high and low. Solid tactics.

Dropping my hand for Goblin to get down, I dropped to

one knee and fired. I had fourteen rounds left in the magazine. Despite the heavy garb, they weren't wearing combat helmets.

Bad planning. I fired right through the head of one and into the midsection of the guy behind him. The vest took the hit, but the blood and brain spatter had them falling back a step. Another two bullets into the guy's knee to bring him down and it created a chokepoint of bodies for them to have to get over.

Four bullets, two bodies. Ten in the mag. Another pair fought their way over and I spent the ammo to take both of them. Eight bullets, four bodies. Seemed a little pricey. Six in the mag.

"Moving," Voodoo snapped from behind me and I nodded. Goblin still crouched next to me, his whole body facing forward. I checked the phone cams. We still had a few out back and upstairs.

That meant another team had to be incoming. Time to make that hole. I checked the mag then pulled my knife and murmured a command to Goblin. He moved with me as we stalked across the foyer. We intercepted the guy yanking his buddies out of the way.

Bullet to the head would be faster, but I wanted to preserve my ammo. Goblin nailed the guy's forearm. A stream of curses escaped the man as he released his gun under the pressure of Goblin's teeth.

The fact he went for his own knife had me intercepting now. He wasn't stabbing my goddamn dog. I struck at his upper arm, going for the nerves, then against his collarbone, just next to the vest. The slide of the blade digging into the flesh cost the man the use of his left arm.

Another two rapid blows and I cut his carotid, then I thrust the blade through his throat and twisted. Less than six seconds, his blood pumped out of him in spray. It coated me and Goblin both. Goblin released him on command and I hauled the guy around and used him as a meat shield as bullets struck the door frame and the body.

Goblin darted to the side at my order, and I fell back to press against the inside of the door with Goblin leaning into my leg. The sound of gunfire peppered the silence along with a splash of displaced water as something hit the pool in the back.

A rush of boots over the paved drive carried. Yep, they really were way too into us. Glancing down at Goblin, I wiped the blade on my jeans. My hand was still slick, but I could make it work.

Upstairs, something exploded. I'd worry more if it were anyone other than Lunchbox up there. Rolling my head from side to side, I used my phone to check the front door cams. Two more teams of five.

There was aggressive and then there were these guys. Touching the comm in my ear, I activated it. "I really think someone should explain consent to these guys."

"Well, we never have been fond of safe words." Voodoo's dry comment made me grin.

"We don't have a problem with them," Lunchbox argued. "We just never use them."

This was also true. "Two more fresh teams are incoming," I warned them. "We need to make the call now."

I heard the rip of a pin coming out as I locked my gaze on the screen. I could see the guy and I twisted, using the phone to target so I could literally point and shoot. Man and grenade went down together.

The muffled boom following my safe retreat back inside almost made me laugh.

"Okay, so only one fresh team now. The other is a little scattered."

Lunchbox actually laughed then. "You're a comedian." Not that it sounded like a complaint.

"I'm here all day," I promised. The other five were being a little more cautious on their approach. Four bullets. Five guys. "It's about to get sticky. We still good to go?"

A split-second moment of silence cleaved by a harried exhale. "What the fuck," Voodoo said finally. "Do it."

"Understood."

I rolled my head from side to side. "Cover fire incoming," Lunchbox said and a moment later there was a shattering of glass right before something heavy hit the ground. I went low and covered Goblin as a fresh *boom* echoed from outside. "Holy shit, that's a mess."

"We're going," I warned them, then gave Goblin a soft follow command before I climbed over the bodies with him right behind me. I went after the guy closest to us who was struggling to his feet.

He had glass shards embedded in his face. That just wasn't pretty. I went with the knife slashing his throat open. He was already staggering so it didn't take much to put him down. Blood sprayed me and Goblin both. We turned to the guy racing toward us and he actually stumbled.

"Not a fan of horror movies?" I asked and the quip felt good cause it made the guy blink. I pistol-whipped him with the gun and he went down. Then the next pair came staggering toward me, gun raised. "Time to go," I told Goblin. This was our opening. "*Reveiren*, Gracie, Bones."

As much as I wanted him with me, I wanted him and Grace safe more. He didn't hesitate, sprinting toward the drive and the road as I used the last four bullets in my magazine to pin the two heading at me. Goblin was around the corner and out of sight before I used the gun as another projectile and threw it.

It struck the guy on the left right in the face and then there was just one.

I spun the knife in my hand and beckoned. "Let's go..."

FOUR

GRACE

We drove north on the A7. It was early afternoon by the time we reached the Place Bellecour in Lyon. We parked on a side street, facing away from the square. I'd been to Lyon before, a couple of times. It seemed almost strangely familiar and yet utterly alien.

Though he'd stopped for food and coffee on the way up, we'd said very little. The whole of the drive, all I'd wondered was when would we hear from them? The farther north we went, the more I worried we weren't going to hear from them at all.

And I couldn't focus on that right now. When Bones put the car into park and blew out a breath, I twisted in the seat to look at him. "Is it okay to ask a few questions now?"

He rubbed a hand over his face, then frowned at me. Only instead of looking annoyed, he actually appeared puzzled. "Yes."

That eased one major concern. "Are we staying in the car or going with you?"

Another brief frown and then he glanced toward Goblin in the backseat before he looked at me again. "With."

Real relief spilled through me. Staying in the car was definitely not safer. "Second question?"

One corner of his mouth inched higher, but he nodded.

"Where are we going?"

To my shock, he actually chuckled. I didn't think I'd heard the man laugh before. No, not even a little laugh or hint of humor. He barely smiled. Glower? Glare? Frown disapprovingly? Those he definitely did.

"There's a small bank just off the plaza back there where we have a safe deposit box. We can pick up some papers, more currency, and keys for a safe house outside of Lyon." He checked his watch. "We have a little under an hour before it closes."

"Okay. We can take Goblin inside?"

"Yep," he said with far more confidence than I felt. "Just need to gear him up." Gearing him up turned out to be putting him in a work vest. For me, it was just buttoning up the oversized shirt I'd dressed in, rolling up the sleeves and accessorizing it with a chunky belt. I wanted to stay in my sneakers, but he was right, the sandals would draw less attention.

For his part, he was dressed in basic black on black, with a sports coat thrown on. The man looked elegant in what was essentially combat gear. He removed his weapon with care and secured it in the car. Then he held his hand out.

"Taser."

At my hesitation, he straightened and met my gaze.

"We're not going into a fight. This is just to get to the safety deposit box and come back out. But we don't have time to work around the metal detectors."

That made sense. I passed it to him. I still had my phone. Once he locked up the car, he passed me Goblin's leash then set his sunglasses in place. I followed suit. When he took my hand in his, I didn't fight the grip, just fell into step.

The warmth of his palm on mine offered a kind of comfort. It also helped to settle my racing heart. As we followed the road up to the boulevard, I stared across at the huge Place Bellecour—the pedestrian square was huge and old. There was a statue of Louis XIV in the middle.

"They installed a guillotine there during the French Revolution."

"Well hopefully, not something we need to worry about today." His dry response almost made me smile.

"Hopefully. It's not there anymore."

Bones led the way around the corner, Goblin trotting neatly at my side. "I'd be more concerned if it was *still* there."

"Fair," I admitted, scanning the area and the people making their way. The French language settled over me like a familiar blanket, though I caught snippets of Italian, German, and English from the passersby. "Think it would send a message if they did put one back?"

At the door to the bank, Bones pulled the door open. "Definitely. And it would only be popular in some quarters."

I couldn't really disagree with that. It was cooler inside the bank. Light filtered through the glass windows. Some were fashioned in deeper hues and offered an almost golden light to the bank's interior.

Nudging my sunglasses up, I scanned the area. There were conversation areas along the front wall of windows with comfortable chairs and low tables. Along the other wall, heading toward the back, were a series of offices.

Two guards were readily apparent, one right there in the lobby, where visitors could approach the bank counter. The other was stationed closer to the main doors. We'd passed him on our way in and when my gaze collided with his, I smiled automatically.

Bones gestured to the desk to the left of the bank counters, so I followed him with Goblin firmly at my side. He was such a good boy. Thankfully, no one commented on his presence nor urged us to take him back out.

We had to wait a moment before the concierge was free to speak. Bones approached him to sign in, "*Parles-vous anglais?*"

"If he doesn't," I said softly. "I can translate."

"*Oui,*" the man said. "How can I help you?"

"I need to get into—"

The doors at the front slammed before Bones could finish his sentence and there was a distinct bang from a gun even as the metal detectors shrieked. Goblin snarled next to me and I looked back to see three men, all in ski masks and wearing all black and sporting weapons stalking inside.

This was not happening.

The guard closest to the door was already down, one of the men struck him with their weapon as another one fired his gun again. The sound reverberated through the building.

"*Allonge-toi sur le sol!*" The one still on the move yelled as he headed straight towards us and the concierge. I dropped. They wanted everyone on the floor, so I got on the floor.

Bones didn't. He stood there, eyeing the men as they approached. Goblin's lips peeled back as he snarled at the men. "No," I whispered to Goblin. "Down. Please." I patted the floor next to me because one of those guns was swinging toward the dog.

The man near the door locked them and then stalked forward following his friend and he had his weapon down but a black sack in hand. "Téléphones dans le sac ! Baissez la tête ou vous êtes le prochain!"

For all his blustering, the man sounded terrifically young. The closer he got, the more I could see his eyes. He was jittery and almost painfully lean. Bones still hadn't gotten down, he glanced down at me, then back at the men. The concierge was down as well, his hands over his head.

"Stay here," Bones told me and I stared up at him. Was he *insane*?

"*Téléphones!*" The man repeated, thrusting the bag at others, he wasn't quite to us yet, but they were getting devices from the others. We weren't in the direct line of sight but...

Movement jerked my attention back to where Bones had been. Where the hell had he gone? I didn't want to twist around, so I focused on the men. Three of them were hustling people out from the counter. Fortunately, the bank wasn't that busy, or maybe not so fortunately.

The other guard was also down, then one of them stalked closer to me and Goblin, but he just dragged the concierge up and muttered at him. As the man stumbled away with them, a pen hit the carpet and rolled toward me. It was one of those very fancy, metal pens.

I palmed it and pulled it closer to me and really wished I had my taser or Bones had his gun.

Or something.

The three masked men were split up. They hadn't moved everyone together so they were trying to cover all of us. The man who'd dragged the concierge away was currently threatening him near a door that went behind the bank counters.

Bones was… there. I caught him crouched near one of the sofas. He was just a few feet from one of the men. That was two, the third—the one who'd been screaming for telephones—paced back and forth between me and them.

If he kept looking in that direction, he'd see Bones whether the man moved like a shadow or not. Goblin's low growls vibrated against me. Another shout from the man with the concierge and there was the sound of a blow.

A woman near the desks began to cry and I swallowed hard. How the hell had we walked right into a bank robbery? This couldn't be real, right?

The man nearest Bones swung his gun around, his movements were getting even more nervous. He yelled at them to hurry. No doubt they were worried about getting caught. The man closest to me yelled at the other and Bones stayed absolutely still.

Okay, this wasn't working. The tension stretched so tight, I wanted to vomit. I pushed myself upward, fanning myself like I was too hot.

That got me noticed. Mr. Telephone Man whipped around and waved his gun right at me.

"Revenez sur le sol!" He was bringing that gun up toward Goblin but I shifted in front of him. It wasn't hard to pretend I was faint. My heart was racing so fast, I wasn't sure I wouldn't pass out.

When the man leaned down to yell at me, I jammed the pen right into the soft spot below his jaw. Gazes locked, he stared at me, puzzlement clear in his eyes as his mouth opened. Blood flowed down the metal pen and onto my hand.

The guy dropped without another word. Bones was already on his feet. He disarmed the robber closest to him in a blur of motion before he slammed the man headfirst into a column.

The clatter of a gun to the floor yanked my attention back to the man collapsed in front of me. I reached for the weapon, wrapping my bloodied fingers around it. Then Goblin lunged upwards, sinking his teeth into the third man's arm.

I hadn't even seen the guy move, but his weapon also went flying as Goblin wrenched him down. Bones was just there, finishing the man with two brutal hits—one to his throat and the second to the back of his head.

Then they were all down.

I slid my gaze back to the man with the pen in the soft part beneath his jaw. He was dead.

I was almost certain of it.

Sirens wailed in the distance. It was like someone unmuted the sound and it all rushed back in. Bones glanced down at me.

"You didn't stay put," he said.

"You didn't leave me behind." To be fair, he had moved across the room, but I got it. He wasn't abandoning me.

When he extended his hand to me, I clasped his. "We need to go," he murmured and I followed his glance around the room.

"We didn't get the box."

"There are others," he told me. "C'mon." With my hand firmly in his, he headed for the doors and jerked his head to Goblin. The good boy trotted right along with us.

"*Monsieur!*" One of the others called, but Bones just unlocked the door and let us out. Then we were striding down the street. It took no time and forever, then we were back in the car with Goblin.

The sirens were getting closer. I caught the sight of flashing lights behind us as Bones started the car and we pulled away.

"Seatbelt," he murmured to me and I glanced at him and then down at the gun I was still holding. He covered the weapon with one hand. "Seatbelt," he repeated.

My hand was still sticky and red, so I used the other to pull the seatbelt over and buckle it in. Then Bones reached to flip open the console and pulled out a pack of wet wipes.

I cleaned my hand, then the hilt of the gun. Another glance behind us showed we were navigating our way from the Place Bellecour.

Away from the bank.

From the robbery.

"Not staying in the car wasn't safer."

"No," he said easily, covering my hand on the gun once more. "But you did good."

Did I?

CHAPTER

FIVE

GRACE

Instead of leaving Lyon entirely after the bank incident, Bones took us across the river Saône, through a quieter neighborhood, to a little boutique hotel called *Étoile du Matin*.

Morning Star.

The name was as lovely as the centuries old building housing it. Though the hotel also offered valet, Bones drove a block over and booked a slot in a parking garage. It also came with a charging station for the car. Smart.

He passed me his blazer to carry over my arm. It hid the blood on the shirt sleeve. The weapon, he tucked into a larger tote that would double as a purse for me.

Bags in hand like a pair of travelers, with Goblin walking with us, we made our way back to the hotel. A light rain had begun to fall, the clouds crowding out the thin sunlight. It was almost as depressing as the day had grown.

"Ask her to book the suite on the top floor?" He handed me a black credit card and a passport.

Having a task grounded me. The woman's cheerful

35

greeting made me smile. I asked her about the suite on the top floor and she checked to see if it was available.

"Oui, on a cette chambre de dispo. Vous comptez rester combien de nuits ? Et vous serez bien que deux ?"

"She said the suite is available. How many nights?"

"Two," Bones said, his cool gaze seemed to constantly be on the move, sweeping the area, though he rested it on me at the moment. "We might need to extend to three."

I nodded, then looked at the pretty receptionist with her warm smile and well-styled hair. She looked so put together and I felt like a bag lady. *"Oui, nous serons deux, avec notre chien. Nous aimerions rester deux nuits, peut-être même une troisième si tout se passe bien."* I made sure to include Goblin in the booking. Because he was definitely going to the suite with us.

Her smile warmed. *"Je vais laisser une note pour la troisième nuit et on pourra prendre un dépôt pour la réserver, que nous pourrons vous rembourser si vous n'en avez finalement pas besoin."*

That would work. Not that it was my money, but a deposit they would refund if we didn't need the third night made sense. Because Bones had already handed me the card, I passed it over along with his passport. The name on both read Caylon Gwyar.

She took both and began the booking process. When she asked for a phone number and email address, I blanked for a moment. Bones, however, offered me two easily enough and I translated.

Once she had us all checked in, she provided two cards to access the room, then asked, *"Souhaitez-vous que je vous fasse monter une bouteille de champagne ? Nous pouvons aussi vous proposer un repas si vous préférez vous concentrer l'un sur l'autre."*

Why would I want her to send champagne up to the room? But her playful nod toward Bones and conspiratorial smile had heat scorching my face. Apparently, I'd been a little too suggestive in saying we might need a third night if all went well.

"Non, merci beaucoup. Peut-être demain. Pas d'interruptions ce soir." I almost stuttered the words, but my nervous laughter seemed to garner me some sympathy.

She passed over the cards, along with Bones' passport and credit card. *"Sois patient avec celui-là. Les plus silencieux sont souvent les plus observateurs et cachent le plus de passion."*

This time, I didn't have to pretend a smile or a laugh, but rather than respond to her advice about how passionate the quiet ones could be, I just thanked her. *"Merci."*

Thankfully, the ride up in the gated elevator passed swiftly. The suite was the only room on the top floor. His desire for it made a lot more sense when we let out on that floor. The building narrowed toward the top.

The hallway smelled of lemon cleaner and a hint of rain. The windows at either end were closed, but they'd likely been open earlier. The door opposite the elevator was the only one on this floor. The sky had darkened even further while we'd been checking in and the rain fell steadily.

I swiped the card and the door unlocked. Goblin went in first and wiggled his way around sniffing. Thankfully, he'd peed on our way from the parking garage to the hotel itself. Though in fairness, we needed to get him some food and water.

Probably a real walk too.

Bones locked the door once we were inside. Deadbolt, privacy lock and a lock for the handle itself. He set our bags down then moved across the sitting room area of the suite, closing the blinds and the curtains before he disappeared into the bedroom.

The blinds snapped closed in there and a soft yellow light came on before he returned. All the cheer and amusement from downstairs bled away. It was like I'd been playing a role but I didn't need to anymore.

Setting aside his blazer, I glanced down at the gun I was still holding. My right hand seemed permanently shaped around the grip. Goblin came back from his sweep of the room and looked up at me, tail wagging.

It was those soulful eyes that decided me. I put the gun down carefully on the side table and then crouched to remove Goblin's leash.

A toilet flushed from beyond the door to the suite's bedroom. Water came on, then off and a moment later, Bones reappeared sans shirt, hair wet, and drying his hands with a towel.

"Can I take off his harness?"

Focus on Goblin, I reminded myself. Leering at Bones was not cool. Particularly because, he hadn't really had time to change since we'd begun this odyssey. Of course, he'd take the first chance to clean up. The broad muscular frame of his hadn't changed, though he seemed almost as wiry as he was thick in the chest. The muscle definition reminded me of how he'd taken people down with his bare hands.

The skin over his right pec and to his shoulder seemed mottled and discolored compared to the rest. There was also a tattoo off a dagger dripping blood on his side under his left arm.

"Go ahead, I'll take him out later for a walk but we should stay in for a while." Outside, sirens passed by. A reminder that the city was still out there. The city with its bank robbery and jittery robbers and the man I killed.

Yanking my mind from that path, I focused my trembling fingers on unsnapping the harness. Once I took it off him, Goblin went a little wiggly nuts. He raced around the room and rolled, rubbing his back against the carpet.

It was just so—canine.

I laughed. Still wiggling, Goblin flopped over and bounded back to me. I barely got to pet him before he slurped me and raced away. He dashed past Bones and into the bedroom. Then he was back.

More laughter escaped me at his antics. It was like he needed to shake off all of his own tension and, God, did I understand that.

"Here,' Bones said, holding out a hand to me. "I want to look at those cuts."

Cuts?

I frowned and reached up to touch the one hidden by the shirt on my collarbone, then spotted the one on the inside of my arm. It was a slice along the side of my arm. I hadn't even realized I had cut it, but the moment I looked at it, it stung. Clasping his hand, I let him pull me to my feet.

"Come, sit down." He tugged me over to the sofa. His gruff tone wasn't unkind in the least.

"It's really nothing," I told him, but he just opened one of the duffels and pulled out what looked like a small first aid kit. He set it on the table as Goblin finally settled from his running around to lay there panting as he watched us.

Boring humans, not playing with him. I shot him a sympathetic smile as Bones disappeared back into the bedroom. The water kicked on again and he returned with a fresh towel, a damp washcloth, and a glass of water.

"Drink this," he told me and knelt after I took the water. He cleaned the cut with quick, efficient movements. I sipped the water, and it showed me just how dry my mouth was. The cut stung and I still couldn't figure out when I did that.

"This wasn't part of the plan," I murmured.

"Neither was you stabbing a guy in the neck with a pen." He flicked a look at me briefly before returning to the cut on my arm. "Effective though."

I huffed out a laugh though the humor dried up when he undid the belt followed by the buttons on my shirt. "Um…"

"Just getting to the cut here." He didn't tease or soften the words, just kept it straightforward and blunt. It wasn't like I was naked under the shirt, the bikini top was more than enough coverage but…

A hiss slipped past my teeth as he continued cleaning the cut. Why it was stinging so much now, I had no idea. My back and my shoulders were starting to hurt too. He replaced the cloth with his fingers, and applied some ointment with gentle touches. It didn't erase the pain, but it definitely helped to lessen it.

"Why didn't you stop me from taking the gun?" I was staring at it sitting on the side table. Not once after we left the bank had he tried to take it away or keep it from me. Even when we got here, he put his coat over my arm so I could hide that I still had it.

"Because you didn't freeze."

"That's it?" It seemed almost too easy of an answer.

He spared me a look, something moved behind his pale gray eyes. Something… I couldn't quite define. An emotion piercing the cool veil, but what precisely it was, I had no idea.

"And I don't need a passenger—I need someone who'll

fight." Of all the things I half-expected he would answer with, those words were *not* it.

He finished with the ointment then lifted my wrist to study the shallow cut on my arm.

"You don't trust me," I said. It wasn't a question. Not that I could blame him.

"Not yet," he said, adding the ointment to my arm now. "But I don't trust anyone. You're not special."

The most indelicate snort left me as I scoffed at him. "Liar."

He just shrugged then eased back before he rose. The steely silence had been replaced by something more brittle, and then a deep snore punctuated it and we both looked at Goblin. The puppy was out.

All at once, worry for Alphabet, Voodoo, and Lunchbox slammed into me. They were still out there. We still didn't know how they were or where they were. "Do you have another plan?" I had to know.

"Not yet," Bones answered as he turned away. There were more scars on his back. Whiter slices that seemed weathered into sun darkened skin and dotted in places by rough puckers of flesh that made me think of bullet wounds.

Yeah, no comfort in that either. But I would rather he told me the truth even if I didn't like it.

"Can I do anything to help?" At my question, he stopped at the doorway to the bedroom.

"Don't open the door. Don't call anyone. Try to rest. I want to shower. I imagine you want one too. For now, we lie low. You can do that to help." The rough tone was back, but it didn't seem as cold or as distant as it had before.

"Okay." I rose and retrieved the gun before I went back to sitting on the sofa. Goblin had cracked an eyelid at my motion, but he closed them again once I was seated. "I can do that."

Silence rushed back in to fill all the empty spaces between us, drowning the cracks and fractures, but not quite filling them in.

"I'll be quick," he said, the three words almost startled me and I jerked my head up. I hadn't realized he was still in the doorway. "Thank you, Grace."

Then he was gone.

SIX

LUNCHBOX

Monaco.

Of all the gin joints, in all the towns, in all the world... Our hunt had brought us to Monaco. Our original plan had been to interrogate the assailants or to follow and gather more info...

Maybe if we hadn't been quite so efficient with the teams sent to reclaim Gallo, we could have played this differently.

Oh well.

Our bad.

Technically, we were collecting more information via a different avenue. And yes, arguably, this was more about precision chaos than pure extraction, but always play to your strengths.

The elevator ride to the lower level took several seconds longer than I thought it should. Then again, I trusted Alphabet's work to get us the credentials. Well, get *them* the credentials. I was just here as the rogue arm candy.

When the panel flashed from red to green, I blew out a breath. Three seconds later, the elevator car glided to a stop and the doors slid open to reveal *The Marquess,* a lavish underground casino tucked below a luxury hotel in Monaco.

Exclusive, elite, and accessible only by invitation. Voodoo and Alphabet gripped my biceps and marched me out into the lush lobby area with its expensive furniture, imported marble floors, and ancient artifacts—three of which I damn well knew belonged back in Greece but had *disappeared* during a repatriation from the British Museum to Athens.

Good to know.

Cameras were likely tucked into every fixture. Security on these levels would be ruthless and swift. They wouldn't bother with questions. In addition to the gaming tables and private rooms for whispered deals, *The Marquess* played host to the real action that brought us all the way here. Trafficking auctions masked as "discreet services."

From what Gallo had said, Grace was nearly sold here. This would have been her destination before he picked her up—at a considerable *markup.*

Jackass.

While we stopped her from being brought here, so many others were still being trafficked through the facility. I took all of it in on our way across the lobby. The staff and security all wore similar high-end suits, distinguished only by the presence of weapons.

Two members of security, including one wearing an ankle holster from the way his pant leg draped, stepped forward as we marched toward an area marked off by velvet ropes.

Meeting the gaze of that man, I bared my teeth and had the satisfaction of him narrowing his gaze even as he rocked his weight back a half step.

Made you blink.

Voodoo waved the other guy back, the action would have revealed his own weapon. "We're already late, get out of the way." The cold dismissal in his voice would have made a new recruit piss their pants. Maybe it didn't have quite the same effect here, but it did prevent them from blocking our access.

The man who rose as we cleared the lobby and into the rear hall was older, harder eyed, and wore his intellect as fiercely as his skill. The flat line of his mouth and set of his shoulders said he would not be moved by a stare alone.

"What is this?" He motioned toward me. Yes, I was bruised, and the split in my lip had reopened though it wasn't bleeding. The zip tie around my wrists declared I wasn't here willingly. Not that they would care.

In addition to the sex and service options they trafficked in, they also dealt in security assets. I was a rogue, and ideal for the right bidder who may want to use my skills for muscle, personal revenge, or just training for their own security.

Under the right circumstances, I might almost do this for fun. Taking down these arrogant pricks could be a good time.

"He's not listed," the steely-eyed man stated. He tapped one thick finger to a clipboard on his desk.

"That's because this isn't on the list," Alphabet drawled the words, smacking the gum that I'd actually forgotten he'd stuffed in his mouth on the way in.

"If he's not on the list..."

"We didn't say *he* isn't on the list." Voodoo spoke in a far more precise, impersonal tone as though detailing directions. "We said *this* isn't on the list."

"Papers," the security chief demanded.

Alphabet snorted. "Papers? How fucking new are you? All invoices and manifests come in electronically. Physical papers are trackable, dumbass."

Color bloomed in the man's face and his nostrils flared. "I want identification. Now. Or you can join your delivery in the chute."

Physically suppressing the urge to roll my eyes took every ounce of my strength. What a tool...

"You want to clear this with management?" Voodoo said, still a picture of dispassionate patience. "Or would you like to explain why you delayed delivery?"

A vein throbbed in the chief's forehead. I didn't have to glance behind me to know he didn't have the backup right there. If anything, the lack of audience reduced his posturing. Still, I might need to stage a "break" for a distraction—Alphabet tapped morse code against the inside of my arm.

Oh, that would work.

The man went to round his desk and I made a "lunge" that had Voodoo elbow me, before he slammed me chest down over the desk and bracing a forearm across my back.

"Can't you control him?" The chief had retreated three hard steps.

Wimp.

"Clear us or call management," Voodoo ordered. The tone said obey or *else*.

Snarl in place, the chief stormed back to the desk and I had a closeup look at his password as he keyed it in. Yeah, this guy was not used to real threats walking in the door. Doubtful the rest of the staff would be so easy.

An alert beeped and the chief frowned. The angle only let me catch a little of the screen. The priority notice with my details was right there and the words *urgent delivery* flashed.

Nice. I hadn't even seen Alphabet slide in the thumb drive or remove it. He had a gift.

"My apologies," the chief ground over the words as if they stuck to his tongue like garlic frosted donuts. "I didn't know he was marked for a private buyer."

Not bothering to answer him, Voodoo and Alphabet hauled me upright before bypassing him and heading to the next set of doors. We were a half-step from them when the locks released with a buzz.

This door opened into a whole new level of sin and debauchery. It was an open casino flooring, with nude women and men delivering drinks and providing other *services*. Security was also placed strategically about the room, but they barely glanced at us.

Sometimes, threat-level swagger was all you needed. The layout we'd mapped needed filling in, so that was exactly what we did as we made our way across the floor toward a new bank of elevators and doors.

"Peacock," Voodoo said almost under his breath. "Suitcase. Diamond. Sickle. That's four."

So four of twelve were already here. Two points to Gallo, he'd been straight with us about that. Maybe we should have killed him a little faster, but he'd been real hesitant about sharing.

Once inside the elevator, Alphabet said, "Thirty seconds."

I snapped the zip ties with one hard jerk. Then traded with Alphabet for a weapon and jacket. He raked a hand through his hair, smacked his gum, then pulled out his phone.

When the doors opened to an executive level, Voodoo took point with Alphabet shuffling next to him and I shifted to the role of bodyguard. Meetings often occurred on this level, not sales. Though one of the primary bidding rooms was located here.

A guard stepped out of a door ahead of us. He frowned and said something in French, but Voodoo already had him in a headlock and back through the door. He was out ten seconds later and we had a working security badge.

"I have the cameras on this level," Alphabet said. "It's not going to last long, so I'm going to have to roll them along with us, just lock the view on the ones we have to pass while we pass them. They have a lot of fail-safes in place."

"We'll make it work," I said, joining Voodoo in a swift search of the room. The table had binders on it with digital pads inside them. No paperwork. Each pad required a fingerprint to open.

Not helpful.

A remote turned on the television screen. The view overlooked a room, stretched long and cold. Industrial lights casting a sterile glow over rows of metal cages. Inside each one stood a man or woman, dressed to impress—sleek suits, tight dresses, every detail curated to draw the eye.

Their bodies were posed like mannequins, expressions vacant but inviting, as if frozen mid-catwalk. The air buzzed with the sound of footsteps—spectators moving slowly, snapping photos, muttering judgments. It was a runway stripped of glamor, a showroom of human display where allure met captivity in a parade of unsettling elegance.

"Bidding will start soon," Alphabet said. "We need the 'in.'"

The guard Voodoo dragged in with us wasn't tall or broad enough for us to use his clothes. We'd just have to fake it. "Then we go downstairs, find the targets, follow them." We could lift credentials if we had to.

Because we needed the guard to stay quiet and out of sight, I found a small maintenance closet in the back of the room and we stuffed him in there—bound hand and foot, and gagged.

Not perfect, but it would have to do.

"Security camera angles on the main room," Alphabet said and I joined them to study the images on the screen. "Comm check."

I pressed the small device just behind my ear. It was flesh-toned and would short out after a day or two, but it worked for quick missions. "Check."

"Check," Voodoo said. At the door, I exited first, sweeping the hall before stepping out and letting Voodoo and Alphabet fall back into their roles. We headed back to the casino floor.

For the next hour, Voodoo gambled, flirted, and "drank," while Alphabet smacked his gum and I drifted along with them. According to Gallo, this section of the operation fell under the control of twelve high level bidders. They were the ones who extended the invitations, as well as ensured there was plenty of "stock."

He had *some* of the names.

We needed the rest.

It was with this in mind that Voodoo made his way around to the pai gow table where the peacock, one of the first targets we'd marked, sat playing. A silver-haired woman in her mid-sixties, she'd embraced her age and wore it like an ethereal crown.

Enormously attractive and fit, she seemed absolutely certain of her appeal. She also knew what she liked. One glance at Voodoo and she gestured for the man next to her to leave, freeing the seat up for him.

"Madam," Voodoo said before he took the seat and settled his chips on the table.

"Hmm," was all she replied before she took a sip of her wine. "You're new."

"I am." Voodoo spread his hands. "Since we're offering facts, allow me to say, you're exquisite."

She laughed.

Damn, the man had skill. I kept my face expressionless and scanned the room.

"I warn you," she told him as the dealer began. "I do not have a soft side."

"That sounds like a challenge," Voodoo drawled. "What do I get when I find it?"

When, not if.

Not even a full minute and he had her charmed. There was more than one way to skin a cat. Now to make sure when she went into that auction, we went with her.

CHAPTER
SEVEN
VOODOO

Marva Duvall, also known as the Peacock, seemed to enjoy pai gow as much as she did flirting. Her somewhat careless attitude, playful glances, and gentle caresses with her free roaming hand seemed at odds with her reputation.

Each time she patted my left thigh, she landed somewhere slightly different. The artless brushes of her hand down my shoulder and arm were as much a pat down as anything else. It wasn't difficult to understand how she'd avoided detection. As attractive as she was in a gilded lady manner, she didn't radiate "underworld menace."

In my book, that made the stories about her all the worse.

"You must tell me…" She eyed me expectantly as we played the next hand. I had as yet not given her my name and I had no intentions of doing so.

"Tell you what, lovely lady?" I increased my buy-in with each game, though the last three had all ended in a push with the dealer. Madame Duvall had also increased her wagers as I did, but she'd lost two of the past three and only pushed on one. Neither of us had beaten the dealer since the first hand when I joined the table.

We were now on our fifth game, and the other players had dropped out as the stakes climbed with each game. It was akin to playing chicken with an asp. You just had to be comfortable with the idea that you might get struck and have to deal with the venom.

Amusement kindled in her honey brown eyes as she set the stakes for the next game, raising the initial bet to five thousand. "You are a dangerous one, aren't you?"

"That depends," I said, affecting a careless shrug as the last of the other players at the table ceded their position rather than place a bet. It was down to just us and the dealer.

"On?" She dared me as I debated both progressive *and* fortune bets. The progressive pot had also significantly increased with each game with no one taking the prize. That was far more like baiting the hook. I could respect it.

"What game I am playing—fortune bet?" We had not placed this side bet even once.

"Based on our current odds, that would seem unwise."

Though there was no denying the flash of interest in her eyes. The private guard attending her backed off as she waved her hand at him. I lifted a finger and Lunchbox also retreated a couple of steps. It gave us an illusion of privacy.

"Odds have never impressed me. Odds are designed to intimidate the foolish and challenge the daring." I picked up the aged Scotch I'd been nursing since I sat. The ball of ice had begun to melt and water it down. Not that one drink was going to do me in.

"What are the current odds up to?" she asked the dealer.

"At the moment, fifteen thousand to one. The progressive is now up to three hundred thousand." The dealer waited, not urging us to continue or demanding we start. Whether that was down to the fact it was just the two of us or because she was one of the luminaries in their dirty little world was anyone's guess.

I'd wager it was some of column A and some of column B. Still, the past hour had given me some insights, and there was a mental clock ticking down in my head. When she withdrew, the auction would begin.

When it started, we needed to be in that room. We needed to identify, tag, and question the members of Nocturne. The pretentiousness in the name was enough to make me ill.

Still, I met Duvall's gaze evenly and raised my brows. "Live a little..."

"How about we make it a little more interesting?" The low throaty invitation coupled with her hand squeezing my thigh was all about sex.

"What did you have in mind?" She wanted it? She was going to have to spell it out.

Head canted, she crooked a finger, beckoning me closer. Keeping one hand on the table, I braced the other against the back of her chair. While I trusted the guys to have my back, I dipped my chin to protect my throat even as I leaned toward her.

The barest of touches as she pushed my hair away from my ear. The woman just could not keep her hands to herself. No wonder she was one of their highest bidders and earned a seat at that table.

"We'll wager the money—it's only money. But I want you to add something to the Fortune pot for me. A private wager, just between us."

"I'm waiting."

For a moment, her eyes narrowed and her lips compressed. I was definitely playing with her, but not ceding even a little control. I wasn't agreeing to anything without details.

"If I win, you spend the night with me." Her lips brushed my ear, and that was no teasing mistake. It was more than just the whisper of her breath, she was definitely trying to come onto me. "All night, until dawn...and we can let whatever happens—happen."

Lifting the glass of Scotch, I swirled it then glanced at her. "And when I win?"

A throaty laughter escaped her. "I do admire your confidence."

"That doesn't answer my question," I countered, then knocked back the rest of the drink. The warmth hit my system, and helped to smooth down some of the bile burning its way up thanks to this game.

She stroked her lower lip with her tongue. The deliberate move offered a suggestion of eroticism, but I didn't even pretend to let it affect me.

"You intrigue me," she said finally. "Enough for me to agree to a great deal more than I would normally. So I will ask you this... what do you want?"

I met her stare and held it. There was the faintest dilation of her pupils. Her nostrils flared. Yes, she was very turned on and invested. Somehow, I suspected she would very much agree to whatever I asked.

With that in mind, I leaned forward and whispered next to her ear. "An invitation."

She blinked, straightening and taking a deeper breath. But it was too late to cover her more tremulous reactions. Settling back, I tapped one of my chips against the table as the dealer and I both awaited her decision.

"That's it?" She appeared to be turning it over, looking for the trap. One would assume if I needed an invitation that I didn't already have one.

Or, more likely, because I was here, I did have one. What I wanted was access to the upper echelons. Of course, the latter was far more accurate.

"That's it." I agreed. "One night."

Some of the tension left her. So just this evening. I could almost see the rationalization play out on her face. This wasn't permanent. No more permanent than her getting me to stand stud for a night.

Not like *that* was ever happening.

"Done." She put her chips in with a flick of her wrist. I didn't smile or crow. I just ante'd up and motioned to the dealer.

I divided my cards into the high hand and low hand. Yes, they would definitely do particularly after a little sleight of hand.

The dealer laid out his tables. A pair of aces and eights in his high hand. Five and seven in the low.

Marva smiled. A straight in her high hand. Three and two in her low. A push. It wouldn't win anything, but she didn't lose.

Yet.

They both eyed me and I flipped over my high hand. Royal flush. Pair of nines for the low hand.

I beat them both.

"Well," she said with a long exhale. "Well done, sir. Well done."

"Thank you."

The dealer passed the markers to me. The progressive win was mine as was the hand, and the fortune. A total of just under three million. But not under by much.

I passed the dealer a five hundred dollar chip as I rose. Then I tucked the markers into the inner pocket of my jacket. It would be nice to clear the money but that was not the primary mission.

A server came by our table and presented a card to Madame Duvall. "What excellent timing." She rose, ever graceful. "Would you be so kind as to join me?"

"I would be honored."

She took the arm I offered. "Both of yours with you?" She waved her invitation toward Alphabet and Lunchbox.

"Absolutely. I presume you're taking all three of yours."

A flash of irritation danced through her eyes, but she shuttered it away swiftly. I probably shouldn't enjoy tweaking her so much, but I hadn't missed any of her security. Better for her to understand that I was not an easy mark.

"Of course." She let out a soft laugh. "This is what happens when I let a pretty face turn my head." She made a show of fanning herself as we headed toward the elevators. Unsurprisingly, the Nocturne would be meeting on a different floor.

The man we'd already identified as Suitcase was already at the elevator bank with his own retinue. He surveyed our little group with cool eyes before he nodded to Madame Duvall—Peacock. When the doors opened, he and his went in and they rode alone.

Alphabet hit the button to summon the car back once the elevator was on the move. Another elevator opened. We boarded the empty one. Removing her hand from my arm, she pulled a key from beneath her dress. While it looked like an old fashioned skeleton key, she merely pressed it to the tap and a secondary keypad opened.

She chose an unmarked floor for our destination. The

elevator's motion told me we were going up. Not down. So wherever we were headed, it wasn't below where they were actually hosting the auction.

That made sense. They probably wanted to do their bidding with creature comforts in place. Based on the seconds passing, we climbed six levels. So we were back in the luxury hotel's private area most likely.

Above ground.

That would make exfiltration easier.

When the doors opened, it was to thickly carpeted hallway that muffled even the suggestion of steps. The walls were done in varying shades with expensive artwork serving as general decor.

The one with the young girls as ballet dancers offered a disturbing surrealism to this macabre drama we were unearthing. Madame Duvall gestured with one hand the directions we needed to follow.

At the end of the hallway was a pair of double doors standing wide with guards in place. Movement in the room showed Suitcase was there well ahead of us. Diamond passed the doors with a cigar in one hand and a whiskey in the other.

The room was quite full with bidders, the Nocturne, and their various parties. I just gave the room a bored sweep of my gaze before glancing at Madame Duvall.

"My table is there." She motioned to one near the back. "I don't like to be crowded."

"Would you care for a drink?" It would allow me to disconnect and put me on the back foot with her. The offer of service seemed to brighten her mood.

"Romanee-Conti Grand Cru 2019," she said, with a slow smile. "The bottle. Two glasses."

Taking her hand from my arm, I cupped her palm as I

lifted her knuckles to my mouth for a kiss. "Of course." I held her gaze for just a few seconds longer than necessary as lips brushed over her skin. When her pupils widened again, I smiled and then stepped away.

Her people converged on her as Lunchbox and Alphabet did with me.

"Pretty sure she would have skipped this entirely if she'd won that hand," Alphabet commented.

"I'm sure she'll manage her disappointment." I waited for my turn at the bar.

"I've got four more," Lunchbox said, barely moving his lips.

"Two more arriving now. That's eleven, there were five in here with Peacock stepping in." Alphabet had tucked his phone into his pocket, but he had a lapel camera in place and he was photographing the room and had been since we settled in the casino.

"Find your seats," a man near the front said. "We will begin in five minutes. Guest lists and menus have been delivered to your tables."

Guest lists?

I slid a look at Lunchbox. His expression didn't reflect the grimness in his eyes. Not one drop. But I felt every ounce of the darkness sliding through him.

Guest. List.

"Oh, well," Alphabet said. "That could be a problem."

I'd just ordered the wine bottle and turned to see what had snared Alphabet's attention and locked eyes with Reznik, Captain T. The last time I'd seen him had been five minutes before all hell broke loose.

"You," he snapped as recognition rippled over his face.

Yeah, why should it be any different today?

CHAPTER

EIGHT

ALPHABET

"You still limping, Kelly?" Reznik said in a dark snarl as his gaze traveled past Voodoo to lock on me. Yeah, he was *definitely* going to be a problem.

So many ways we could play this.

So. Many. Ways.

For one long moment, I let my gaze sweep the room. I'd identified and photographed eleven of the targets.

We were waiting on number twelve.

Riveting my attention back to Reznik, I straightened to let the camera on my lapel snap his image. Not that I could forget it. Then again, sometimes you had to see it to believe it particularly when it came to this former captain, dishonorably discharged and disgraced.

"Well, you're definitely still ugly."

His dark snarl turned into a smirk just in time for the bartender to set out the twenty thousand dollar bottle of wine. There was timing and then there was timing. Taking a page out of Gracie's book, I hurled the bottle and took enormous satisfaction out of it colliding with the man's face.

The nature of the premium glass used for expensive bottles added heft but it still didn't prevent it from smashing as it slammed into his nose. Pain exploded over his expression along with the wine and he staggered.

Voodoo flipped the table closest to us, sending glasses flying and catching one of Reznik's guards in the face with the wood. Knives flashed in hands and he sliced his way through the men stampeding toward us.

I yanked the bartender toward me, and relieved him of his gun. A single blow with the weapon knock him out. I aimed low and took out the knees of any security racing toward us. Lunchbox had Reznik up and slammed his head into another table repeatedly.

Marva Duvall—Peacock—and Diamond along with her, were already rushing out the doors as their guards split up. Half came toward us, while the others hustled them out. Voodoo cut through the crowd, lethal, fast, and more than a little reckless.

There was a reason he was the only one who could keep up with Bones in hand-to-hand. Another door opened on the far side of the room.

"Fuck," I swore as more of our targets sought to escape. I yanked a ball vial out of my inner pocket and threw it. It arced over the room and I shot it. It rained glass and a uv-traceable liquid down on those rushing out.

It was better than nothing, so I headed for the main doors as metal coverings slid down over the windows. Yeah, we weren't going to be locked in here. I took out the two guards in my way, then smashed open the control panel.

"Time to wrap this gentlemen," I said, taking control of the doors to hold them open. Voodoo and Lunchbox converged on me with Reznik and two other key bidders in hand. Once out, I let the doors shut and caught up to Suitcase and his men before their elevator could close.

The gun in close quarters would deafen the man, but I wanted his guards down. Then we had all four of them in the elevator. One elbow to Suitcase's jaw and he went down. The other three collapsed at our feet.

"Switch," Voodoo said to Lunchbox who was already pulling out the darts he'd readied for this. He stabbed each one of them swiftly, one in the neck and two others in their arms. He glared down at Reznik, then stabbed him behind the ear.

It was hardly going to kill them. As much as I wouldn't mind beating Reznik to death, I'd rather see him spend the rest of his life in a cage.

Soon, I promised myself.

We took the elevator down to the control room level and the guys were out, leaving our passengers in the wedged open space. I passed the gun to Voodoo and trusted them to have my back as I got the control room open.

The techs inside weren't top level security and they ran as soon as they saw us. "Server room," I told Lunchbox and he corralled them in there. I spat out the gum I'd been chewing and used it to secure a magnet under the console.

It was a fast job, but I ran wires to it from the three nearest consoles. The screens were all playing a saver. Smart techs had already logged us out.

That was fine. I slid a flash drive into a server rack at the back, leaving it while I wired another magnet to the front console. As soon as I was done, I yanked out the thumb drive before I smashed the button over the fire alarm and yanked it.

The sound was ear splitting, but it would ripple upwards to the hotel and down to the casino.

"Done," I called and we left the control room and headed past the open elevator and to the service stairs. We took them three at a time, and climbed back up to ground level, then up three more levels to guest floors.

I used one of the keycards I'd collected to open the door to the hotel room hall. We were stripping suit jackets and ties. With one hard tug, I pulled the bloodied shirt off over my head.

There was a laundry cart mid-way down the hall and we deposited the clothes in that one. Weapons went in a trash cart farther down. Voodoo grabbed a master key off one of the maid carts wedged into a door. The alarms hadn't gone off up here—

Then right on cue, they sounded. We were already in another room. I went through the closet. "Nope."

We gave it a beat then went to another. The search turned up fresh shirts. They would fit. No pants.

That was fine, I'd rather wear my own. There was a baseball cap in the suitcase and I tucked it over my head. There was also a jeweler's box and I popped it open. The sapphire bracelet inside was stunning.

Tempting.

But I left it. I could buy Gracie one of her own. I snagged the backpack though and shoved a couple of fresh shirts inside it and the shaving kit. At the rate we were going, we were going to need it.

I made sure there were no trackers in the bag then slung it over my shoulder. We needed to move. As long as the adrenaline was pumping, the aches in my right leg were tolerable.

Lunchbox opened the door and scanned the hall before he motioned to us. "Let's go."

The fire alarm would lock down the elevators, so we

headed for the fire stairs on the far end from where we'd come up and we fell in with the other guests descending to get out.

Going up was always easier on my leg than down, but I ignored the jolt shooting up from my knee with each step. Security was everywhere on the ground floor trying to keep the chaos in check.

We split apart, moving steadily but separately. I took a woman's elbow and her bag to "help" her. Lunchbox was ushering an older couple ahead of him, particularly the man who seemed to be struggling to catch his breath. Voodoo had his phone to his ear and a violent expression that kept everyone away from him.

It took us less than fifteen minutes from leaving that room to walk away from the hotel, the security, and the crowds as local authorities poured in. They were going to have a hell of a time explaining this mess.

Opening another piece of gum, I popped it into my mouth and limped my way toward the Monte Carlo station. They might be looking for three guys, they wouldn't be looking as closely at individuals. While Reznik had our IDs, he'd also been unconscious, with a broken nose, and probably nursing a concussion.

Couldn't happen to a better guy.

We had twelve out of twelve bidders photographed. At least half that many were already ID'd. I'd have the others as soon as I could sit down and decrypt the images I'd taken. The uv-reactive serum made them traceable, at least for a time.

If they were smart, which everything pointed to them being, they'd check themselves for something and the reactivity would keep them on lockdown for a couple of days.

Enough to buy us some time to regroup. By the time I

got to the station, Voodoo sat at a table eating a burger and looking like a Magnum PI reject in his Hawaiian shirt, dark sunglasses, and smirk. He must have grabbed it on the way in, cause there were no cafes in here.

Shaking my head, I snagged my own meal *after* I hit the ticket office. There were three trains departing over the next ninety minutes. I booked the one leaving after those three. Lingering would send any trackers in the wrong direction and on the wrong trains.

I found the Starbucks right outside, and got a coffee and a sandwich before I headed back in. The lack of my laptop had me itchy. Still, we'd get it back after we got to Marseille and picked up our gear from that station.

Three hours later, I settled into my seat on the train and stretched my leg out. It was definitely aching like a bitch now. Lunchbox turned up and he dropped into a seat on the other side of the aisle. Voodoo wasn't far behind. The train wasn't loaded. At least this car wasn't. That was nice.

None of us relaxed, though. When we crossed from Monaco back into France, some of the tension knotting my back eased. But not all of it.

I kept turning the idea of the bracelet over in my head. I really liked it. In Marseille, we left the train and the limp damn near dropped me. My knee wanted nothing to do with me.

"Here," Lunchbox said, bracing me. "Lean on me."

"Fuck," I swore under my breath. As much as I didn't want to need the help, if I didn't take it, I'd be crawling after them and that wouldn't do anyone any good. Voodoo slanted a look at us, then nodded.

"I'll get the car. Meet at the south exit."

I waved him off. Lunchbox and I made our way to the train lockers. Once there, I sat my pitiful ass down and rubbed at the rock hard cramps twisting my thigh. Sweat beaded along my back and my shirt clung uncomfortably to me.

"You're hurting," Lunchbox said after he pulled out their duffels then pulled mine from another locker along with my laptop. Our overall luggage was a wash, but we had everything that was necessary.

"Yep." Wasn't even going to lie about it. "I'll survive."

He shot me a look and I shrugged.

"I will," I reminded him. "We got the job done. Identified bidders. Marked a huge spot on their little trafficking super highway. And I broke Reznik's nose while you got to break the rest of his head. As ops go, this was a good one."

A smile ghosted over his mouth. "Did not see him coming."

"He didn't see us coming either. But I'm not gonna be the one who tells Bones." At my comment, Lunchbox grunted.

"We'll make Voodoo handle it."

"Seems fair," I agreed. "That everything?" Because I needed to get up again.

"You got it?" He watched me warily and I nodded.

"I can handle it, let's just get the hell out of here. We still need to track down Bones, Gracie, and Goblin." It seemed like it had been days since we last saw them.

To be fair, it had been. At least three, if I hadn't lost count. Probably closer to four or five. Definitely five by the time we caught up. We'd had an extraction plan and designated meetups.

We just needed to catch them now.

Voodoo waited, SUV running when we got there. Lunchbox waved me into the back and I took it, I wanted to stretch my leg out. After everything was loaded and Lunchbox was in the passenger seat, we pulled out.

"We were just supposed to get the info," Voodoo said, almost conversationally. "Mission briefing had to change while in op."

"We did get the info," Lunchbox reminded him. "We also got to beat the shit out of a few assholes. As ops go, that worked."

With a snort, Voodoo shook his head then he glanced back at me. "You good?"

"Not even on my best days," I said, closing my eyes. "But I'll live. I want a couple of hours. Then wake me so I can start decrypting the data."

"You got it?" Lunchbox jerked to look over his shoulder at me.

I held up the flash drive. "Grabbed it on the way out. Once I decrypt it, we'll know what they know."

Buyers. Sellers. The people on the menu.

Everything.

I yawned. Everything, I hoped. Better to amend that and keep my aspirations low.

For now.

"Two hours," I repeated, folding my arms and tucking my chin down. Two hours, then I'd get back to work.

CHAPTER

NINE

GRACE

Our first morning in the hotel dawned gray, wet, and early. Goblin nuzzled at me, pawing the side of the bed. Everything hurt as I sat up and blinked slowly. When had I gone to bed? I hadn't even remembered going to sleep.

Another soft plea from the puppy had me rubbing a hand over my face. "I'm coming," I murmured. "Sorry." After my shower, I'd put on clean clothes, t-shirt and leggings and I was still in them.

That was something. The half-light from the windows seemed muddy. Probably street lamps still. There was no clock in the bedroom. The light in the bathroom's water closet was on. The dim illumination was more than enough to make my way from the bed, to the sitting room.

It seemed even darker in the sitting room, when I nailed my little toe on the corner of *something*, I swore. "Mother. Fuck. Ing. Puss. Buckets. Shit. Damn."

Each word fired off like a bullet as I tried to not scream. Holy shit that hurt. Bones rolled off the sofa and to his feet,

67

a gun in one hand and a flashlight in the other. I barely had time to register him before the halo of light blinded me.

He swung the light from me to the door, then back. Still dazzled, I blinked as he lowered the weapon. It was hard to see anything now with a big white blur seared into the center of my eyesight.

Abruptly, the light dipped. "What happened?" The soft question in Bones' gruff tone soothed more than it should have.

"I kicked the chair." Sad fact, but true.

"Probably shouldn't do that." The deadpan response had me glaring at him, mostly so I wouldn't laugh.

"Really? Captain Boy, that's what you have for me?"

"I could have said maybe curse quieter next time unless you need me to shoot the chair. If the chair needs shooting, I'll do it." The offer startled me nearly as much as it entertained.

Maybe because he made it as he sounded serious about it, I shook my head. "Not the chair's fault."

"Right." The light was on my foot now. "No blood."

Goblin bumped against my leg, a not so subtle reminder as to what had gotten me up in the first place. "Good, I just need to get my shoes and his harness. Goblin wants to go out."

"I'll take him," Bones said, and I blinked over at him. He was in boxers and very little else.

"You're not dressed," I told him, smothering a yawn. "I'll take him down the stairs the way we did last night." No elevators, because that meant the lobby. The stairs opened next to external doors away from the reception desk.

The location was about fire safety, but it also offered us privacy. Bones didn't want anyone tracking us coming or going while we were here. A part of me was certain the only reason he'd chosen a hotel was me. They offered room service that could be delivered to the door and we never had to open it to them.

"You shouldn't go out by yourself," he said, the rustle of him pulling on his jeans followed me as I tracked down my shoes. Once I slipped them on, I lifted Goblin's harness. He let me slide it on him without any argument.

I smothered another yawn, as I glanced back to find Bones dressed and ready before I finished snapping Goblin's leash on. "Okay. Then come with. Can you grab me that hoodie?"

He brought it over and held it up so I could slide one arm, then the other in. I meant to hand him the leash so I could zip it up, but he did it. Then slid the hood up over my hair.

"Cute," he said and I blinked.

Wait... had he just said cute?

But he didn't give me time to ask before he opened the door and stepped out ahead of us. I struggled with another yawn, but followed him down the steps. It was definitely looking like a dreary day by the time we got downstairs.

Damp. Chilly. It seemed so utterly at odds with the past few days on the Riviera. We walked in a comfortable silence along the sleepy streets. There was a park not far from the hotel where we could let Goblin do his business.

One perk to Bones coming, he totally took care of cleaning up the poop. We were circling the far side of the park when the scents of fresh baked bread wafted out like on some cartoon cloud to wrap alluringly around me and tug.

My stomach registered its interest with a very noisy gurgle. Yeasty goodness and sugar twinned with the buttery notes to just make me hungrier. Not just bread, but pastries.

"We can get some pastries and coffee before we head back," Bones offered, already detouring away from the route that took us back to the hotel. In no time at all we arrived at the *boulangerie*. "What do you want?"

When he opened the door, the sweet and savory rushed out to surround us. "Just coffee," I said as Goblin and I stepped in. There were no other customers present, and someone called out from the back to wait just one moment.

Bones frowned at me. "You need to eat."

"This is just a lot of carbs and sugar and we're—" I broke off as a woman bustled out. Her cheeks were flushed and her hair a little frizzy. She was clearly in the middle of baking, but she had a warm, wide encompassing smile that was irresistible.

At her welcome, I greeted her with a good morning. Bones was still staring at me then he said, "Let's do two loaves of the bread, then we'll do two of each of these..."

I ordered the bread but frowned at the different pastries he was discussing. That was almost too much for one person and too much sugar altogether. When I didn't translate, he shook his head.

"*Deux de ceux-là, s'il vous plaît.*" He tapped against the case and held up two fingers as he gestured to each item.

He spoke French?

The corner of his mouth curved upward when he spared me another look as the shop mistress began to load up bags. "*Je voudrais deux grands cafés, s'il vous plaît — un clair et sucré, l'autre noir. Et s'il y a quelque chose pour le chien, je prends aussi.*"

I swore my mouth fell open as I continued to stare at him. If he spoke it, why had he made me translate? The woman beamed at him and she had the pastries and breads boxed up, then added the coffees before she slipped into the back, then returned with another box that she told us was for Goblin.

After Bones counted out the cash for the purchases, he picked it up, coffee cups and all and nodded to the door. A part of me wanted to be irritated, but I was too busy being flummoxed by his charming tone and smile.

Once we were back on the street, he passed me the coffee he'd ordered for me. Sweet and light. It was— perfect. Not a flat white, but definitely worth the walk and the wait. "Thank you," I murmured.

"You're welcome," he said. "As for whether the food is too sweet or has too many carbs, you need to eat when food is available."

The brisk tone demanded I pay attention and when I glared at him, he just met my gaze blandly.

"You need to eat, Grace. You starve yourself far too often."

"I don't," I protested.

"You do," he countered without hesitation nor did he raise his voice. "A lot of models do. I used to think it was a stereotype and you shouldn't judge others based on an idea."

"So why are you doing it?" Great, now I was a *stereotype*. Oddly, that stung. Especially since I thought we'd been getting along.

"Because I'm judging based on my observations of your behavior. You turn down meals more often than you eat them. When you do eat, you choose very small portions. You've protested sugar and carbohydrates. You don't want to risk gaining any weight even if you are far too spare as it is."

Far too...

I snapped my mouth shut on my own retort. Too spare. So now, I was too skinny. No, I couldn't keep quiet on this... "The camera," I began.

"Adds five pounds," he finished for me. "I understand. It's likely something you've heard from photographers, your managers, everyone. Here's something they don't tell you—starving yourself might be good for the camera, but it's absolute shit for your health. You need your strength. One way to keep that up is to eat. You need energy, something we collect through eating and sleeping. Right now, you're limited on both."

He wasn't wrong and didn't that just grate even worse. I took another sip of coffee as we walked through the misting rain toward the hotel. As we let ourselves in that side door, then made our way up the stairs, he continued to say nothing.

Though the torture of inhaling the luscious treats all the way to our floor and suite made my stomach gurgle almost rudely. No amount of coffee sipping managed to shut it up. At all.

In the suite, he set the food down, then we stripped out of the jackets and hoodies. Finally, he grabbed a towel to wipe down Goblin before he removed his leash but left him in his harness. Once all of that was done, he stepped right into my path.

"Grace..."

There was just something in the way he said my name that had me freezing before he touched a finger to my chin, nudging it upwards until our gazes met.

"You have very little you have been able to control over the past few weeks. Even less these last few days. I may not agree with your reasoning, but I understand why you want to maintain here. You want to eventually go back to your work, to what you know."

I swallowed. Because that was extremely true. I did want to go back to my life. "I get that it might not happen." It was the first time I admitted it to myself.

"Maybe. Maybe not." He shrugged, letting the barely there contact of his fingers to my face fall away. "I can't answer that. What I can tell you is that starving yourself seems to be more than a habit for you and that concerns me."

I glanced down at my coffee. "It's not starving myself, it's just..." A sigh escaped me. "I don't have an eating disorder."

"Are you sure?" The blunt question jerked my head back up. "No judgment here."

"Are *you* sure about *that*?" Because it sounded like judgment to me.

That rare, faint smile returned. "I'm certain that you need to eat. That each person needs a standard number of calories per day to survive. The more you undercut those, the more likely it is you will lose energy, and muscle mass. It can also affect your internal organs and more. If you continue to do so, even if you are aware of how it affects your health because you're compelled by some drive to do so—what would you call it?"

Between the silence ballooned, filled with all the things he wasn't saying and I wasn't arguing. I didn't have an eating disorder. I didn't.

Except...

"If I eat something will you let this topic go?" Wow that came out petulant. This time, I raised a hand before he could say anything. Eyes closed, I clamped down on the irritation at being called out because I could see *why* he was doing it.

Goddammit, he was even being *nice* about it.

"Sorry," I said, as I opened my eyes and met his gaze. "I didn't mean to snap."

"I can handle you," he murmured, but went quiet when I glared again.

"Maybe you can. The point is—you are making a good argument for me to eat, so, I'll eat something because I am hungry. That doesn't mean I'm going to stuff myself with sugar."

"I wouldn't presume," he said, the corners of his mouth curving upward again.

"Oh yes, you would," I said, wrinkling my nose.

"Not as long as you do eat." He motioned to the boxes. "Help yourself. Pretty sure a couple of those were stuffed breakfast sandwiches. So if you don't want to go for the sweet, go for the savory."

With that, he toed off his shoes then picked up the box she'd packed for Goblin. The smell coming off those was downright divine. Meat pies.

Goblin was already sitting up and looking eager. Bones took the time to feed Goblin and let me pick out what I wanted. I did get a breakfast sandwich, and I chose a raspberry tart looking pastry with cream cheese. It was small, terribly sweet, but small.

I told myself I'd only eat it *after* the breakfast sandwich if I was still hungry. Once I moved over to a chair and sat to eat, Bones helped himself. He carried almost a full box over and tucked right into it.

"How long are we going to stay here?"

"At least another day," he told me, after wiping his mouth. "We're holding here to give them time to catch up."

My head snapped up. "Really?"

He nodded. "If we have no word by tomorrow, we move again."

My heart sank.

"There's a plan, Grace," he said almost gently. "They know where I'm going and where I'd take you."

That... helped. "Why can't we call them?"

"Because we don't know their status. If they aren't secure and I call, it could endanger them."

Oh.

I took another bite of the sandwich. It definitely helped to fill my growling stomach. "You think they're all right then?"

Because I needed that hope.

"I think they'll get the job done, then we'll rendezvous."

While the answer evaded some, it said we *would* see them again, not *if*.

Once I finished the sandwich, I washed it down with the last of my coffee. While the sandwich had been good, it was the coffee that really tasted like more, even if we didn't have the option to make more here.

"Bones?"

He flicked his gaze up and it wasn't hard to read his surprise. If he could use my name then I'd use his. "Grace?"

"Thank you."

Not asking me for what, he just said, "You're welcome," and oddly, that really was enough right now.

TEN

GRACE

Right on schedule, we left the hotel the next morning without going by the desk. Checking out remotely let us slip away unnoticed. The night before we'd watched three different news programs. The aborted bank robbery in Lyon turned up on all of them. The bank video that had been made available didn't really get a good look at either of us.

I hoped that was a good sign, but Bones had only shrugged. "If they have cleaner video with a clear way to ID us, they'll use it first *then* share with the rest of the world."

When I made a face, he'd merely chuckled.

"Whatever they have," he'd continued. "We'll handle it."

He punched up the confidence in the last three words so much that I just nodded. "Okay."

"Okay?" Surprise danced beneath those two syllables.

I spared him a look as I pulled on my hoodie. "Would you rather I argue?"

He didn't answer immediately. Then, later after he

collected our bags and we were out of the hotel and heading for the parking structure, he said, "Maybe."

The single word left me stumped for a response. A suggestion of a smirk touched his face before he put our bags away and opened up the back for Goblin to climb in.

It was early and rather than stop at the *boulangerie* he put miles between us and Lyon before choosing a small place an hour outside of the city. "You walk Goblin, I'll get us all some food and coffee."

"That sounds like a plan—"

He caught my arm before I could climb out of the car. Then beckoned me to face him with a curl of his fingers. When he slipped his hand inside my hoodie, I blinked. The weight of a weapon slid into an inner pocket.

"Taser," he reminded me. "Your gun is still secure, in a case beneath the seat. This isn't quite as illegal here."

I put a hand over the familiarity of it. "Thank you."

"Of course." Then he leaned back and slanted a glance toward the green area. "Stay in sight."

"Yes, sir," I said with a salute that I only meant partially in jest. The fact it made his eyes narrow was just a perk. I slid out of the car and let Goblin out. Poor guy was more than ready to go for a walk.

I needed to stretch my legs as well. We made our way through the drizzling rain. Despite the lack of sunshine, it was a lovely morning. A mist rolled along the green and around the trees. It made me think of some kind of fanciful story with magic and wonders rather than something dark and ominous.

Maybe it was the hints of light piercing the drizzle and giving a suggestive glow to the mist itself. Goblin was efficient with his business, and clearly, he'd waited long enough. But even after I'd cleaned up behind him and disposed of the poop bag in the garbage, we didn't head straight back to the car.

It was just nice to walk and think. The weather seemed like a barrier to the rest of the world and for these few minutes we didn't have to worry about anything. Bones' reminders to let Goblin alert me to any potential threats whispered in the back of my mind.

There was a comfort in being able to trust his instincts, Goblin's, Voodoo's, Alphabet's, Lunchbox's—and Bones' too. As if summoned by the thought, he reappeared from inside the shop with two large boxes, three bags, and two huge cups of coffee.

Gawking, just a little, at the sheer volume of food he purchased, I shook my head. I would still keep any complaints to myself. I'd eaten both lunch and dinner the previous day. Smaller portions than either him or Goblin— the pair could *eat*, but I had eaten.

It seemed to satisfy him and he kept any other potential criticisms to himself. Thankfully, he also helped to make sure I had options that weren't overly sweet or loaded with carbs.

He joined me with the cups of coffee. "Fifteen more and we need to move." With that word, he passed me a cup and I savored the sweetness. It was nearly as good as the one we'd purchased at the *boulangerie* in Lyon.

"We can go now," I offered. "If it's important." The hood protected my hair for the most part, but both Goblin and I were more than a little damp. "It was just nice to take a walk."

"Agreed. We can take fifteen more minutes." He paused and glanced at his watch. "Make that thirteen and a half minutes."

The dry delivery pulled a snorting laugh from me. Goblin

seemed to be enjoying the walk as much as I was, but Bones seemed far more vigilant. Maybe I hadn't noticed it before, but he seemed to constantly survey the area around us.

To be fair, we hadn't spent a lot of time in public spaces, just the two of us. Our interactions usually took place in private or in lockdown—or when he hauled me up to my room and locked me in there.

Jerk.

Oddly, the memory sparked a laugh in me and while Bones shot me a curious look, he didn't ask. Yeah, I wasn't going to tell either. That I could look back on it at all fondly was a boon to me.

He didn't get to share.

Eventually though, we were back in the car. Goblin ate his bacon, eggs, and croissants greedily. "He's going to be irritated by kibble if we ever get back to feeding him that."

"He'll be fine," Bones said, getting us back on the road. "Foraging is a fact of life, as is eating a regular diet."

I snorted and he shook his head.

"That wasn't a dig."

"I believe you," I said, saluting him with my coffee cup. "But it's still funny to think of croissants and bacon as 'foraging' versus kibble as a 'regular' diet."

He was silent for a beat then grunted. "I concede the point." A flash of smile warmed his whole expression, the sun coming out from behind dark clouds. But I barely got a chance to even register it before it vanished again.

The drive took a good portion of the day. He didn't stay on the motorways entirely. France had a significant number of toll roads. We got off frequently and took country roads and routes.

It was how we ended up eating lunch in a field while

Goblin played and we basically had a picnic. Also how we stopped at a quaint pub in an incredibly small town for coffee and chocolate tarts for *quatre-heures.*

Frankly, the chocolate was divine and it boosted my mood so I didn't protest it one iota. The lengthy detours had to be keeping people from tracking us, or maybe to kill time. Since Bones didn't offer any other explanations, I didn't ask.

Three hours later, he pulled us into a hotel just outside of Villefranche-de-Rouergue, if I was reading the signs right. We'd basically taken the most circuitous route ever to turn back south again.

This time, Bones checked us in and I stayed in the car with Goblin until he had the keys. He also wanted to check the room out. It was a sleepy area, with little foot traffic and not a lot of nightlife. I wanted to go and explore, but that wasn't really an option at the moment.

Thankfully, we got to stretch our legs before he ushered Goblin and I upstairs. "I'm going to get us food and charge the car," he told me. "Keep the room locked, tell Goblin to guard if you need to shower."

That was fair, we weren't really in a suite this time. Just a small hotel room with a single bed and a couple of chairs. Well, one rather uncomfortable armchair and another desk chair.

"Gun," he said, touching the weapon he'd unpacked once we were in the room. "It's loaded. Safety here. Flick it off, point, shoot."

Yeah...

My stomach rolled at that one.

"Taser here." He patted that and something far more like relief crept through me. "And your phone. Any issues at all, call me. Even if you can't say anything, just call and leave the phone line open."

An icy kind of sweat seemed to coat me. "How long are you going to be gone?"

"No more than an hour. That's my plan. Anything in particular you'd like for supper?"

"Honestly?" At the question, he just gave me a bland look. Of course, he meant honestly. "I'd kill for spaghetti."

Pasta. So. Many. Carbs.

Yes, I wanted all of them right now. I ducked my head as I ran fingers through my hair. It felt kind of grimy. Honestly, all of me did. A shower was a good idea.

"Grace," he said, touching two fingers to my chin again and I lifted my gaze before he even nudged. "You're going to be fine and safe. Goblin will look after you and I'll be back."

He seemed to search my face, and I blew out a breath. He was waiting for me to say it. "I'll be fine," I told him, summoning up a smile even if I didn't feel it. "And I think a shower sounds awesome." Fake the cheer until you make it, I reminded myself. "I'll even try to leave you some hot water."

Warmth touched those chilly eyes and he nodded. Then he slipped out of the door like the ghost he often seemed to be. I glanced at Goblin who just stared up at me and thumped his tail once.

"I'm going to shower," I told him. "Guard?"

It came out more of a question than a command and he cocked his head, but when I pointed at the door and repeated the word with a little more emphasis this time, he thumped his tail twice and rose.

When he settled this time, he lay right across the door.

Okay, that worked.

At forty-five minutes, I was spreading the hotel's lotion

over my legs when Bones called through the door. I didn't quite hear the words, but then I recognized the voice.

So did Goblin, cause he rose a split-second before the door opened. It was dark outside the windows, but I'd drawn the curtains and I only had a low lamp on. The smell of the spaghetti and red sauce hit with the force of a freight train.

"Oh..." I rose as he set the bags and a bottle of wine down on the desk. Before I could finish the thought though, his phone made a vibrating noise. Excitement spun through me as he pulled it out and answered it.

"Status." One word, not even a hello, but a part of me didn't care as I leaned forward, straining for the response.

"Twelve bidders." Voodoo's voice was a revelation. Bones had put him on speaker.

Tears burned in my eyes as all the tension drained out of me. He was okay. He was okay and he was calling. Bones had said there was a plan but hearing him just made all of it real.

"Photographed. Marked. Most in the wind, but we're working on IDs. Picked up fresh intel, including a list. Grace's name was on it." The last five words came out hard and fresh tension coiled in my stomach.

"They're still looking." Bones glanced at me. It wasn't a question. He also didn't take Voodoo off speaker either.

"We improvised," Lunchbox volunteered and I scraped my teeth over my lower lip. That was two of them. "Took a little longer than anticipated but burned them in that location. Almost literally, but we ran into a familiar face."

"Casualties?" Bones set the phone down as he reached for a corkscrew and began to open the wine.

"None on our side. Definitely more than a few broken bones and faces on theirs."

Alphabet!

Goblin's tail began to wag happily and when I patted the bed next to me, he leapt up. We were both excited to hear them.

"The list told us something else," Alphabet continued. "Amorette's name isn't on it."

Bones pulled the cork out and it gave a distinctive pop as he set the wine to breathe.

"Reznik is also involved in this organization," Voodoo said. "He was one of the high end bidders."

Bones scowled. "He got away?"

"Not without considerable pain." Lunchbox seemed pleased. "We'll deal with him."

Silence fell. I didn't know who Reznik was, but his presence seemed to piss all of them off.

"Gracie..." Alphabet said.

"I'm here," I answered.

"Amorette isn't in any of their data that I've sifted so far. The good news is that means they don't have her." The bad news he didn't have to say was that meant we still didn't know where she was.

"Are you guys okay?" The fact they said no casualties on our side was good.

"We're fine, Firecracker," Voodoo said. "Barely even a scratch."

"Good work," Bones stepped back into the conversation. "If you're clean, take the scenic route. Go dark for forty-eight, make sure everything cools off. We'll meet at Perrault in the wood."

"Copy," Voodoo said, then the call ended.

They were okay. They were okay and they'd found out that Amorette wasn't being held by the people here. I was going to hold onto that good news with both hands.

Bones poured two glasses of the wine and brought one over to me.

"What's Perrault in the wood?"

"Weapons. Supplies. Safe house."

"Does it have to be forty-eight hours?" That was another two days of us just wandering around? "Not complaining..." When he raised his eyebrows, I made a face. "Okay, I'm not complaining much. It was just—really good to hear they were okay."

"Yes, it does." He touched his wine glass to mine with a light clink. "Come eat your spaghetti and you can ask the rest of the questions I can see burning in your eyes."

I sipped some of the wine, it was excellent. "Does that mean you're going to answer all my questions?"

There was no mistaking his smile when he glanced over his shoulder at me. "No."

Figured.

CHAPTER

ELEVEN

GRACE

ood coupled with relief from hearing from the guys relaxed me to almost boneless. That was my only excuse for not fully registering our surroundings until weariness had me yawning.

"You should get some sleep," Bones said. "I'll take Goblin out for a last walk."

"I'll go with," I volunteered, already standing up and reaching for leggings to drag on. I hadn't bothered with a bra after the shower and didn't intend to now. Shrugging into a hoodie, I finger combed my hair. It was still damp, but I wanted to be able to pull the hood up anyway.

Rather than argue with me, Bones just pulled on his own jacket and clipped the leash onto Goblin. Then they both waited patiently for me to stuff my feet into my shoes.

I forgot my taser, briefly, but Bones just gestured to it. Right. I stuffed it in the inner pocket of the hoodie. It created a slouchy, saggy look, but who really cared? Smothering a yawn, I shuffled out with the pair and down the stairs.

At least I'm getting a lot of steps in.

87

I snorted a laugh at the thought. Both of my companions just shared a mild look at me but I waved them off. Outside, the night had turned cooler and the drizzle had all but stopped.

Lights gleamed off the damp streets and puddles decorated the walk. It added a little magical flourish to what was a rather quaint location. "So many places here and in Germany look like they belong in a fairytale," I said before covering my yawn with my hand. "Sorry."

"You're tired," Bones said simply, seemingly accepting the apology without any other comment. I didn't argue with his assessment either.

While I was tired, yes, I didn't want to stay in the room by myself. Neither of us said much as we walked. There was a park area not that far. The quiet blanketing the area was occasionally disturbed by the sound of a car passing in the distance. Somewhere else music spilled out into the night air. Dogs barked and laughter trickled along the breeze.

It was—nice.

Just nice.

I zoned as we walked, just—existed. In the park, it occurred to me I needed to be paying more attention. So I tried to shake myself back into wakefulness. It wasn't going well. Bones seemed ever vigilant though and maybe that was why I didn't have to worry.

He wasn't going to miss anything.

Once we were back at the hotel, I stripped the shoes, taser, hoodie, and leggings with more efficiency than I'd put them on. In the bathroom, I emptied my bladder, then washed my hands, face, and brushed my teeth on autopilot.

The hotel lotion smelled way too much like gardenias. I needed to moisturize but the scent just made my nose wrinkle. One night wouldn't kill me. Shuffling back out, I said, "Bathroom is free."

"Thanks."

I crawled into the bed and dragged the blankets over me. It was a little softer than I liked but it could have been a marshmallow or a brick, I didn't care. I just wanted to sleep. Sinking fast, I burrowed into the pillow.

A gentle hand against my back nudged me. "Shift over, darling." The soft voice practically crooned the words. I didn't want to wake up, much less move. The lightest sound of laughter touched his voice. "Alright, you sleep. I'll take care of it."

The warmth of the blankets went away, but before I could protest I glided over onto cooler sheets. That was even worse. I wanted to retreat back to the warmth.

"Shh, Grace." The hum of sound wrapped around me as neatly as the blankets did and then there was warmth all along my back.

Oh, that was better. Much better.

Another huff of laughter. "So," he murmured. "You're a cuddler. Good to know."

Those words meant something, but what little awareness I'd reclaimed evaporated as I sank like a stone.

"C'mon," he continued. "Get up here." Weight hit the edge of the bed, then shifted until something heavier settled against my legs. The tuck of a head to my calf.

Oh, that was nice.

Then I was out.

The next time I surfaced, it was dark and the warmth wrapped all around me, securing me like I was wrapped up in a blanket burrito. Too early if it was this dark and I closed my eyes again.

Breath whispered against my throat and my eyes flickered open.

Breath?

"Shh," the soft voice had deepened into a mellow rumble. A hand on my hip massaged a slow circle against the fabric of my t-shirt. "You're safe. Sleep."

The casual comfort eased some of the disturbance of realizing Bones was in bed with me. A yawn cracked my jaw and I rubbed my cheek against the pillow. The arms around me tightened and the shifting weight near my legs reminded me of Goblin.

Trust Goblin's instincts. That little voice wedged right through the sleepy cloud and I nestled into the warmth again. Warm.

Safe.

Sleepy.

The next time I snapped my eyes open, it was still dark but the cozy comfort had gone away and taken all the heat with it. My heart raced and I fisted my hand against the blanket. Worried, I reached behind me and felt only empty space. The sheets were still warm, so he hadn't been out of bed long.

Where...?

I sat up abruptly and glanced at the bathroom as the toilet flushed, then the water ran. Disquiet tangled around me. The flash of the light from the interior blinded me in the split second between Bones opening the door and him flipping the switch off.

"Hey..." The gruff, sleep-roughened voice soothed the jangle of nerves that were all rattling like we were being visited by Marley's ghost or something. "Didn't mean to wake you up."

"You didn't." That came out a squeak. Grimacing, I coughed a little to clear my throat. "I just woke up." Better.

"Need the bathroom?" The question poked at me, jarring me out of me staring into the darkness. Did I need the...

"No," I said. "Sorry." Then I scooted some, though Goblin gave a little groan and shifted his own weight so I could move over farther to let Bones get back in the bed.

His weight depressed the bed and then he was under the blankets. The furnace of heat suddenly present chased away the chill that invaded in his absence. With one hand, he groped around until he found me and then he tugged me back toward him.

The fact he'd rolled until my back was snugged to his chest again and he caged me in his arms was kind of embarrassing. Okay, the act wasn't what got me—it was the little sigh I let out and the fact the knotted tension in my shoulders and back gave way.

"Go back to sleep," he ordered, though his voice lacked any of the punch he usually gave to snap commands. "It's still early."

And we had what? Forty-eight hours? Even as I let my eyes close, my mind began to race. Less now. He said forty-eight hours from when we spoke to them.

They still had to get to wherever the rendezvous point was and until then, we had to lay low or keep moving...

Bones sighed. "You're safe," he murmured, as if needing to remind me.

"I know," I said and I did know. That wasn't what had my mind starting to race. It was all the other...

"Tell me." Two words. A simple prompt. A suggestion. I could ignore it, but even the gentle prompt had a fresh set of images and memories surging through my mind.

The weight of a hand clamping over my mouth.

The drag of a bigger body jerking me off my feet.

The loom of the dark eyed man ordering me to ride him.

The men invading my apartment.

The loft in the barn, the men climbing the ladder.

The man in the barn, his hand clamped around my throat—

"Grace," he said my name with his lips pressed against my ear. "Stay here."

"What?" Oh, my teeth chattered and made that one syllable jitter and jump.

"You're here," he said, then bit my ear as if to prove it to me. That sting of pain seemed to tear away some of the haze. "Feel that?"

As much as I didn't want to stutter, I pushed out the answer, "Yes."

He bit my ear again, this time the sting became a throb and I dragged in a deeper breath. Oh, I'd been panting.

"Better," he said. "Nope, keep breathing. Just because I give you a compliment doesn't mean you get to stop." I wasn't stopping? "There you go. Deep breaths."

He shifted a hand to rub against my stomach, stroking over my abdomen through the fabric muted the contact. Each slow circuit of his palm moved in time to my breathing.

Tingles prickled over my skin. It was like ice slicked up my spine and heat flushed up against it. I wasn't sure whether to try and get closer or push the blankets off. Restlessness burned in my muscles.

"Grace." This time my name landed like a verbal smack, knocking me back out of the tempest my wild thoughts seemed to be lost in. "Stay here."

"I'm not going anywhere." Oh that came out a miserable complaint. "What do you want me to do?"

"I want you to go back to sleep and be able to sleep." he all but growled the words and a fragment of hysterical laughter broke off in me. Right. There was Bones. "What do you need?"

The tone said I'd better answer or else. Honestly—I needed it. "Help me think about something else."

"Like?" Fired like a bullet, no patience softened the blow.

"Anything..." I groaned, because the shaking was now everywhere. My hands trembled. My heart seemed to stutter. Everything quavered. I made my eyes stay open because I didn't want to see any of those men if I closed them... "Please."

I'd beg if I had to.

His grip shifted abruptly. The hand on my belly glided down to my panties even as he cupped my breast with his left hand. My nipples strained and I made the most pathetic sound as he slid his fingers beneath the fabric.

"If you want this to stop... tell me to stop." Another damn order. The man could do nothing but tell me what to do.

Thank fuck.

Right now, I needed to be told.

"Okay," I whispered, almost afraid to say anything because the last thing I wanted him to do was stop. He slid two fingers down to glide right over the seam of my cunt.

I swore my inner muscles clenched so hard, that I was torn between grinding against him with my ass or just riding his hand. He kneaded my breast, but only until he encountered the peaked point of my nipple.

Then he pulled his hand from my panties and let go of my breast.

"Wait—" The protest burst out of me.

"Shh," he said. "You didn't say stop."

But he fisted my shirt collar in each hand and then it just ripped open all the way down and fresh shivers raced over my skin.

The rough calluses of his palms glided over both of my breasts now and he didn't tease or toy, he just tormented both nipples with tugs, pinches, and pulls. When I tried to roll my hips, he sank his teeth down on my throat. It wasn't a bite so much as a hold. The promise of pain and a sting to ground me in reality.

"Please." The shudders cascading through me now had nothing to do with fear or loathing.

Thankfully, he dropped his right hand back under my panties and he went straight for my clit. The roughness of his thick fingers were barely blunted by my own wetness. The pressure was absolute, his strokes demanding my absolute acquiescence and I just let it go as I bucked upward to ride those fingers.

When he eased the pressure just shy of my first orgasm, I wanted to scream. Then the bastard chuckled. The pinch of fresh pain on my nipple as he twisted it almost too much had me groaning for real.

The slip of his hand cupping me as those thick fingers found my entrance and he pushed inward. I clenched around them, so damn needy for the touch that one graze from the heel of his palm damn near set me off.

He adjusted his hand, stroking my breast and then across to the other as he began to thrust and then he added a slow, torturous circular stroke from his hand to my clit.

I tilted my head back, pressing it against his shoulder as he increased that delicious pressure. The tension threading me began to coil tighter and tighter.

"That's it, Grace," he said, his rough voice its very own caress. "Give it all to me. Every fucking drop. You're going to come. Right now…"

He coupled action with order and the first orgasm burst over me. I clenched my teeth together to keep from making a sound, but he abandoned my breast to wrap his hand around my throat. At some point, he'd stopped biting.

My eyes were open but I strained to see him in the dark. He stroked his thumb along my pulse even as it rabbited while I shuddered from the release. He still had two fingers inside of me and his palm rested against my clit. Every little jerk from me seemed to add electricity to the contact.

"You're going to come again." Why did that sound like a threat *and* a promise? "This time, you're going to let me hear you."

He flexed his hand, the warmth of it held me captive but without any sense of terror. I'd much rather feel his hand than anyone else's.

Suddenly, his mouth was right at my cheek, then the corner of my mouth. "You think of nothing else right now, just this—me touching you, and you soaking my hand as you come. I want to hear you Grace."

Even if I couldn't see him, I could feel him and he wasn't kidding. He teased, stroked, and rubbed my clit until I was shaking and he didn't let me come until the first cry burst from my throat.

Then he made me come again.

And again.

The light edged toward gray on the windows when he

finally let me float. Not once had I gotten to do more than hold onto his forearm as he controlled everything—controlled me.

That's how I finally slept again, wrapped up in Bones.

CHAPTER

TWELVE

GRACE

With just four hours to go on the clock, Bones drove us up toward a stucco and clay house with shuttered windows painted a dull blue. It perched at the edge of the Rhône, south of Arles. While it seemed isolated, it was close enough to the city to keep it from being truly isolated.

Bones didn't bother with Goblin's leash here, just opened the door and let him get out to run. The puppy was the happiest I'd seen him in the past few days. He rolled, wiggled, and dashed around. Not that he went too far or ever got out of sight. No, he checked on us frequently and kept coming back before ranging out again.

"It's almost like he's scouting," I said, shielding my eyes from the sun. It had put on an appearance after a couple of truly gray days.

"He is." Bones hadn't retrieved the bags yet. "Give me a moment to clear the house."

He didn't wait for a response. Frankly, he didn't have to. I waited close enough to use the car for cover. I also had my taser in the pocket of my hoodie. The night before, I'd gone to sleep with him wrapped around me. Different hotel, still with only one bed.

We hadn't discussed how he'd held me or how he'd wrenched orgasm after orgasm out of me until I'd finally slept and slept deeply. Nope, we just got up and acted like nothing happened. I wasn't sure whether he didn't want to talk about it or if it wasn't that big a deal or what.

Maybe I was being a coward, but I didn't want to be more of a girl than I'd already been. He'd helped me. And it *had* helped. Maybe that just had to be enough. But when we got to the new hotel, we didn't follow up then. He just wrapped around me and settled me in place and then—I was out like a light.

"Clear," Bones said from the door and I sighed.

"On my way." I detoured to the back of the car and opened the trunk. I'd barely gotten one of the bags out before he took it and the other from me. He whistled and Goblin came trotting back.

Inside it smelled like dried lavender, hints of lemon, furniture polish, and linseed oil. The furniture was sturdy wood and very clean. The curtains were closed, but they weren't dusty. While it looked lived in, it didn't look like anyone was there now.

"Whose place is this?" I asked, more to add some sound to the silence than because I wanted to know. Though, I wouldn't mind knowing.

"A friend."

Helpful. A direct non-answer. I had to admire it.

"Rooms are upstairs," he said. "Three up, one down here. You can take your pick. Two full baths up there, just a water closet down here."

Take my pick.

He set the bags on the old oak table in the corner, then

moved around the kitchen taking an inventory. Someone had stocked it with food. There was fresh looking items in the fridge too. The place had to have a caretaker of some kind. Made sense.

I licked my lips. "Do they have laundry machines?"

"They do," he said, twisting to glance at me. "Good idea. Probably need to wash what clothes we have. I'll take care of it."

That wasn't what I meant but he was on the move again. "I'll go check the rooms…"

"Sounds good. I'll start coffee soon. We have supplies for sandwiches."

"I'll make something when I come back down." Not waiting for his response, I took the stairs two at a time. Goblin trotted right along with me.

As promised, there were three bedrooms upstairs. One of the bathrooms was an old school Jack and Jill with a door to the hall too. The third bedroom had an ensuite and it jutted out over the kitchen below but the ceiling seriously slanted on this side.

The bed was a queen. They were all queens. Like below it was clean, dust-free, even if the linens were a bit frillier than I would expect for the guys. Who said they had anything to do with the decorating?

Honestly, I didn't care where I slept. I guess we wouldn't have to share tonight and he probably wasn't getting a lot of sleep with babysitting me. Voodoo would be here… so would Alphabet.

"You're going to like that, aren't you?" I asked Goblin. For his part, the dog sat there tail thumping as he watched me. I finally went for the ensuite because at least then I didn't have to worry about running into someone in the bathroom in the middle of the night.

Yeah, that's why you're picking it. My inner snark was not impressed. Well, she could just shut up.

I took some time to wash my face and hands in the bathroom. Then I eyed myself. There were shadows beneath my eyes. I could pack for a fortnight in the luggage I had there. My hair was more than a little wispy, and looked kind of sad.

The cut on my neck had mostly closed. The other bruises and bumps I had were fading to a sickly yellow-green or had finally begun to disappear. Hiding in the bedroom was not a good plan.

One, I already felt like a coward. Two, I really was hungry. So, Bones and I should talk *before* the guys got here. Having sex with Voodoo and Alphabet when they both not only knew about the other but seemed very okay with it was one thing.

Bones and me? Well, that wasn't a thing-thing. At least, I don't think it was a thing. We were just starting to not hate each other. Goblin bumped my leg.

"Right, I'm circling. Let's go find food." The scent of coffee drifted upstairs. "Coffee too."

Bones was in the kitchen, shirtless and with his gun holster prominently displayed. Coffee brewed and hissed. He had food set out on the counter—sandwich fixings— and he moved around like a machine getting things done.

"Can I help?"

He just shook his head at the offer. When the coffee was ready, he set out two mugs and filled them but his phone rang. The sound was enough to make me jump. Worry immediately plunged through me as he pulled it out of his pocket and scanned the screen.

"I have to take this."

Coffee cup in one hand, phone in the other, he disappeared into the other room and then a door closed distantly. The downstairs bedroom? Maybe.

I set up my coffee how I liked it, then got to work assessing what we had for sandwiches. I started building different types—roast beef and cheddar along with ham and swiss. There was horseradish so I added that to about half the roast beef sandwiches and left the other half free. I used butter on some of the ham sandwiches, and some spicy brown mustard on the others.

When I had four plates of sandwiches halved and stacked, I covered them up then started cleaning up the debris. I'd used all the bread and most of the cheddar. I'd also finished my coffee, so I poured another cup and there was no sign of Bones.

It was the better part of an hour before he emerged once more—once more wearing a shirt—and I had a fresh pot going. Bones eyed the sandwiches then me.

"I swapped the laundry too." Since the washer had buzzed.

He nodded once, but said nothing as I leaned against the counter, arms folded and watched him. I'd had plenty of time to stew. Whatever this was, we should talk about it.

"You're not going to say anything?"

Bones paused, then glanced at me. "About?"

"Us? The weather? Food? The call? I don't know. Something more than the stony silence."

Hands stilling on the sandwich, he paused to study me. I would give a year's damn salary to know what the hell was going on in his head. Just a little peek would be worth it.

Goblin stood abruptly from where he'd been flopped at my feet. A door rattled and there was a knock. It carried from the front of the house. Unlike most dogs, Goblin didn't start barking like mad. No, he went right behind Bones as the man stalked out of the kitchen to head for the door.

As frustrating as it was to be interrupted, excitement kindled in my belly.

They were here.

I lasted all of three seconds before I pushed away from the counter to follow. He hadn't told me to wait and that was good. I didn't want to wait.

The door swung inward just as I got there. The guys were just there, filling the doorway. Mud on their boots and looking a little bruised and battered. Voodoo's hair was disheveled, but his eyes warmed the moment they lasered onto me.

Tension bled off of me like static.

They were here. They were safe.

Blowing out a breath, Voodoo strode across the open space in three strides. He pulled me into him, a fierce embrace of adrenaline-fueled intimacy. Yet, it was with infinite care that he pressed his forehead to mine.

"You good?" Two little words to sum up the past few days of separation.

"Now," I admitted in a voice as low as his. I'd been okay. Bones had kept me okay. But I was so much better now that I could see all of them. Now that I could feel him.

He traced my jaw, the contact featherlight but it grounded me. The connection between us just sizzling back to life with a surge of power.

Goblin barked once, bolting across the space as Alphabet stepped inside. Dropping to one knee, he welcomed Goblin's excited yips and rough play as the sweet puppy seemed determined to maul him with affection.

Still leaning into Voodoo, I drank in the sight of Alphabet's laughing smile and the relief that seemed to radiate off both him and Goblin. When he glanced up at me, stripped-down tactical calm barely hid the fire in his eyes.

"I'm sorry, Gracie." The apology caught me off-guard, and it must have showed because he rose with care still petting Goblin. "I'm sorry we didn't have time to read you in. I'm even more sorry that we didn't find Amorette."

My heart squeezed.

"Just—wanted to tell you that," he said, exhaling a sharp breath like a man who could finally take a deep one again. He didn't reach for me, but that was okay. Goblin was radiating happiness and I could see them both. It was enough.

As for his words? I planned to hold onto them as tightly as possible.

The last through the door was Lunchbox wearing a weary, but genuine smile. His knuckles were raw and scraped. There was a shadow of a bruise along his jaw. He dropped his bag, then closed the door behind him.

Gaze fixed on me, he nodded slowly then cut a look at Bones once before returning to me. "We need to eat. Kitchen stocked?"

"Yes," I said, then added, "And I made sandwiches."

His expression transformed into a kind of startled surprise. "Did you?"

"Don't look so impressed," I mimed a warning, even as Voodoo shifted, but only to stand with an arm around me so we could face them all. "They're just sandwiches."

"It's food," Alphabet declared with a laugh. "Let's eat."

"Status report," Bones ordered as we adjourned to the kitchen.

The coffee was as much a siren for the guys as it had been for me. They made short work of transferring the plates of sandwiches to the scarred farm table in the kitchen along with a carafe of coffee before they started another. Lunchbox opened the fridge and pulled out large slabs of meat, then added some vegetables before he joined us.

It was fascinating to watch them move and split the story between the three of them as they brought Bones—and by default me—up to date. They covered the details of the attack at the house.

The men had been Gallo's but they'd expected something like it and had planned for it. While Bones had indicated as much, I buried my irritation on the subject. Telling me wouldn't have changed anything except, I'd probably have been on edge the whole time, so—not telling me was the way to go.

For now.

Alphabet picked up on the tracking data he'd put together just before the attack. "We knew that at least some of the sales had to be in Monaco, it just made sense and I'd gotten my first real bite. It took time to decode after that."

"Gallo admitted that while he often participated in the auctions, he wasn't one of the high bidders—twelve people who split the action between them, be it region, type of stock, or original location. He admitted Grace was supposed to go through those channels and he'd put in the request for you specifically." Voodoo's expression darkened on the last. He drifted his knuckles down my cheek.

"He's dead now," Lunchbox assured me.

"We should have made it hurt more," was all Voodoo had to say on the subject.

"From Gallo we had the location of the auction and the time. We headed there directly," Alphabet took up the story again. "I'd gotten a good chunk of it decrypted, at least the *where*. We just needed to get in."

"Took a little finessing," Lunchbox said with a shrug. "Some intimidation. Cracked a couple of heads, and Voodoo seduced the high roller—or pretended to let her seduce him and we were in."

"I'm still working on names for all of them," Alphabet said in between bites of his second sandwich. "We have IDs for some, they also know they were compromised but not how much."

"Reznik," Bones stated.

"Yes." Voodoo rubbed a hand against my thigh, whether to soothe me or himself, I had no idea. Maybe both of us. "He's a problem and one we will need to sort. It also means they'll have our IDs and that could make problems for us getting to him."

"Maybe," Lunchbox said. "Maybe not. Depends on how we do our approach this time."

"If we do an approach at all," Bones said, his expression deeply thoughtful. "Hit and run might be a better option with him."

"I have no doubts he's got legitimate financial assets tied up in this mess." Alphabet washed down his second sandwich with a long drink of coffee. "Once I pull those strings, we can start draining their nasty little pool."

"We're going to take them down?" I had to ask, I had to be sure because that was what it sounded like.

"One thread at a time," Alphabet assured me.

"Or scorched earth and just blow the whole thing up," Lunchbox said the last with a kind of feral smile. The glee in it made me want to smile at him even if he was referring to bloodshed and mayhem.

Yeah, I could totally smile about that.

"Just need to identify the best access point with the most leverage," Voodoo stated. "Easier to get them if we can force them back together. Might be harder to manage that with the current situation."

"We'll figure it out," Alphabet said.

"You just need bait," I murmured. All four of them looked at me, the weight of their regard settled like heavy storm clouds filled to near bursting.

I didn't shy away from any of them. Not the hesitation in Lunchbox's eyes or the respect in Alphabet's or the worry in Voodoo's. The silence in Bones' gray eyes held me though.

"I'm already the reason we're in this," I reminded them. They were in this because of me. Because they were helping me. So this was a *we*. "Let me be a weapon now, too."

Bones pursed his lips, but he didn't say no.

And he didn't argue.

CHAPTER
THIRTEEN
GRACE

The rain had returned, the soft patter of it added to the soundtrack of the old farmhouse. The air inside was still thick, the walls practically sweating with all the unsaid things after I suggested that they use me as bait. None of them liked the plan, but not a single one shot it down.

Not even Bones.

I wasn't sure what made them more unhappy. That I suggested it or that they didn't have a counter argument for it. Instead of pressing on from there, though, the whole tide of conversation shifted until the decision to call it a night had broken us up.

Laying on top of the covers, I stared up at the ceiling. It was too warm to crawl under them. I wanted to crack the window, but the guys would probably deem it a security hazard so I'd left it alone. As tired as I was, my mind would not settle down. Every creak in the hallway made my heart jump.

It seemed even stranger to be in the room by myself. For the past few nights, Bones had always been within reach and closer still for the last two. Heat swept through me at the memory of the way he'd stroked me to distraction. While I had no regrets, I did have questions. Questions I wasn't even sure I should ask. His silence left me wondering if he just didn't want to discuss it or if it was just simply that he had nothing to say at all.

We had enough issues right now? Didn't we?

Rolling onto my side, I stared at the window. The darkness outside, the flicker of exterior lights visible through the sheer curtain, the spatter of rain against the glass should all lull me into sleep. Or at least, I thought they should.

But the silence pressed in like a second skin, weighing so heavily it should crush me all the way through the floor. Yet, no matter how many times I told myself to sleep, I couldn't even bring myself to close my eyes.

A soft knock brushed against the door. So soft, it took me a moment to recognize it as a knock and not another creak of the floor in the hallway. Had I heard it? Then it came again. Not urgent. Not hesitant.

Just... intentional.

I sat up and then slid off the bed. Opening the door, I stared up at Voodoo. He leaned against the frame, his dark eyes unreadable.

"Can't sleep," he said simply.

"Me neither." I pulled the door wider and backed up a step to let him come in.

He followed, slow and quiet and then closed the door behind him. I half-expected him to scoop me up, but he didn't. All he did was stand there, watching me.

"This plan—" He seemed to consider his words. "The next stages of this are going to be messy."

"Is this your way of saying 'you might not come back'?" Because the "plan" was still in the building stages.

"Firecracker..." The sigh as he exhaled my nickname seemed equal parts exasperation and affection. Thankfully, when I held out my hand, he glided his palm over mine. "I try not to say things I don't mean."

When I tugged, he followed me easily back to the bed. Without waiting for me to invite him, he dropped his hands to my hips and just picked me up to put me on the bed. These men were so damn tall. I was used to being short, but they made me feel so fragile.

"Whatever happens, *whatever* plan we go with..." And no, I didn't miss the stress on the "whatever plan", but I let it go. "Believe me when I say *you* will make it out."

"I know," I said, not letting go of him. Thankfully, he slid onto the bed with me. When he stretched out, I curled up to him and hooked one leg over his as he wrapped his arm around my shoulders. "Bones told me you all had contingencies for when things went wrong."

"Did he?" The soft question made me smile. "Good."

"I just—I don't want to be the reason something happens to any of you. Or that the plan to make sure whoever is closest to me gets out with me while everyone else covers means that you'll be down a man who might make all the difference." I'd been turning that one over in my head since Bones' reveal.

He was right to remind me that every moment I argued then might cost them something, I could argue against it now.

"Knowing you weren't in the middle of that," Voodoo murmured before he pressed a kiss to the top of my head. "Knowing Bones already had you out, he just had to keep going—that did help us. We focused on what was in front of us and not on who or what might get past us."

I made a face. "I hate that that makes sense."

His chuckle was delicious and low. "I'd say sorry, Firecracker."

"But you're not," I finished for him and he just let out a hum of agreement. His breathing deepened and his heart beat steadily beneath my fingers. When I tipped my head back, I had to smile. His eyes were closed and his breathing deep and regular.

Settled, I snuggled closer and told myself to drift. If he could sleep, maybe I could too.

IT WAS ALMOST three when I slipped out of my room and left Voodoo still sleeping. I'd dozed, but worry continued to nibble away at me. About Lunchbox, Alphabet, and Bones? Yes. About Amorette? Also, yes. Worry about where we were and what came next?

Absolutely, yes.

I didn't want to wake Voodoo up since he'd seemed so exhausted. It was to let him sleep for as long as he could.

The soft spit and patter of the rain had grown fainter and fainter until it vanished altogether. The other upstairs doors were all closed. Hopefully, that meant the guys were all getting sleep. Cooler air greeted me as I descended the steps on bare feet.

A soft clink of china told me someone else was awake. Alphabet was in the kitchen, dressed in sweats and a t-shirt when I slipped inside. He was stirring something in a mug and turned at my arrival to hold it out to me.

"Hot chocolate," he said. "Probably not as good as yours, so don't judge me."

A laugh escaped me at the offer. "I'm sure it's perfect." The smell of the chocolate was an invitation. He just gave me a faint smile before moving back to the stove and pouring more milk into a pan.

Goblin sprawled on the rug beneath the farm table. He glanced up briefly to look at me before his eyes drooped closed once more. Sipping the hot cocoa, I sighed. It was definitely made with powder, but it was double-chocolate, sweet, and very warm.

When he finished his, he waved me over to the table. It was hard to miss his faint limp as he came to join me.

"Are you really okay?"

When I nodded toward his leg, he flashed a smile. "Just sore. I get stiff, the joint can get a little raw. We pushed it. I'll be fine."

So matter-of-fact.

"Well, if I can help or do something, tell me." It didn't seem like much of an offer, but I wanted to make it anyway. "I was really glad to hear you were all fine."

"Did we worry you?" The note of teasing in his voice seemed to be an invitation to play, but I lifted a shoulder.

"You did. All of you did. Bones because he wouldn't let me go back. You guys because you were in the middle of it." I ran my bare foot along Goblin's back to pet him. "Goblin because he was covered in blood when he came racing down the street."

Alphabet grimaced. "We were planning on the fly. We knew something like that *might* happen. If it did, you and Goblin needed to be elsewhere."

"Because they could have hurt him." Goblin wouldn't have let them be taken prisoner.

"Yeah." He sighed. "I'm sorry, Gracie. I didn't think about the blood on him—it wasn't mine. It wasn't any of ours."

"Well, that helps—*now*." I wrinkled my nose. "But apology accepted. Even more because you guys made it back."

"You scare me a little." The admission surprised me.

"I do?" That was so not what I expected to hear.

"Yeah, you do." He toasted me with his mug. "You're stronger than I thought you were when we first met. You seem to get stronger every day. Not sure we planned for you. Not like this."

"I didn't plan for any of you." Admitting that wasn't remotely difficult. "How could I? I didn't plan to be kidnapped or to end up in the middle of some international trafficking ring. All I planned to do was just survive. Then... you guys showed up."

"Well, that's not totally true," he said, tilting his head as he turned sideways. He'd taken the seat next to me rather than across from me. "You planned to go home."

"You did take me home though—and I know, I was a bitch about the fact you had to pull me back out and then you kept me."

"You were *not* a bitch." He scowled and when I shrugged, he cupped my chin and pulled my gaze to his "You were not. You were struggling. We weren't really taking the time you needed and we didn't feel like we had the time. That's on all of us."

"Fine, so we're all at fault." I didn't think that was wholly true, but if he wanted to jump under the bus with me, I wouldn't let him take all the blame.

"Better." He nodded, then tapped my lower lip with his

thumb. "Here's the thing though, you haven't fallen apart. You haven't asked anyone to save you—"

When I would have protested that, he pressed his thumb to my lips again. At my sigh, he nodded.

"You want to find your sister. That's what you asked for. You wanted help finding her. You wanted help getting to her. You aren't asking for you..."

Oh.

"I used to ask for things," I said slowly. "I used to want a lot of things." Sometimes, I still did. "I used to think that becoming a model and making it—making a lot of money, it would pay for all the things Amorette and I wanted when we were kids. I wanted to do things for our mother—buy her all the things she had to do without because our father was such a dick."

It was the first time I'd admitted that out loud. At least to someone who wasn't Amorette. I'd never felt so far away from her as I did right now. It was also the first time I didn't want to abandon where I was to go to her.

I cleared my throat. "I wanted to do all those things. I used to plan it in my head. This is even before I got my first job modeling. But the modeling seemed to be an answer to that original dream. But *Maman* died and then it was just me and Amorette. She would never have let me spoil her the way I would have wanted."

A half-laugh escaped me and Alphabet brushed his knuckles to my cheek. I hadn't even realized I was crying.

"Sorry." I downed the rest of the chocolate like it was a shot. "I didn't mean to just dump all that." I wasn't even sure where it all came from.

"You have nothing to be sorry for Gracie." He took the empty cup from my hand and set it aside before he turned to face me fully. There was nowhere to go to escape the depth of emotion in his blue eyes.

The intensity pinned me in place. The warmth in his hands penetrated the ice that had seemed to coat me.

"Can I?"

His question pierced through the fog and I tilted my head. The action had me rubbing my cheek against his palms, but I wasn't trying to pull away.

"Can you—what?"

A slow smile curved his lips. "Can I kiss you?"

Could he— "Yes." The answer just burst out of me with a smile of my own. "Of cour—"

He didn't let me finish the thought, he just kissed me. Not a storm or a tempest. Not a raging fire. But a firm, slow, deep kiss that held promise and hope. He teased my lips apart with a steady application of pressure. With tiny licks of his tongue, he sampled and invited me to do the same.

The thunder erupted in my pulse as it seemed to crash in my ears. I leaned into the kiss, straining to give even as I took. Missing him had taken on texture and weight, all of it seemed to disintegrate almost effortlessly under his kiss.

When we broke apart, he didn't leave but merely pressed his forehead to mine.

"You don't know it yet," he said, the soft whisper as much a soothing caress for my senses as his kiss had been for my heart. "I'm going to be someone you can count on, you can trust. We all will be. But I'm telling you right now, you can depend on us, Gracie. We're not going to let you down."

That was the thing.

I did know it.

Maybe he didn't understand how I knew. But I did. I

was going to be someone they could trust too. I covered his hand on my cheek and closed my eyes as we existed there.

Together.

It was close to five when Alphabet and Goblin went back up to bed. As tempting as it was to go up with him, he really needed the sleep.

And I...

I needed to think.

Standing at the sink, I stared out the window into the quiet dark of the French countryside. The drag of a step alerted me to someone else coming down. It hadn't been that long since Alphabet went up.

"Gunning for my job?" Lunchbox asked as he padded into the kitchen.

Not that he made a sound as soft as his steps were. No, I'd heard him only because he'd let me hear him. Watching his reflection in the window made me smile.

"Your job?" I twisted to face him.

"You made sandwiches last night." He raised his brows. "Don't tell me you're down here to start prepping breakfast."

"Okay," I said, managing to contain my own amusement. "I won't tell you that."

His eyes narrowed. "You're giving me shit, aren't you?"

"Maybe." Deadpan took discipline, because I really wanted to laugh. "Though, I try not to cook too much when there are no fire extinguishers around."

His lips twitched. "You and Alphabet will get along just fine."

"I actually know that. We had a very similar discussion

about not cooking in your kitchen. Though—I did make hot cocoa in it. That I can do."

Like the others, he'd dressed for sleep. Though instead of sweatpants, he wore shorts and his t-shirt seemed a little tight. His biceps were on full display.

So was the tattoo on his right bicep. He had several others that I'd glimpsed, but this one looked like some kind of chemical compound.

"Hey," he said, drawing my gaze back up to his.

"Hmm?"

He narrowed the distance between us, bracing his hands on the lip of the sink on either side of me. I had to tilt my head back to meet his gaze.

"You scare the shit out of me, Grace."

"Why?"

"Because I find myself not wanting to let you out of my sight ever again."

That didn't answer my question. Or at least, I didn't think it did. But he didn't give me the opportunity to comment, not really as he dropped his hands to my hips and lifted me up even as his mouth came down.

His lips were hot and firm, the kiss searing as he took possession of my mouth. It wasn't gentle or just a brush. It wasn't a tease or a taste. It was deep, claiming and tasted like salt, smoke, and all the things that could never be spoken aloud.

When he wrapped his hand around my nape, and tilted my head to the side, he took the kiss even deeper. The strokes of his tongue staked his possession even as his lips branded mine.

The world crumpled up into ash, devoured entirely by the flame he fanned. It lasted forever and not long enough. Then he pulled back, just an inch and stared into my soul.

"Don't volunteer to be the damn bait," he said.

"I have to," I whispered. "This is about me."

"I don't want you to risk yourself."

"But it's okay for all of you to take the risks?" I licked my lips, savoring the taste of him lingering there. Him. Alphabet. Voodoo.

They were all stealing away pieces of me and it was really hard to care.

"Yes," he said, almost defiant. "We take the risks because we have the training. We know what we're doing and if anything happened...you'd still be safe. Because one of us is always going to be with you."

His words dug in, fisting my heart, and squeezed the tears from my eyes.

"I need you to be okay. *All* of you." I didn't want any of them to sacrifice themselves for me.

"And I need *you* to be okay."

Blowing out a breath, I pressed my hands to his chest. "Lunchbox...I *need* to do this."

He took my mouth in another kiss, a little longer, a little rougher, and a lot *more* than the earlier one.

"I know," he whispered, when he finally released my mouth. "I'm just *never* going to like it."

CHAPTER

FOURTEEN

BONES

I should be the one inside with her right now, instead, Alphabet and I were in the van, a half-klick out from the chateau outside Avignon.

We had video, grainy as it was, because they had it shielded. Alphabet was trying to clean it up.

We had comms up, letting us hear her and everyone else. Voodoo had shaved, trimmed his hair back, and shifted his appearance so he wouldn't stand out. Lunchbox had done the same.

With Reznik in play, we couldn't risk anyone spotting them. It was why Lunchbox was in as a waiter. Staff gave him access to the back rooms as well. Security was tight. Ridiculously tight.

"Breathe, Cap," Alphabet murmured. "You're giving Goblin heartburn."

The soft words had me glancing down at the dog. He'd parked himself between me and Alphabet. I was close enough to slide right into the driver's seat if necessary and I also had video feeds for the front and back of the van.

No ambushes.

119

"I'm breathing, focus on her."

"We are focused on her," came the way too relaxed reply. "She looks damn good in that dress."

"What there is of it," Lunchbox muttered and Alphabet snorted.

The outfit in question didn't seem to possess enough fabric to be labeled a dress.

"What the hell is that?" I'd asked when she'd walked out in it.

"A bodycon mini." Her smirk dared me to dispute it. "They are very trendy and they get noticed."

She'd be noticeable in a burlap damn sack. As much as I wanted to tell her to change, I shut up. Bait. The whole point of this exercise was to lure those bidders back out. To lure *Reznik* out. Knowing he was part of the operation made snaring him a two-fold goal.

Removing him from the board was business, but I would take no small amount of pleasure in the act. My gaze tracked to where Grace descended the steps into the ballroom like a queen. She moved with—grace. Like so many others present, she was masked.

The plunging cowl neck gave the illusion of bared breasts while the bare back with the single spaghetti string offered a far sultrier promise. The sheer mesh of navy blue fabric seemed to flow like it had been painted on and was still liquid.

Or maybe that was just her movements.

"I have eyes on her," Voodoo said patiently into comms. We all had eyes on her. I'd have eyes on her if I was dead.

She moved through the centuries-old estate all dressed up in its velvet corruption like she belonged there and everyone else were the guests. Chandeliers gleamed and champagne flowed amongst the masked patrons as violence whispered its way through the ball.

Ball.

It was another goddamn auction. Dressing it up in all the finery and coating it in a cloud of sweet perfume didn't change the ugliness of the whole damn thing. A monitor to the left of my screens detailed her heart rate and respiration. The data flashed like a countdown. Each time it started to race, she found a way to slow it again.

The monitors hummed. A beep indicated she was close to one of the others. It had to be Lunchbox because Voodoo's camera hadn't moved from where he listened to some woman drone on about the newest addition to a formula one team.

She was impossible not to watch. Her arrival had snared attention and her drift through the ballroom snagged more. Bait.

We were dangling her like bait to see what swam up to the surface to take a bite. The tightrope was too narrow and there were no safeties if they got their teeth into her. Baiting a trap only worked if you were willing to lose the bait.

"Comm check," I said, because Grace wasn't talking. Lunchbox and Voodoo seemed to get what I wanted because they just each sent a beep.

"I can hear you," she said, though on the screen she had the champagne flute lifted to her lips. The dark feathery mask hid the upper half of her face, it made her ruby red lips even more appealing. They glistened under the lights. "Loud and clear."

She smiled as she lowered the glass and my left hand curled into a fist. On the monitor, even with the grain of interference, she was a vision. Every step she took a sinuous stride that made all kinds of sensual promises.

No doubt existed within me that she commanded considerable fees for her work. She owned that room right now and the people in it, they just didn't know how much. Watching her from too damn far away magnified every moment like a slow bleed draining my life away.

If you didn't know where she was going, she would look like a woman just drifting from group to group. Wandering. Bored. She presses into one group. Laughter. Flirtation. A man gestured to her empty champagne flute, passing it to a waiter, but she waved off another. He set his hand against the bare skin of her back.

Head tilted, she doesn't throw the drink in his face, stomp on his foot, or break his goddamn hand. No, she looks at him like she's sizing up prey, not potentially dancing into the wolf's maw.

"Persistent son of a bitch," Lunchbox muttered. "Need me to remove him?"

"No," Grace said. "You mustn't." Whether she was talking to the putz or to Lunchbox, I wasn't sure. "I need to mingle."

Then she strolled away from her admirer. I stayed focused on him for a moment. What would he do? His hand also curled into a fist and he stared after her. Adrenaline spiked into my system as he looked like he would follow, but another man approached and then he was distracted.

Good.

"You've got a tail," Alphabet said. "Slim suit. Scar near the temple. On your five o'clock, Gracie."

I shifted my attention to the interloper. Alphabet was right. The man moved on a direct angle to intercept her. There was no mistaking the purposefulness of his stride.

"I see him. He looks very determined."

He was also smiling. I wasn't.

The man wore a much thinner mask, it barely covered his face. "Are we getting facial rec yet?"

"No," Alphabet said. "Harder with this quality."

"Mademoiselle," the man said. "You are… exquisite."

Grace laughed, a practiced sound that seemed to match her slow smile. The man crowded right in, stepping closer than was even remotely appropriate.

"You will come with me. I will get you a drink and then we'll talk. I have many questions." The command in his tone was impossible to miss. He wasn't speaking French, though his English was very accented.

"Go with him," I said through gritted teeth. "Don't drink anything he offers."

The man gripped her elbow, tugging her toward the stairs for the ballroom mezzanine. Grace's breathing hitched, just a sharp inhale, but noticeable. The man wasn't slowing for any other group. When he moved his hand from her elbow to the curve of her back, just above where the fabric curved over her ass.

"I've got eyes," Voodoo reminded them. "Right behind her."

He'd broken away from his own group. Good. Still, my left fist tightened as I said, "Let her lead."

The man's hand continued to drift lower, but they moved out of range of the primary camera as it glided toward the curve of her ass.

Grace's soft laughter carried easily over the comms. Alphabet was scanning the cams, looking for a better angle as Voodoo followed, but had to maintain distance so he didn't *look* like he was following.

Tactically sound for intelligence gathering. Bad fucking

idea to not have him right there letting others know they took their lives in their hands putting a finger on her.

There...

The angle wasn't great, but we could see them standing in the archway leading into a room off the mezzanine. He towered over where she leaned against the wall. He had his hand on her bare shoulder and glided down her arm.

"Tell me," she murmured. "Do you always touch things you haven't bought yet?" Was that a quaver in her voice?

The mark laughed, though his expression was difficult to read at this distance and I couldn't see Grace's at all.

"You okay?" I asked, keeping my voice low. The whole team could hear her, hear me, but I needed to know she was still in this.

"So far..." Her response trailed off as the man handed her a glass, presumably with alcohol, taken from a waiter who approached them and then retreated once more.

She accepted the offer, but didn't drink.

Good girl.

When she blew out a breath, the low sigh echoed too damn close to the way she'd exhaled after she came. Those two experiences did not belong side by side in this.

"Heads up," Lunchbox said abruptly. "North stairwell."

"What the hell—?" Alphabet exhaled shock with each syllable.

The camera angles updated on my second screen. My stomach dropped sickeningly. For the first time all evening, the feed was almost crystal fucking clear. No static. A clean-shaven man dressed in a dark gray suit approached along the mezzanine. His measured pace was as familiar as my own.

Worse, the military cut of his dark brown hair was high and tight. It added to the harsh angles of his face. Not even the tailored suit could detract from the wide-shoulders or the barrel like chest. The man was a tank.

He'd always been.

The last time I laid eyes on him had been only a few seconds before a collapsing building buried him in what should have been his tomb.

"Not possible." Each word broke off like ice cracking.

"Declan O'Rourke." Voodoo sounded even quieter, colder, and I had no doubts, as furious as I was. Declan had been his "friend" before.

Ex-special forces. Former ally. Mercenary for hire. Reported dead. Killed in action.

Traitor.

He sold us out. Him and Reznik.

Only, we hadn't known he'd been just as much a part of it as Reznik before three years ago.

And now?

The man walked out of the past, heading straight for Grace.

"Grace. Abort. Now."

But it was already too late. O'Rourke was there.

O'Rourke glanced at the man who'd taken Grace upstairs The other dropped his chin, a nod as he withdrew. He stepped aside as though he knew his place.

As if he'd already lost the bid.

O'Rourke?

He lifted Grace's hand, brushing a kiss to her knuckles.

"We need a better angle," I growled, though I'd pressed mute on my comms. She didn't need to hear this part. Not when she was the one standing right in front of that son of a bitch.

"Working on it," Alphabet gritted out.

"Did they send you?" The silken tone barely gloved the

measured violence in the traitor's voice. "Or are you the gift I've been promised?"

She didn't respond, not immediately. All I could see was the way she tilted her head. The seconds passed like hours.

"Lunchbox, get us a better goddamn angle."

Blowing out a breath, I unmuted my link to her comm. "You breathe my name, Grace, and I'll burn that goddamn building to the ground."

We wanted to know who else was involved.

O'Rourke was not on my bingo card.

A new screen opened, Lunchbox was on the mezzanine and that was a much better angle. Fuck.

Grace's smile was still there, and the tilt of her head was almost playful. Yes, the mask still hid the upper part of her face but the stubborn lift of her chin was defiance.

Defiance and terror.

I'd seen that fear on her face the night we'd been run off the road...

Again when I made her leave the guys.

In the bank.

The same defiance had burned to life.

One word from her...

"I have a shot," Voodoo said.

"Ready to move," Lunchbox concurred.

"I have eyes," Alphabet reminded them. "Exit mapped."

The only one who mattered right now needed to make the call.

What was our play?

"Now," Grace said in this slow, teasing tone that dared a man to test her. "Why would I ruin the surprise?"

FIFTEEN

GRACE

The wall behind me was almost too cool. The chateau's old-world style housed far more than blood-soaked secrets amidst the history built into the framework itself. From the moment I'd ascended the steps, my pulse had begun to race. Lunchbox and Voodoo were here, but I hadn't seen them and I didn't dare look at them. The fact I was burning up made the chill of the stone all the more desirable.

I'd never been good at gymnastics and yet here I was, navigating this balance beam to dangle myself out here like chum for the sharks swimming in this oversized tank. Though, calling the wealthy men and women who made their trade in trafficking *human beings*, sharks might really be unkind to the animals.

Bones' calm, almost detached voice kept me grounded. Nothing seemed to ruffle him. I might want to give him shit about it, but I also really needed the steadiness so I wasn't going to complain.

The man they called O'Rourke, studied me like I was a mystery he needed to decipher. He'd dismissed the other like he wasn't remotely an issue and not only had the man retreated, he'd left the playing field entirely.

It was just me and O'Rourke. The man smelled like designer cologne, the musk rich and overpowering. It seemed to complement his expensive violence but it did nothing to disguise it. His hand on mine was warm, firm, and perfectly rehearsed. This man knew exactly who and what he was. No pretense existed for him and that made me far more uneasy than I'd been when I woke up shackled in hell's waiting room.

When he let his gaze linger on my lips, I softened them to hint a smile. The seconds seemed to just go on for infinity. Surely one of us should have said something by now, but he'd barely responded to my tease.

"Come," he murmured, pulling me from the wall. "Let's talk somewhere quieter."

"Stay in public," Bones ordered. His clipped tones soothed my rabbiting heart. "Don't let him isolate you anymore than you already are."

I could have lived without the last part.

"Only if you promise not to bite." I played coy, dropping my voice to something huskier. In the low-light of the mezzanine, O'Rourke's eyes were shadowed. But his nostrils flared and that gave me the boost I didn't realize I needed.

O'Rourke chuckled, bringing my hand back up to his lips and this time, he pressed a kiss to my palm. When his mouth lingered there, I braced for the feel of his teeth. He didn't disappoint, scraping the kiss down to the heel of my hand then my wrist.

The bite wasn't erotic or inviting, it was pain. Pinching pain and daring me to say something. I clenched my teeth, refusing to give him the satisfaction. A mockery of a smile twisted his lips as he straightened.

"No promises," he said finally, as if he hadn't just proven his point. "Now, come this way."

He didn't wait for me to agree, pulling me through the archway and into a room that was decorated with velvet couches, heavy curtains, a hearth with a lit fire waiting along with glasses that had been poured.

O'Rourke closed the door behind us and it gave me the opportunity to move away from him and study the room. I also spared a glance down at my wrist. The rip of skin was visible as was the livid bruising already appearing.

Great. I probably needed shots after that.

"You have me at a disadvantage, Mr..."

"Declan," he said, easily enough. His American accent was relatively generic and it didn't betray any region. "And I know who you are, Grace."

My spine stiffened as a new shock registered.

His smile was not friendly. "You don't mind if I call you Grace, do you? I feel like you and I know each other very well."

"Do you?"

"You're the girl they pulled from the New York ship-ment. The reason Gallo has gone missing and Dubois is raging all about Monaco regarding the raid and other events. You are one half a gorgeous set, but you were the one meant to be nothing but a memory."

His voice was smooth. Like a scalpel.

"He's baiting," Bones said, the crisp note in his voice hard. "Keep control."

For all the distance in Declan's eyes, he wasn't unaf-fected by me. Spreading my arms, I added just a little sway to my step as I pivoted to face him. Yes, his gaze went to my chest, then to my legs.

"I'm a girl with options, *Declan*." The name was so much more sexier than the man. Pity. "You planning to make me one?"

Amusement filtered through his expression as he moved to where the wine and the glasses waited. "Not exactly. You see, Grace—I really do love your name. Simple. Elegant. Like you. Then, there is you and you've already made yourself... very interesting."

He took the time to fill each glass with the red wine. It looked like blood in the firelight. When he held out to me, I had to prowl closer to accept it. Avoiding touching him while I took the glass was a win.

"You're doing fine," Bones said, the razor-wire tension in his voice an anchor "You see a weapon, you give me the word."

They were out there. Voodoo. Lunchbox. Alphabet. Bones.

I wasn't alone. "Tell me something, Declan," I coated the words with a little honey. Nothing but some sweetness to own the moment. "What do you want?"

"To—"

"What do you want, really?" I cut off whatever charming response he was about to offer. "You asked if *they* sent me or was I a gift that you were promised—then you say you know who I am. So let's cut to the chase. *What. Do. You. Want?*"

It was like channeling my sister as I fired off each word. Amorette could put a person on the spot, deconstruct their arguments and never let them get off the subject she wanted discussed.

Declan's smile faltered. A brief crack in the facade of his

charm. Brief but real. "Death is expensive, Grace. Some of us learn to leverage it."

Ice slid down my spine.

"I wouldn't be in such a hurry to demand things from me." He stepped closer, close enough to feel the heat that rolled of of him. Close enough to let me see the scar just beneath the open collar of his unbuttoned tux.

A bullet wound.

I'd seen similar scars on the guys.

"You don't have to run anymore," he told me, brushing the hair off my shoulder. "I can make you disappear the right way. Set you up so you will always be taken care of…"

The urge to vomit was right there.

"I swear if he fucking touches her again," Voodoo swore.

"Hold," Bones said, his confidence pouring into me and helping me to lift my chin. "She's got this."

"I'm not running, Declan." I made his name a taunt as much as anything. "I'm shopping."

Honestly, I was making this up. The guys knew him. He was tied to the syndicate or whatever that hosted the auctions in Monaco. Moreover, he knew who I was. That had to be enough right?

Not that I thought whatever we had would get him arrested so much as confirmed as the bad guys.

"We've got company," Bones said. "One of ours?"

"Nothing here," Voodoo said. "Lunchbox?"

No response.

Declan chuckled, tracing his fingers down my arm to my hip. His light grip didn't offer any kind of threat.

Yet.

"Lunchbox. Where the hell are you?"

Nothing.

My pulse sped up as Declan set his wine glass down then took mine and put it to the side. Neither of us were drinking. Why wasn't Lunchbox answering?

"South wing." His calm voice nearly made me sag. "Setting a low-level flash burn on the backup grid. Just in case we need a scene."

"Goddammit. That wasn't the call." Bones wasn't happy. Why did his snarling make me feel better?

"Neither is letting her go dark with a ghost in a suit." Dislike kissed each of Lunchbox's words. "I want her out of there."

"Grace," Declan asked, his lips practically stroking my cheek. "Are they listening to us?"

I laughed. Really laughed.

It was almost a hysterical giggle that burst out of me, refusing to be contained. "Wouldn't that just ruin the fun?" I slapped a hand against his chest and pushed myself away.

"Grace, full abort. Get out. Now." Honestly, I was with Bones on this one all the way. I wanted out of here.

The lights flickered all around us, the chandelier dimmed and then there was a pop as the lights themselves went out. O'Rourke dragged me back toward him even as he turned.

One distraction was all I needed. I slammed my knee upward right into his groin. He swore, but I'd already wrenched myself away. The doors exploded open, guards crashing into the room. Shouts came from downstairs. Screams.

"Gracie, drop."

Something hit the floor even as I registered Lunchbox's warning. I dropped. Then a flashbang exploded. The light dazzled and the smoke made me cough.

Lunchbox and Voodoo appeared through the smoke like

something right out of an action movie. They each took out a guard. The wild grin on Lunchbox's face captivated me.

"Hey Dick-lan," Lunchbox said as he held out a hand to me. When I clasped his, he pulled me to my feet. "So not glad to see you again. Next time a lady tells you she wants to go, accept it and get the hell out of her way."

I didn't even get a look back at Declan before Lunchbox threw something else and it detonated against the bar. Flame licked out over the old wood and made a path straight for the alcohol.

"Get back-up up here, *now*," Declan shouted from somewhere, but Lunchbox pulled me with him as we moved. He weaved through the smoke and the chaos. I lost track of Voodoo. I lost track of where anything was.

We were out on the mezzanine then into another room, then out doors where crystal clear air filled my lungs. Smoke billowed from inside and people screamed. The evacuation below was chaos.

"Time to go," Voodoo said as he arrived next to us. The doors closed and they both glanced at me. "Lose the shoes and climb on Lunchbox's back, Firecracker."

I slid right out of them and made a leap even as Voodoo helped. Then we were all going over the edge.

Closing my eyes, I held on for dear life. Then we were on the ground.

"You're clear through the gardens," Alphabet said. "Bones is on the way to meet you. You have one minute, guards are incoming."

"Can you run on bare feet?" Voodoo asked as I wiggled down.

"Yes." Because right now I had no choice.

"Stay with Lunchbox." He nodded. "I'll cover."

Hand in hand, we raced through the darkened garden.

Gun fire erupted sporadically behind us. Worse, there was breaking glass erupting behind us. An alarm went off on Lunchbox's wrist.

"Down," he ordered, pulling me to him and all but rolling me beneath him even as Voodoo landed on top of us. The next boom that came was a *lot* louder. Debris rained down.

"What the fuck was that?" Voodoo demanded as they both pulled me to my feet.

"Boomer on their wine cellar to let their guests out. They're going to be busy and those people didn't need to be down there."

"East gate," Bones growled. "Now."

Thankfully, that wasn't that far and as sore as my feet were, I was almost floating by the time we got there. Four men lay in a heap just inside the gate.

Guards.

None of them were moving.

Or breathing.

Bones held out his hand. It shouldn't have surprised me that he picked me up and sprinted with me. He'd done the same when we'd had to leave the guys before. But this was different.

The guys were with us for one.

They didn't slow down as they raced through the dark and I held on, trying to make myself small. When we got to the van, he set me down inside it.

"You did good," he murmured, touching a hand to my cheek. "You did real good."

I blew out a breath. Lunchbox was climbing in the driver's seat as Voodoo slid into the back with me. Then the vehicle was starting and I sagged into the seat.

"Nothing went to plan," I said, panting. "How did I do

good?" The plan hadn't called for them to extract me with *bombs*.

"You adapted," Voodoo said, cupping my cheek. "Went with it. Followed orders. That's why you did good, Fire-cracker."

"Always did like it when a plan has some wiggle room," Lunchbox said almost cheerfully.

"Even if we have to make it ourselves," Alphabet commented drily.

"Exactly."

Another laugh bubbled out of me. They were crazy.

We were all crazy.

CHAPTER

SIXTEEN

GRACE

A new day, a new problem, and a new safe house. It was like being on some cracked world tour, only instead of playing a venue or hosting a party or just being seen—we did all of that with extreme prejudice and blowing shit up.

This place was colder, had less charm. The floors were concrete, the windows covered in black-out and framed by heavy curtains. One bathroom, and four rooms total with a kitchen that just made Lunchbox shake his head. There weren't even that many beds and the furniture should probably have been taken out and burnt.

"We won't be here that long," Bones said. "Voodoo, we need to swap out the van."

The van we'd been in was now parked inside a glorified shed. They called it a carport, but it looked like a shed. I already missed the car Bones had "purchased" when we'd been on the run. But I had a feeling, like everything else, it wasn't coming back.

I paced the room, arms folded as much to warm myself

137

up because it was chilly as to work off the wild nervous energy that vibrated beneath my skin.

"We will," Voodoo said, leaning against the wall nearest the fireplace. Lunchbox had built a fire in it, the flames licking over the kindling. It was kind of a promise of warmth but it seemed a paltry defense against the ice spreading within me. "But not yet."

"We need to debrief," Alphabet said as he and Goblin came in. "I want to know why in the past few days we've run into Reznik and now O'Rourke. One should be in a prison and the other in a grave."

I shot him a sympathetic look as he took a seat. With all the chatter on the comms, he'd actually said little. He'd said even less during our subsequent flight.

"I want to know how deep their ties are," Voodoo said in a grim tone of voice. "In fact, I vote we pick one or both up and take them out behind the woodshed and beat the information out of them."

"I could get on board with that plan." Lunchbox stood, then sliced a look toward me. "You're cold." He stripped off his jacket and stepped right into my path before he draped it over my shoulders. It was still warm from him, even if it smelled like smoke.

"You didn't know him," Bones said as I shifted my stance and our gazes collided. "Right?"

"No, I didn't know him. I'd never seen him before tonight. To be honest, I don't think I knew anyone there, not that I lingered in the main party that long and most of those people were masked." I rubbed my right arm. The cold seemed to be settling in my bones and everything had begun to hurt.

Maybe that was the adrenaline wearing off.

"You should eat," Lunchbox said, worry deepening the

grooves at the corners of his mouth. "Maybe change your clothes?" Without waiting for my response, he diverted toward the bathroom. "I'm going to see if we have hot water. Then you can shower."

Alphabet let out a sigh, then pulled out his phone. "I've uploaded everything, but it's going to take time. The servers are secure, but the decryption programs will need massaging. If we're not staying here longer than a night, I'm going to wait until we get to the next place."

"How long will you need?" Bones might have been talking to Alphabet, but the weight of his gaze rested on me. Did he want to talk? Fight? Yell?

I had no idea. Since I could go for all three right now, I resumed pacing. The idea had been mine. I had no one to blame for the past few hours, that wasn't me. The guys hadn't liked the plan, but they'd supported me and I wasn't in there alone.

The rational argument being waged against the emotional upheaval tearing me apart wasn't doing me any good.

"Best case? Forty-eight hours, but we won't have best case here. I need my equipment at base for that. What I have here, seventy-two and that's generous. If I knew what we were looking for specifically, I could parse that way but we don't." Alphabet sounded so damn resigned and I could practically feel the apology.

A bang came from the other room and I jumped.

"It's just Lunchbox," Voodoo said, his tone soothing even if the words were just an explanation. "Sounds like he's beating on the water heater."

My ribs felt bruised from the beating they were taking from my heart. I tried to get my breathing back under control.

"We could backtrack to Arles, but if they are trying to follow a trail, I'd rather not be somewhere they can trip over us." Bones wasn't asking, he was talking aloud. "Seventy-two hours in one location is a hard push."

"Not," Alphabet said slowly. "If we split up. I take Goblin and make straight for Paris. Stay at one of the high-end places. Use their wifi and security to mask what I'm doing."

Split up?

When I pivoted to face him, Alphabet gave me an encouraging smile. "That way, you have the three of them with you. They'll be in a better position to move if I get something actionable."

"I still think we need to just pick up Reznik," Voodoo said. "Definitely want O'Rourke. That fucker—"

A slicing motion from Bones silenced him and I glanced between the two. "I already know you have hard feelings since you didn't know he was alive."

"It's more than hard feelings," Bones said, evenly.

"Gracie," Lunchbox said as he emerged wearing a very real smile. "We have hot water. Want a shower?"

He looked so damn earnest, and his smile so wide that it was impossible to not smile back at him. Unlike his crazy smile back at the chateau this one was far warmer and richer.

"Thank you," I told him and I meant it. "Not sure I'm ready to shower yet. I'm—"

I extended my hands forward to show them how hard they were shaking.

"Maybe in a few?" After I calmed down, if I could calm down. I went to fold my arms again but Bones caught my right wrist and turned my hand over.

"What is that?" He stared down at the livid bruising

and torn skin. Voodoo pushed away from the wall to stalk over to where I was standing. He stared down at it and then he jerked his gaze up to me.

Lunchbox and Alphabet were just there, I didn't even hear them move. The four of them formed this almost insurmountable wall of testosterone. My pulse sped up again at the way they closed ranks. It was like being trapped all over again except...

They won't hurt me.

Those four words played on a loop even as my anxiety see-sawed violently despite the whispered confidence from my more rational side. It probably only worked because I did believe they wouldn't.

"He bit me."

"He fucking what?" Lunchbox's voice dipped into a dark place that sucked all the lightness out of him. "O'Rourke bit you?"

I met his hard-eyed gaze. "Yes." I could soften this. I should probably ease it somehow. "I think it was a test because I said he had to promise to not bite or whatever stupid thing it was that I said."

"It wasn't stupid," Alphabet said, resting his hands on my hips. I don't know which of us shifted, but he was just a solid wall of muscle now at my back, and it helped to begin to fracture the ice spreading through me. "You were being charming, thinking on your feet."

"You handled it," Bones said when I lifted my gaze to him.

"I'm going to gut that son of a bitch and feed him his own entrails." The explicit and very violent reaction from Lunchbox had me shifting my attention to him. His lips had compressed into a tight white line. His jaw tensed, and a muscle leaped in his cheek. I swore I could see a vein throbbing in his forehead. "You should never have had to even see him, much less let him touch you."

I shrugged. "I don't care about the touching."

"Liar." Voodoo delivered the accusation in a gentle voice that robbed it of any pique. "Handling it, being *able* to handle it, doesn't mean you wanted it, enjoyed it, or don't care."

"If I'm the one who allows it then I still have control." That was something they needed to understand. "I say who and I say when."

Except he bit me when I asked him to say he wouldn't. He'd done it and then... I tried to swallow against the sudden dryness in my throat. Bones traced the area around the wound.

"I'll get the first aid kit," Voodoo said. "Clean that out and we can bandage it before you shower."

I didn't want to shower.

"He knew you guys were listening." I wanted to face this all head on even as they crowded around me. Tilting my head back, I rested it against Alphabet's chest and found him gazing down at me with a fierce light in his eyes. For one moment, he flicked a look toward Bones before he looked at me again.

Bones sighed, the long exhale slicing through the silence. "Do you need to know who he is, Grace?" That question caught me off-guard and I straightened to meet him head-on. Those gray eyes which so often seemed cold seemed to shine like armor at the moment. Steel maybe. "Intelligence can be a double-edged sword. What you know, someone can try to take. We haven't discussed what happens when we erase the people after you and dismantle the organization."

Erase.

Dismantle.

I swallowed.

He rubbed his thumb against my palm, the slow, even strokes easing the tension and letting my fingers relax.

"O'Rourke and Reznik, however, are tied to us. To our past. Not yours."

"Except O'Rourke knows who I am and he knew about Amorette. They may not have her. She may not be in their network or whatever they call it. But he knew about her." I licked my lips. "He also seems to know I'm with you or the other way around."

He nodded. "Potentially. Or he was fishing for information. Reznik recognized them in Monaco. If O'Rourke and Reznik are still in each other's pockets, then it's not impossible for him to believe it involves you."

"We haven't exactly been quiet about looking after you," Lunchbox admitted. Fortunately, some of the dark cloud of anger had eased away. Not gone, but definitely not storming anymore. "If we were identified by any of their scoop teams..."

He shrugged.

"Good," Voodoo said. "I hope those assholes know we're involved. It means maybe they won't keep trying to take her."

"Except I walked right in there tonight because I wanted to help—to be in this fight. I don't know if what I did made this worse."

Bones closed his hand around mine and squeezed. The gesture had me glancing up at him again. "It helped. You pulled another ghost out of the closet. That's one less to ambush us. We have names. With you inside and distracting them, all three of you got more images of their guests. We can't identify everyone yet, but I meant what I said. We will erase your pursuers and dismantle the rest."

"Hopefully, some of the people I cut loose tonight kept going. They could be dealing with some legal bullshit," Lunchbox said and his smile suddenly returned. "Oh yeah, that will be something for them to have to deal with. They had a full house downstairs and their security was spotty."

"Surveillance was jammed," Alphabet said with a shrug of his own that made me bounce a little. "I left them a lovely little virus that would have made a mess out of everything. So sad for them."

"You set fire to the bar," I reminded Lunchbox and he winked.

"That I did. So yes, Gracie. You helped. Intelligence is never a bad thing. We know more. The more we know, the more we can make our targets hurt." He nodded once. "Oh yeah. Definitely planning some maximum pain there. Now, you need to eat. I'm going to see what supplies we have. Then we can debate where we're going."

Bones said nothing, but his expression said he was considering options.

"Two things," I said before Lunchbox could derail us with food again. Though, admittedly, the longer I leaned into Alphabet the more I relaxed and the hungrier I grew. "One, yes I want to know who they are and what they did to all of you. Not just because it involves me right now, but because they hurt you."

No one had to draw me a map for that. I could read the room and the reactions. Bones *hated* O'Rourke. If he'd been in that room instead of on comms, this whole conversation would probably be moot.

O'Rourke would be dead.

"And two?" Voodoo prompted, though I had all of their attention.

"I'm in this, all of this. With you. I know I'm freaking out and I reserve the right to do that. Tonight scared the shit out of me, but if I helped, then I want to keep helping. Don't keep me out of this." I looked at each of them in turns.

"Grace," Bones said. "You shouldn't want any part of this."

Any part of them. That's what he was saying.

"But I do." My voice was hoarse and raw. I straightened, stepping away from Alphabet long enough so I could turn in a slow circle and meet their gazes one by one. "And you do, too."

Not a single one denied it.

"Right now, I'm going to go shower and wash him off. While I do that, you four can decide how you want to handle this and what you're going to tell me." I cleared my throat. "Then I'm going to change and come back out here and eat. Be ready to discuss when I am."

That was my plan.

"Orders, Grace?" Bones asked in the most mild of tones and I couldn't help it, I grinned.

"Think of them more as guidelines... suggestions really-ly." It wasn't the exact quote, but it worked for me. At the bathroom door, I hesitated and glanced back at them to add, "Please."

After I closed the door, I leaned against it. They didn't move, at least not that I could hear. They didn't speak either.

Then, Bones said, "You heard the lady. Get her food started. Then we'll plan."

SEVENTEEN

GRACE

"Reznik," Bones said once I sat down on the sofa. The "table" in the kitchen wasn't much and the guys all skipped using it. The "living room" was more comfortable. Instead, I got the middle seat on the sofa in between Alphabet and Lunchbox. Goblin sprawled on the floor in front of us while Bones and Voodoo took the seats opposite. "Captain Thomas Reznik went through boot with me. He was always competitive, but with me, it was personal."

Voodoo snorted. "What he's trying to say is they were the top two, and he always lost out to Bones."

"Not always," Bones corrected. Someone else might not have wanted to admit that. Bones, however, detailed the information much as he might a shopping list. These were the facts. "However, I was also competitive. The challenge drove both of us. I climbed the ranks faster, that never sat well with him."

Lunchbox gave me a gentle nudge and nodded to the stew. He'd decried what we had in the kitchen, but then served up a thick meaty stew and crusty bread. It all smelled good, but it was also heavy.

Still, I dunked some bread into the stew then took a bite. Oh, god, it tasted better than it smelled. Moaning in the middle of Bones' *debrief* would be wholly inappropriate so I fought to contain it.

"Regardless," Bones dunked some of his own bread, the guys did too. I guessed they'd been waiting for me to eat. "When assignments to train came up for special forces, we were once again in competition. I made the first cut. He didn't."

"So, he doesn't like you cause he's a sore loser?" Essentially, that was what it sounded like. I was no stranger to competition. I'd endured my share of it and participated in far more. Frankly, I thrived in those circumstances, but fighting for a top contract couldn't remotely be the same as what these guys did.

"More or less," Voodoo answered rather than Bones. "What Cap won't tell you is that Reznik had a hard-on to stick it to him from the day Cap got his first team."

"It was a strike team," Bones offered by way of explanation. "This team." He motioned to Lunchbox and Alphabet. "Along with a couple of others."

A couple of others.

"Doc was one," Alphabet told me and when I glanced at him, he gave me an encouraging nod. "You met him—well actually, he's the reason we met you. It was his people that pulled you out of the truck."

"I remember, he was nice." He'd been very kind. "Who is the other?"

Lunchbox remained mute, but Alphabet just lifted his shoulders. "O'Rourke."

The man who... I jerked my gaze to each of them in turn and every single one wore the same expression. Twisted anger, darkness and rage. "*He* was one of you?"

"He was never one of us," Bones said slowly. "Looking back on it, I can see it. Arrogance prevented me from understanding just how far Reznik would go to prove he was superior."

The self-loathing in his cool, clipped tones was impossible to ignore. My stomach clenched. "What did he do?"

"Betrayed us," Alphabet delivered the two words in a matter-of-fact tone rather than the sucker punch it had to have been. "He and Reznik went back. They set us up, we went in on a mission with bad intel. It cost me the lower half of my leg and Doc got burned to hell and back trying to save me."

"Burned with my explosives," Lunchbox said.

"That you built on my orders," Bones corrected.

"And deployed on mine," Voodoo added. The complex tangle of guilt and grief choked all four men. Well, three, because Alphabet touched two fingers to my knee when I would have said something. At his gentle head shake, I covered his hand with mine.

"We're a unit," Alphabet said, looking past me to Lunchbox. "All of us. What one does, we all do. I don't care which of us built the explosives, we all did it." He shifted his attention to Voodoo and Bones. "We trusted the intel because O'Rourke was supposed to be one of us. I would have bled for him the same way I would any brother. Taken a bullet for him. If any of us had to take that hit, I'm glad it was me."

Pain twisted up inside of me, because the sober declaration wasn't bravado or bullshit. He meant it.

"My only regrets are that Doc got hurt so damn much saving me." Not *helping*, but saving. I closed my fingers around Alphabet's and squeezed his hand.

I swallowed back the tears that clawed at my throat. The suffocating pressure around me seemed to contract. Not for me, but for them.

"I'm glad he saved you, AB." The words seemed far too simple to encompass the depth of emotion overflowing the dam inside. "And going by you four now—I'm going to guess, he doesn't regret saving you in the slightest, no matter what it cost him."

"What she said," Voodoo stated, his own voice thick. "So don't be a dipshit."

A snort of laughter escaped Alphabet, but it was Lunchbox who sighed. "Too late. We're all compromised." Alphabet gave my hand another squeeze then set it back next to my bowl. An action Lunchbox hadn't missed because he said, "You stopped eating."

I made a face, but I dunked more of the hard crusty bread into the thick stew. "You gave me enough for two of me, but I'm eating." I even took a bite and finished it before I asked, "So, O'Rourke was part of your team, he set you up and then what?"

"Then I buried him alive," Bones said in a brusque, almost business-like manner. "Set him up. He had no idea we knew."

"To be clear, we didn't confirm the betrayal immediately." Voodoo had finished eating at some point and set his empty bowl to the side. His expression came across more circumspect. "He'd done a damn good job of covering his tracks."

Bones merely nodded. "We got Doc and Alphabet packed off to the medics, then they were both eventually taken Stateside. The four of us went back and finished the mission. When it was done, so was O'Rourke. He should be dead."

The bitterness in those last four words leaked through the arctic tempo of his tone. Bones was not unmoved by those events. Far from it. Whether I was getting better at reading him or he was letting me see it, Boney Boy had more than just an axe to grind with those that betrayed him.

Betrayed his team.

Why shouldn't he?

"Apparently, he's more of a cockroach than we realized." Acid threatened to etch Lunchbox's words into the concrete floor of this little box we occupied.

"And working with Reznik." Voodoo looked thoughtful. "Apparently, they are both tied up in this syndicate of human trafficking operations..." He tested the words like he wanted to test their veracity.

"They'd have to be considering where they've turned up," Alphabet stretched out his right leg and began to rub his hand up and down his thigh. Goblin let out a grunt as he flipped over onto his back on the floor before he started snoring.

At least *he* could relax.

"But why?" Voodoo asked the question and none of the others answered. "That's the part that bugs me. This doesn't seem to fit O'Rourke's profile, unless we were just wrong about fucking everything."

The emptiness in the last part of that question scraped against me. I hadn't seen Reznik, or met him. I had O'Rourke. I couldn't answer the question for them either. With the exception of the bite, he hadn't hurt me.

He'd *definitely* had time to do more harm if he'd wanted.

I managed another two bites, but the food turned to ash against my tongue the more I turned over all the chances O'Rourke had. Since I was already full anyway, I handed what was left to Lunchbox.

"I ate plenty," I told him at his frown, raising a hand. "I'm stuffed."

He studied me briefly, then nodded once. "Okay." His expression gentled. "You still doing okay?" He dipped his gaze to my hand and I turned it over to show him my wrist.

It was definitely not pretty. "I don't think it's infected, and I scrubbed it in the shower."

"We'll keep an eye on it," Voodoo said. "Does it still hurt?"

"Just like a bad bruise." It stung like hell when he did it, between the pinch and scrape of his teeth. Alphabet shifted next to me and I dropped my left hand down to his thigh to try and massage the twitching muscles. I would have tried to be gentle, but he kept white knuckling when he dug his own fingers in.

"Fuck," Alphabet said, elongating the word with a groan. He tilted his head back and gritted his teeth. "Don't stop…"

"It's hurting you AB." So yeah, I was a little worried.

"It always hurts, Gracie," he assured me. "You're also loosening it up, so don't stop."

Scraping my teeth over my lower lip, I dug back in and twisted so I could use both hands. My bruised wrist wasn't a huge fan, but the fact Alphabet let out another deep groan encouraged me.

"Pretty sure that shouldn't sound as dirty as it does," Voodoo commented with a hint of a smile. Alphabet lifted his left hand and flipped Voodoo off. A rough chuckle spread around the men. "Hey now, I don't judge. Fire-cracker is definitely my kink too."

Lunchbox snorted behind me, but he rubbed my shoulder as he stood. "She's a good kink to have. Anyone else hungry? If not, I'm gonna pack us supplies for the drive tomorrow. We're going to have to avoid the larger motor-ways, which means fewer options to refuel."

"Pack it up," Bones said, leaning forward, elbows on his knees. "We should stay here for the next twenty-four hours." Not that he sounded committed to it. If anything, he sounded less inclined.

"We could hit the road tonight," Alphabet speculated verbally, his words punctuated with hissing breaths and little gasps as I kept loosening up the cramp that kept trying to seize the muscle. "It's late, but we change out the plates. We could change the van's appearance, or just swap it out entirely."

"Four of us," Lunchbox said, rejoining the conversation. "We tag out the driving…"

"Five," I volunteered. "And I do know how to drive."

That got me four frowning looks, but Bones said, "Five drivers. But eight hours is more than enough time to get to just about anywhere we want to near Paris—even taking backroads."

His gray eyes went distant.

"We haven't replaced the safe house there."

Voodoo sighed. "No, we haven't. I was supposed to do that next month, but the work has been piling up."

"I could probably find us a short term rental," Alphabet said on a longer sigh. "Fuck me, Gracie. You have magic hands."

Heat actually scorched my face at that admission. Still I

didn't let up because those muscles were still spasming. "What do you need for a safe house?"

"Good location, preferably with a decent population that we can blend into, but not so thick that they pick up on the fact we're strangers," Voodoo said.

"Good locations would include near transpo, public and otherwise. Also, access to stores for supplies," Lunchbox added.

"Not on a tourist route," Bones said. "While tourists can provide vital cover, we don't want to create too much of a hazard and those areas tend to also involve a lot more in the way of surveillance and law enforcement.

"Need a park or at least some green areas so we have cover for Goblin," Alphabet suggested. "Not a do or die, but preferable. Room for all of us, or if necessary, side by side apartments so we can control who is next to us and we can secure it."

"That's it?" I checked, sweeping all four with a glance before looking back at Bones. He was the final decision maker.

"No, but it's the solid basis and that type of location would do us well and it would put us in a larger city. Harder to track while Alphabet digs into the data. We can retrench, restock, research, and recon."

"How very alliterate of you," I murmured, because it was kind of funny. "Would you be opposed to me asking someone I know if we can borrow their place?"

"Who?" The question came from four different directions, with varying degrees of emphasis and concern.

"A friend," I said slowly. "A photographer that I've worked with. They have a place in Paris, but they aren't always there. It's a lot bigger than they need, so I've stayed there a couple of times."

The hard silence greeting my statement was so thick and tangible, I half worried that it had actually formed in the way an invisible wall would in a movie.

"What is his name?" Bones asked finally, his eyes narrowed.

His name?

Oh.

"*Her* name is..."

EIGHTEEN

GRACE

The drive to Paris took the rest of the night and into the early hours of the morning. I slept far more of it than I thought I would, curled up on a pallet they'd made in the back of the van with Goblin next to me and the guys taking turns as well. Always two of them up and two resting.

The first stretch of the drive Alphabet was on one side of me and Goblin on the other. The second Voodoo swapped spots with him. For the last few miles, Bones stretched out with me. I wasn't sleeping so much then, but took the time to study him as the light outside grew stronger.

The shadows beneath his eyes seemed to have dug in grooves. All night, I'd thought about the story they'd told. About the men from their past that now seemed inextricably tied up with my own horror story. Reznik—the hate for him was tangible and it had teeth.

Yet all of that paled in contrast to the raw, intense, and volatile tones as they vacillated between rage and heartbreak over O'Rourke. I doubted they would see it the same way, but it was there from the first moment Bones said anything over comms regarding him.

Sharp and clipped, with biting, accusatory words or phrases that threatened to crack under the weight of emotion. That was Bones. For Voodoo it was strained, hoarse and edged as though each statement had to be forced past his teeth. Lunchbox's came out guttural and intense, deepening his voice with adrenaline-fueled anguish.

And AB?

His silence screamed far louder and his humor a desperate shield. The pain he suffered then—still suffered no matter how he dismissed it, was deafening. O'Rourke *hurt* these men. Hurt them in a way only someone truly loved and trusted could hurt another.

Betrayal went down like battery acid and I'd hate O'Rourke for that alone.

"You're thinking too loudly, Grace," Bones said in a low voice. "Go back to sleep. We have..." He raised his wrist to look at his watch. "Another hour before we're at the location. Then another hour to do a scout before we go in."

"Then sleep if you can, unlike some people, I got most of a night's sleep."

He cracked an eyelid, then wrapped an arm around me, flipped me over so I had my back to his chest and then snugged me up tight. Goblin shifted over so he could little spoon to my little spoon.

"Now sleep," Bones ordered in a husky voice. Unexpectedly, the way he wrapped me up tight, the warmth of him there, and the hum of the street below us as we rolled along knocked me out.

Three hours later, we were settling into the huge apartment we now had on loan for the next several days. The owner was in Australia and she'd been more than happy to give me the door code and to stay as long as I needed. The only "payment" she wanted was for me to agree to a photo shoot down the road. Not really a hardship. Rachel was wonderful and I'd worked with her a couple of times before.

As for the apartment, it took up the entire top floor of the building. There were four flats below, also owned by Rachel apparently, but they were only let for students and uni was out currently. So we were in luck there. She said the next tenants weren't due for another month.

Whatever we had to do shouldn't take that long.

"This photographer friend must make a bundle," Voodoo mused as they set up Alphabet's equipment. We didn't have as much as we'd had at the first house, but they were doing an inventory so Voodoo could acquire more.

I shrugged. "She does well. I think this place was a gift, if I recall correctly."

That earned me a *look* from Bones. "A yachting kind of gift?"

"Oh, god no." I raised my hands and shook my head. "Rachel is not a yacht girl. Trust me. She'd be more likely to kick them in the balls than get on their boats. No—she's just really tight with some really wealthy friends and when she relocated to Paris, her friend bought the whole building and set it up for her to live in. Cause she wanted her to have something nice with excellent security."

Alphabet nodded. "That explains all the upgrades." The upgrades included exterior cameras. All access points into the building and the apartment itself had cameras. It also took codes to get in the doors below and the elevator wouldn't work without another code.

"I just...I like the story. Because Rachel would never ask for something like this and I got the impression it kind of baffled her. But I also get why her friends did it. They are back in New York and she's here. They wanted her safe. I would do the same for..."

Amorette.

Some of my good cheer just fled.

"Hey," Lunchbox settled his hands on my upper arms and rubbed them. "It's okay. Come help me make a food shopping list. Your friend has a great place, but I don't think she ever uses her kitchen."

Some of my humor spilled back in, but only a little. The ache for Amorette spread like a poison, burning everywhere it touched. I'd forgotten—for just a little while, I'd forgotten. I sniffed once, blinking back the tears.

"You sure you want me to help?" It came out rougher than I intended. "I really shouldn't be let loose in a kitchen."

"I can take care of all that," he said, wrapping an arm around my shoulders. "What you are going to do is tell me what you like and then I'll build the menus from there."

The kitchen was every bit as nice as I remembered it, huge, open space with double ovens, a double sided sink, a pot filler over the range, and stool seating at the kitchen peninsula. The floor was marble, white with black veins, and beautiful. Sandstone countertops and backsplash warmed it up. The cabinetry was all painted bright white, the windows including the skylight, flooded the room with natural light.

"Oh," I exhaled a breath. "Coffee." The espresso machine was a lot like the one they had at base. A snort of laughter escaped me.

"What's funny?" Lunchbox asked from where he stood at the fridge. The door was open and he frowned. What I could see of it made it seem like it was empty. But if she was in Australia, that was probably a good move.

"I just thought of the house in Montana as base."

He flashed me a quick smile. "That's because it is *base*."

"Accepted," I murmured. "We need to get oat milk."

"See, already helping with a list." he stood at the peninsula making crisp notes on a pad of paper for grocery supplies. He added oat milk and underlined it twice. Some items had slashes next to them, others little asterisks.

"Code?" I asked when I leaned against the counter next to him. He had a lot of items on there, bread, muffins, flour, milk, eggs, potatoes, and meat. "And isn't that a lot of food if we're only here for a few days?"

I didn't want to leave anything to go bad in her fridge.

"Slashes indicates we can substitute if necessary, asterisks are absolutely no substitutes accepted and underlined means don't come back without it."

He added whole bean coffee to the list, and underlined it twice as well. Dog food was also added, then toiletries.

"Do you need any—" He eyed me.

"Any?" I raised my brows.

"Tampons or pads or little cup things or whatever?" His expression was perfectly neutral. Perfectly cool and collected.

"No," I said slowly. "I don't. I have an implant. Just easier because I travel so much. It makes my periods almost non-existent. Though I do PMS now and then even without the rest."

"Good to know." He completed the toiletries list and then slid the pad over to me. "Anything else you want?"

I added chocolate bars to the list. Dark, milk, and white, then extra milk. Tapping my chin with the pen, I studied the kitchen then Lunchbox. "Done."

"Good, stay here." He left the kitchen with the note in hand and headed out to where the guys were. Staying as he'd ordered, I walked over to one of the windows and looked down at the street below.

Paris bustled about its morning. The sunshine after days of misting rain seemed to make it even brighter. So weird to see so much... *normalcy.*

Hands came to rest on my hips and I leaned back, trusting that he wouldn't let me fall and I wasn't disappointed. "Talk to me, Gracie. You look sad."

"I'm not really *sad.*" I turned the words over in my head. "I am, but—it's hard to explain."

"Let's try it this way, then." He wrapped his arms around me, and the warmth of his embrace just pulled me tighter. "What are you thinking about?"

"It's so normal outside. People going to work. Going to shops. Just—going about their lives." I frowned. "That feels like a million years ago to me. It's only been a few months, but even that feels a lot longer."

He didn't say anything for a long moment, just held me while I rested against his chest. The steady thump of his heart helped to erode some of my tension. A part of me wanted to just be one of those people out there. I wanted to return to normalcy.

We're never going to be normal again. How can we? After everything? And these guys...

The thought slid out of the shadows in my mind and I couldn't deny it. Wouldn't even try. They weren't normal. How could I want *normal* if they weren't a part of it?

"Gracie?" He framed a dozen questions in my name and I tilted my head back to look up at him. "Come with me for a little while?"

"Anywhere." Easiest answer ever and he scooped me

up. "I can walk," I reminded him even as he strode out of the kitchen. We didn't go back to the sitting room where we'd parked it when we arrived. Not that I saw the guys anywhere.

Maybe they'd left?

"I know you can," he said, but he didn't slow his stride. "This is faster."

I snorted a laugh then frowned. "Did you just call me slow?"

His eyes twinkled, it was the first hint of light to slip into them since he'd crashed into the lounge to get me away from O'Rourke. "Absolutely not."

At the end of the hall that housed some of the bedrooms, he opened one up and then stepped inside where he locked the door. The whole time, he kept his gaze fixed on mine.

"Would now be the time to remind you that I got a lot of sleep in the van last night?" More curious than anything, I studied his expressions. The blinds were closed in here, but there was enough light sneaking in around to keep it from being truly dark.

"If you want," he said, walking toward the bed while still cradling me. My heart did a little fist bump with my ribs. "Or you can just let me look after you the way I want to."

At the bed, he set me down and then reached for my shoes. Wreathed in shadow and stormlight, he glanced up at me from his crouch.

"Did I tell you how magnificent you were last night?"

"No..." I said slowly. "Which time? When I was freaking out at the safe house or..."

"At the chateau. At the safe house. Before we got there. After. You're a grenade with the pin half out, Gracie."

The air backed up in my lungs and made it difficult to suck in a deeper breath. He set my shoes aside one at a time.

"Is that a good thing?" I frowned. "Cause that sounds dangerous."

"It's very good thing," he murmured, then reached for my shirt and tugged it upward. I raised my arms so he could peel it off. "I've always had a thing for explosives."

My mouth opened then closed, then a snort of laughter escaped me. It was such an undignified sound that I had to clap my hand over my mouth. Lunchbox didn't help, his eyes were practically dancing.

"You're beautiful, and you look fragile. Looks can be deceiving. You're so tiny, it makes me want to build walls around you that no one can breach. You've got a hell of an arm on you and nothing about you is glass."

"No?"

"No," he said, undoing the bra from the back and I let it slide down my arms. The room was chilly, and my nipples peaked almost immediately but I didn't think it had anything to do with the cold. No, it was the way his eyes caressed me. "Glass breaks, Gracie. You don't. You burn."

If it was possible to seduce someone with words, he'd just done it. Heat swept through me as he reached for the waistband of my pants. I fisted his shirt and dragged him forward. He wrapped an arm around my waist and hauled me upwards, falling into me like we'd both been waiting for this moment.

His mouth slammed down onto mine, hard, wild, teeth clashing, and desperate. So damn desperate. Was that need his? Mine? Ours? The weight of his kiss was a brand. He might say I burned, but he seared himself into me.

Then he dropped me back onto the bed, and let go of

me long enough to rip my pants down. He paused, staring down at me. Catching my right foot, he lifted my leg and traced a kiss over a bruise, then the next. Some of them I hadn't even realized I had. Yet, he kissed every single one on his way to my cunt as if they had offended him personally.

I was already squirming long before his breath teased my slit. Then he kissed my pussy with the same kind of open-mouthed possession he had my lips. I arched upwards, straining against the feeling as he stroked, nipped, and sucked against my clit even as he alternated between thrusting his tongue into me.

Zero patience.

He had none, he pushed and pushed and that first orgasm ripped out of me with a scream. I shook as he lapped at me, and hummed.

He fucking hummed.

"This," he said against my thigh. "This is heaven. You taste every bit as sweet and heady as I expected." He pushed upwards and I ached at the loss.

"Lunchbox..." His name left me like a groan in a voice I barely recognized as my own.

"Don't worry, Gracie. I am so not done." He stripped off his clothes with the same lack of patience he'd shown to my orgasm, then he was standing there, raw, naked and beautiful.

His cock jutted out, thick and red. The tip was damn near purple with the strain. There were scars on him. They all had scars. Tattoos too and I wanted to study them all, even the one that looked like a chemical formula on his biceps.

"I want you," I told him.

He took a deep breath, wrapping his hand around his

cock and fisting it twice. "Just taking the edge off. I don't want to hurt you."

"You're not going to hurt me." I pushed up and wrapped my hand over his. "I'm not glass, remember?"

He groaned when he relinquished his dick to me and I gave him a couple of solid pumps. Silky, hot, and hard as hell.

"You're right," he whispered. "You don't break." Then I was on my back again and he dragged my legs upward even as he pulled me to the edge. His first thrust is raw, fast, and damn near violent.

But it was perfect. He stretched me even as he locked an arm around my legs to keep them to his chest. It was like being taken from behind except I could see him, feel him and he drove into me again.

Hips thrusting, he pushed deep and withdrew, then drove himself in again. It was like he was trying to fuse us together. I fought to arch my hips up to take him as the strain showed on his face.

Then he struck that spot inside and my head went back as I lost my grip. "There..." The only word to escape me, pushed out with his thrust.

Words were meaningless as I began to spasm around him. His gasp was music, then he let go of my legs and I spread them as he fell. As much as I longed to have his weight press into me, he caught himself on his hands.

"Wrap those legs around me, Gracie."

I happily obeyed that order and then wrapped my arms around his neck as he took my mouth in another kiss. We rocked together and I savored the feeling of him. The drive as he relentlessly took me toward another orgasm.

This time, he jetted over with me. His hips stuttered before he came in a hot rush and then we were just holding each other, slick with sweat, breathless, and it was my turn to cradle him.

He buried his face against my throat and my legs were like spaghetti, but he didn't try to pull away from me. Instead, as we got our breathing under control, he began to nuzzle kisses against my throat.

"Lunchbox..."

"Hmm?"

"I think I'm hungry."

He was quiet for a moment, then he began to chuckle. Finally, he lifted his head. "Are you now?"

"Yes." I licked my lips as I pressed upwards and he rolled onto his back. "I know exactly what I want, too."

He hadn't let me do much before, but now I wanted to explore. I wanted to kiss his bruises. I wanted to taste him.

"Fuck me, Gracie," he groaned as I began tracing a path down his chest.

"That is the plan," I promised. I wanted more of him.

I wanted more of all of them.

CHAPTER

NINETEEN

LUNCHBOX

The slow, sensuous way she moved coupled with her throaty declaration of, "I'm hungry," made the world fall away. Wanting her had been a fever in my blood for days, one I'd had to keep rigidly compartmentalized. We had a mission. We had to protect her. Voodoo and Alphabet had already found their way into her bed, and fuck me if I didn't want to be there too.

At her urging, I rolled onto my back, taking her with me. She straddled my hips, as she sat up to study me. She was so goddamn tiny. Easy to forget because her personality filled a room, even when she was quiet. A tiny tornado that packed a hell of a punch.

I contented myself with stroking her thighs as she began to kiss a path over my chest. Her hair draped over her like a curtain and the strands of it teased my skin. All that hair, that perfect face and mouth...

"I know exactly what I want, too."

A groan ripped out of my throat as she glided against my softening dick. The wetness slipping out of her a *firm*

169

reminder of how I'd just buried myself inside her. She stole a look up at me, those brilliant blue eyes intoxicating. The movement of her lips, each tickling kiss, peeled the moment open for us. That gaze dug into me, stripping away all the barriers.

I'd never felt more exposed. Instead of concern or worry, I wanted to sink into her demand as she drew me closer. The words *claim me* rested unspoken on my tongue. That she'd let me have her was more than enough.

"Fuck me, Gracie." The words rode another groan as she traced one of my scars with her tongue. No matter how slight she might seem, she marked me with every single touch.

"That's the plan." She hummed as she kissed along my abdomen. As much as I appreciated the faith, I wasn't sure I would recover that swiftly.

Then she wrapped that sexy fucking mouth around the tip of my dick and all my blood rushed south. I fisted the covers on the bed to avoid thrusting. With almost agonizing slowness, she rolled her tongue around the tip. It was hedonistic torture. She wrapped her hand around the base of my cock and I stiffened obediently.

Yes, ma'am. If she wanted me hard to play with then fuck yes, she was going to get what she wanted.

"Gracie..." Her name fell from me like a prayer.

"I'm here," she murmured, but she had to release my dick to do so. That was a terrible form of ecstasy, a momentary reprieve from building pleasure and yet too much chill from the heat of her mouth.

"At some point," I said, fighting to remember why I'd tried to snare her attention. "I'm going to fist your hair and fuck you from behind."

"Are you?" Amusement curled in her voice and I couldn't help but grin.

"Absolutely, want to build right up to that if you need some foreplay for it. I love the way your pussy feels on me and that definitely felt like more." Probably good to make sure she was up for whatever I'd like to do. She would always have final say, but if I didn't ask, I wouldn't know, right?

She gave my dick a casual pump and I arched my hips, pushing against her hand. I didn't miss the way she licked her lips or how gratifying it was for her to look at me the way she was right now.

"I love how you felt inside me." Those low, husky notes wrapped around me like velvet smoke. It wasn't just what she said, but how she said it. The words were a secret meant only for me. "I want to feel that again."

The slow stroking had me at full attention now. She flexed her hand against my cock, gliding up to the tip then all the way to the base. In no way was this a substitute for her cunt. At the same time, being touched by her was no bad thing.

"Right now though," she continued, her breath feathering along my cock. "I want to taste you. I want to feel you come in my mouth. I want to give you all the pleasure you gave me."

In that instant, she held me utterly spellbound. Every nerve was on high alert, tethered to the sound and feel of her.

"Anything you want," I promised her. "Absolutely anything."

She lapped at my tip with her tongue. A perfect torture that had my balls dragging up but not quite releasing as she teased me. I fisted the covers again, holding fast so I wouldn't try to take over.

"You smell musky," she murmured, and for a moment, I wasn't quite sure that I registered the words. With every stroke of her hand, she ran her tongue along my dick. She licked me like I was her favorite goddamn lollipop. "There's traces of smoke, but it's not sour or sharp. More like a memory of a fire you curl up in front of when it's cold."

Could a woman really seduce a man with words? Not something I'd ever really contemplated. Frankly, she owned me. She didn't need to convince me but her words were like a warm whiskey sliding over my senses. They slowed my thoughts and every syllable felt like a touch.

"There's also coffee, that dark bite of it—you know the first grind where it's just edged by bitter but there are elements of burnt sugar, traces of vanilla. Not saccharine or too sweet, caramelized and intimate."

I barely had time to process the words before she swallowed me and I swore I could feel her throat closing around me. Utterly tethered to the sound of her, I rocked my hips in time to her motion. The wet, decadent heat of her mouth threatened to drain me of everything.

Groaning, I murmured, "The French call an orgasm la petite mort..."

She gave a throaty laugh that had my eyes crossing at the intensity of sensation. I swore my dick got even harder, I could probably drill steel with it. But she didn't slow her caresses. If anything, she increased the pressure, the suction, and every downward swoop had my cock in her throat.

When she swallowed around me, my balls dragged up so tightly, I could feel it coming. "Gracie..."

Then she wrapped her hand around my balls, cupping

them and rolling them in a massage that destroyed me. The little death was so much more as I came. I slammed my head back against the bed and part of the comforter tore where I yanked at it.

The ripping fabric punctuated it as I shot every ounce of my release into her. She swallowed and there was a choking sound that had me jerking my head up. Cum dribbled out of the corners of her mouth as she drew back. Her eyes were huge, her hair a dark cloud, and she licked at her lips, chasing the drops of me as she swallowed.

Even as reaction shook through me, my dick was already making a valiant effort. "You're fucking perfect, Gracie."

Her lips were already swollen as I dragged her to me. The moment I kissed her, she let out a little sound. "I have..."

"Yes, me on your lips," I said with a growl, and rolled her over so I could blanket her fully. I teased her tongue with mine, savored the way her nails dug into my shoulder. The little kittenish licks she'd about driven me mad with on my cock were just as intoxicating in her kiss.

I bit her lower lip, dragging at it a moment before I lifted my head. She grinned up at me, the soft flush of her face turning even pinker. Stubble burn marked her cheeks. I should shave, but when she cupped my jaw I rubbed against her palm.

Turning my head, I brushed my lips to her palm then paused at her wrist. At the bite mark there. Fucking O'Rourke had marked her and it pissed me off all over again.

"Don't," she murmured, pulling my attention back to her. "Stay here, with me."

I nuzzled another kiss to her palm, then to her wrist. "I hate that he did that."

"It doesn't matter," she said in that low voice and I snapped my gaze up to hers.

"It *does*." I bit lightly at the juncture of her elbow, then up her biceps to her throat. "Biting someone—marking them—it's a way to claim and possess."

"Does it?" She dragged her foot along the back of my thigh.

"Yes." I lifted my head to meet her gaze again. "It's important, Gracie. No one should ever do something you don't consent to. I want to knock his fucking teeth out of his head."

She stretched and I eased up my weight to let her adjust herself. "Okay, but I don't want to talk about him right now. He's not in this bed."

No, he sure as fuck wasn't.

"If you want to be invited to bite me," she continued, tilting her head back and showing me her throat. "You can. I don't mind."

If my dick wasn't already working hard to stiffen up again, those words would have done it. I pressed a kiss over her pulse point. "Do you want me to bite you?" Her breasts rubbed against my chest and it reminded me, I really hadn't gotten to play with them yet.

There were a lot of things I wanted to do, to play and to tease. I wanted to taste and to torment.

"Yes, please." She lifted her hips and ground against me. "Then we can see about letting you pull my hair... Apparently, I'm starving."

That just made me laugh. "Well then," I said, pressing another kiss to her pulse. "We should make sure you get whatever you want."

When I sucked a hickey into place, I swore it was even more tantalizing than when I used to do it as a teenager. Gracie was so much more. But I was hardly done there. I took some time to kiss and nip a path to her nipples.

Those beautiful breasts could be sucked and bitten. Every kiss included a scrape of my teeth or the stubble on my cheeks. Each time she squirmed or let out that breathy little moan, I repeated the action.

"You're so goddamn beautiful," I told her in between longing sucks to each of her nipples. I could palm her breasts, they were firm and high. I loved the way she felt against me. "I used to jerk off to your pictures."

Admitting that hadn't been on my to do list, and I paused to shoot her a look. Her mouth was open in that silent "o," and her eyes were dark, the pupils swollen and huge.

"Too much?" I checked.

"I—" She licked her lips. "I don't think so." It sounded like she was testing those words out for herself. She tilted her head from side to side. "No—which pictures did you like best?"

I chuckled. "I think admitting it is enough humiliation."

"Oh, don't be embarrassed," she cradled my face in her hands. "I kind of like it."

"Yeah?"

"Yes."

"Okay, so that's not so bad then." Still, I bit down on the heel of her palm. A light mark there. "The real thing is a thousand percent better."

"Well, that's because I can touch you back, suck your cock and you're not going to get paper cuts even by accident." The droll delivery was what did it. I laughed.

A deep laugh that came from somewhere in my soul

that hadn't shaken like that in a while. When I met her gaze, I drank in her smile. "You good with me flipping you over and pulling your hair now?"

"Yes, please," she said with a grin.

Perfect.

She was *perfect*.

A light scuff of a footstep in the hall. "Fuck off," I called, rising just enough to flip her over and pull her hips up. Her face was pink and her laughter seemed to glow off her as I teased my dick at her entrance.

"Lunch—"

"I said, *fuck off*," I called back. "Unless there's blood, bone, or a bomb—if none of those are involved, go away."

A snort of laughter carried through the wood of the door, but they didn't knock or say anything else. Grace looked back at me again as I wrapped my hand in her hair.

"You wanna do me another favor, Gracie?"

"Depends," she said with a gasp as I stroked my dick against her entrance. She was definitely still soaking, but I wanted to torture us both.

"Will you scream for me?"

A snort of laughter escaped her. "You want to taunt them."

"Fuck yes—and I've heard you scream. I want to make you scream like that." The moment I said it, I recognized just how true it was.

She bit her lip. "Can I ask for a favor in return?"

"Anything you want."

"What's your real name?"

I grinned. "Whole thing or just the first name?"

"First," she said as I nudged the tip in, just a testing push.

Tightening my grip in her hair, I pressed my lips to her ear and thrust into her as I whispered, "Legend."

Two more thrusts and she screamed. She rocked back to meet me and her hair was the perfect handle. When she came, she screamed more.

When she came a second time, she really let loose.

Hell, yeah.

Definitely felt like more.

CHAPTER

TWENTY

BONES

Sounds of pans on counters, fridge opening and closing, followed by chopping in the kitchen told me he was up. The doors to the rooms Alphabet and Voodoo had taken the night before were both closed. A low whistle kicked up, then stretched into a tune.

I paused, hand on the swinging door, to identify the song. He was whistling *Patience*. Interesting choice. The door swung inward silently. It was still dark outside, the sunrise at least another hour off.

The scent of fresh coffee perfumed the air and there was a whole pot of it that he'd brewed. Dressed in jeans and nothing else, Lunchbox chopped vegetables with his back to the door. The red marks on his neck and shoulders were very visible.

Even if we hadn't heard her for a good portion of the day and into the evening, the shift in their relationship was blatantly obvious. I waited until he paused mid-chop to let the door swing closed behind me and headed for the coffee pot.

Silence rushed in to fill the room. The apartment that Grace had *borrowed* for us was very nice. Too nice. We'd need to make sure we didn't damage it. No sense in leaving her friend holding the bag for our choices.

Voodoo and I had already discussed that when we left the day before to get supplies. We needed another safe house in the area anyway. Locating one and locking it down could fill in the hours while Alphabet worked on decrypting the files we'd taken.

I filled a large mug with coffee, taking about half of what was left in the pot. Downing a long swallow of the strong brew, I let it burn away the cobwebs and the light fog from low sleep. Carrying the mug, I settled at the kitchen table with my phone.

Aware of Lunchbox's stare, I opened my emails and flipped through the responses that had come in through the night. I'd tapped some sources I still had in intelligence. Reached out to other contacts we'd cultivated over the past few years.

We'd done more than one black bag job that couldn't have official fingerprints. Beyond the actual Network itself, we'd developed other—connections through intelligence sources and local resources in the region.

The chopping resumed without the whistling this time when I took another swallow of coffee. I spared him a look. His jaw had tightened and he glared at the vegetables he was chopping like they were the culprits.

"You want to hit me or just make that face until it cracks?" The question pinged off the walls like we were sitting inside a game of pinball. It whooshed past me, grazing but not quite scoring the hit he was going for.

Lunchbox stared at me steadily as he finished chopping an onion then scraped it all into a bowl. The lack of pretense was probably a good thing. We needed to address this issue. All of us.

But we had to be controlled because I wasn't going to risk destroying this kitchen to solve it. Leaning back in my chair, I turned the phone facedown.

It shouldn't *have* to be said, but here we were.

"She's not yours," I told him. Not clenching my jaw took effort. Where his opening salvo had sailed past me, mine struck. His knuckles went white on the knife handle before he shifted to rinse it and the cutting board off.

"She's not *yours*, either." That landed. More than I cared to admit, that sliced. But I could handle the blow. It took a lot more than a cut to stop me.

He pulled out a basket of potatoes in a strainer from the sink and went to work cutting them.

Blowing out a long breath, I weighed my options. Direct would be better for both of us, no matter how much it might cost. "Do you really think this is about territory?"

"Nope, Cap, I don't." He didn't look up as he halved, then quartered, the chopped until he'd made solid square shaped potatoes for frying. "I think this is about the fact that you're terrified of needing her."

I ignored the accusation. Fear had no place in command. Fear could choke. Fear cost lives. I wouldn't let fear cost me any of them. "What about what she needs?"

He spared me a look before swapping his knife to his free hand and picking up his coffee. "You've been fighting this since Pennsylvania. Watching her bleed, letting her carry it, pretending you don't give a damn and that she needed to be treated as nothing more than a client."

After emptying the mug, he returned it to the counter then began to chop again.

"You might like to think you're stone, Cap. But you're

not." He shook his head, making steady progress through the potatoes. "I've let it slide. At first, I got it, she's been through hell. She's not all the way through it yet. Voodoo—he's already invested and even when it pissed me off, he helped her."

"Something you made clear when you punched him." The dry delivery stopped Lunchbox mid-chop and he just stared at me. "Fortunately, the shifting nature of the relationship hasn't disrupted the team too much."

He snorted. "You do realize the only one who has ever sounded jealous is *you*?"

I didn't bother to deny it. "Then you haven't been paying as close attention as you claim."

"Do you think keeping our distance is going to protect her? Do you think *not* touching her is a noble sacrifice?" He shook his head. "They took a lot from her. A hell of a lot more than she will admit to herself. That need she has for control, you should recognize it."

"I do." I had. Too damn well.

"Then you have to know what she needs isn't a saint or saints? She doesn't need us to parachute in and out. She needs a *pack* around her." He pointed the blade at me. "A pack that will defend her and let her defend us. She told you herself, don't you remember?"

"She said to use her like a weapon." I remembered. "We did. It put her in O'Rourke's crosshairs."

"She was already in them." Lunchbox huffed out a breath. "We'd have to be pretty fucking stupid to think his appearance there has nothing to do with Reznik's in Monaco. Reznik is involved. Grace is on their lists. We were there. It's not a huge stretch to link us to her."

"After the chateau, O'Rourke has his supposition

confirmed." If I'd been closer, I could have just ended it right there and right then. Eliminating him took a lesser priority than getting Grace out.

"Well, we can't exactly put the cat back in the bag." He finished cutting up the last of the potatoes and rinsed off the knife, then the board before he washed his own hands. Only when he was done and drying them did he face me again. "Even if we could, I wouldn't."

"No?" I raised my brows. "Tying her to us only adds fresh targets to her back." For anyone who wanted to get to us, she would be the leverage they needed. We'd kill them. All of them. But it wouldn't take the target off.

It wouldn't let her go home.

"No, I wouldn't. Because A, the guys want her. They want her and they care. B, I'm not backing off. Not now. Not after she's let me see her. All of her." He sounded damn near reverent. "I wasn't interested in retreating before, I damn well won't now."

He went to the cabinet and pulled out a bowl before he retrieved eggs.

"So either you step up or just get the fuck out of the way, Cap. Don't make us choose between you and her." He cracked the first egg into the bowl. "She needs us. We need her. If you were honest with yourself, you'd admit that you aren't immune. It's that simple."

We both wanted to protect her. That was obvious. But he wanted to dive in with her. No tempering with restraint or caution. He was as lost as Voodoo and Alphabet were.

"She's not ready for this," I said, rising with my empty coffee cup. "She's not ready for what we are."

Lunchbox laughed. "None of us were ready." He spread his arms. "Yet here we are."

"They key is we *chose* this life."

"You think she hasn't?" He looked genuinely shocked as I split the remaining pot between his cup and my own. Then I took the time to set up another one. "You're not that blind, Cap. You can't be."

"She didn't choose," I reminded him. "She was kidnapped. Assaulted. Raped. Kidnapped again. Physically abused. Then she's been attacked repeatedly—that's not choosing, Legend. You damn well know that."

We didn't generally rely on the names we were born with, choosing to be the team we were.

"Cap, Alphabet didn't choose to have his leg blown off. He didn't choose to be so wrecked that he needed a dog to help him with episodes and to manage his PTSD. Doc didn't choose to—" He cut off there and sighed, hands braced against the counter.

"We signed up," I reminded him. "Each and every one of us signed up, trained, and went into our service with our eyes open. Were we betrayed? Yes. Did it cost us? Yes. Doc went into that conflagration to get Alphabet. There isn't a single one of us who wouldn't have done the same damn thing."

Facing him across the island, I met his gaze and didn't flinch.

"Everything that's happened to Grace... everything from the time they took her until we got to France, even some of it here, has not been because of her choices."

"She asked for our help."

"I know she did. We're going to help her." That wasn't even a question. "But she wouldn't be here out of choice. She's here because the choices of others have forced her hand."

Lunchbox bowed his head, his throat convulsing once

before he snapped it up to stare at me. "Look me in the eye and tell me she doesn't belong with us. That she doesn't *burn* for every single one of us in a different way."

I couldn't. I wouldn't.

I'd held her when the nightmares came and the fear tried to tear her apart. I'd fought that fear, using her own body to wrest her free of it.

"You care about her. I get it." Lunchbox's voice was deceptively quiet. The coffeemaker hissed and spit as it brewed. Outside, the sky grew lighter. "You're just trying not to drown in it. But me? I'll drown. Happily."

I sighed. He wasn't telling me anything I didn't know. They'd all go over that cliff and into the rapids. They'd let the water sweep them away.

After a moment, Lunchbox went back to cracking eggs as he cleared his throat. "So now we've got a problem. We've got Reznik and O'Rourke, alive and hunting. And we've got Grace, running hot and not stopping to breathe. So what's our move, Cap?"

With a whisk, Lunchbox began to whip the eggs.

"The way I see it, we go after Reznik now. He's one of the big bidders, a lynchpin. We pull him and we strike loud. We send the others scrambling for cover." That was definitely one way to handle it. "Not like we don't owe Reznik some pain. Or... we ghost now and get Grace back stateside and to base. Let things chill here."

She would never agree to the second, he had to know that.

"We can't do both," Lunchbox pressed on. "She's not bulletproof."

All facts. He wasn't wrong. Going after them with her would risk her. Securing her meant letting them go for now. She wanted to be used as a weapon. "If we pull her," I reasoned. "We could lose him. We might not get a second chance."

That was one risk.

"If we stay, and use her, she might not make it out." Real concern edged that fear.

That was another risk. That fear would push them to take the hit for her and it wouldn't be Grace we lost—or not her only.

"It's your call."

I didn't snort, because after all that, it was still my call. Whether they agreed with me or not, they would follow my lead. That curbed some of the irritation and the anger souring my gut.

Another choice.

We had friends.

We had Doc.

"We get her out." I didn't like it. I didn't like trusting her safety to someone else, but putting distance between us might be the best thing. "We get her safe. Then we burn Reznik and the rest of those bastards to the ground. Quiet. Smart. Permanent."

"She's not going to like it." As if I didn't already know that.

"She doesn't have to." The simple fact was as long as she was secure, we could focus on the mission. Destroy this whole arm of it. Then we could work on finding her sister. "She just has to live through it."

"And when she finds out we made the call without her?"

"She'll forgive us." I shrugged. She could forgive them. She had at almost every other step.

The skepticism in Lunchbox's expression was almost laughable. "You think so?"

"No," I told him, taking another long drink of my coffee. "But I'll take that hit if it keeps her breathing."

The creak of the door saved me from the sympathy in Lunchbox's eyes. The light shuffle of steps was Grace.

She was perfect, and composed. Except for her eyes.

They were on fire.

TWENTY-ONE

GRACE

When I woke up it was still dark. Though I was alone, the spot where he'd slept was still warm. Stretching, I'd tried to ease the soreness between my legs and threading throughout the rest of me. I really did ache but in the very best of ways.

I lost track of how many hours *Legend* and I spent in bed. Even when we took breaks or he went for food, he had me stay there. Asked me, really. At one point, he'd even encouraged me to take a bath and when he'd come back he had wine and a charcuterie board.

Delight had curved through me at the board with its bits of cheese, fruit, and jams. There were little crackers and hard bread. The wine was sweet, the cheese sharp, the fruit rich, and Legend sitting on the floor and feeding it to me while I bathed was heavenly.

"Just tonight," he said. "You need a break from every-thing." While that might not have convinced me, his long sigh of, "Fuck knows I need it," had. So, we hid away in this room and after the bath, he took me back to bed. We'd nap, fuck, cuddle, fuck, and basically, just savor this little bubble of escape.

At some point, I must have just crashed entirely because I slept deeper than I had in a while. There were only a couple of nights I could think of in recent weeks that I'd slept like that. They all involved multiple orgasms.

Probably something to that. Smothering a giggle at the thought, I made myself roll over and get up. Oh, I was definitely walking funny. Another giggle escaped me as I got the water going and slid into the shower.

Thankfully, the apartment was well stocked with good bath products and one of my favorites for hair care. The bath the night before along with the wine and the food had been decadent. The near boiling hot shower while working good product through my hair and combing out the snarls while also smoothing out frizz? That was hedonistic.

I took my time. Washing, buffing, and exfoliating in turns. I would need a laser appointment soon. That little nugget gave me pause. When was I going to get to a laser appointment?

It made me look at my nails. They weren't painted. They weren't even that long anymore. I'd broken nearly all of them at one point or another. Filing to keep them neat and somewhat rounded was the best I could do.

Glancing down at my toes, I wiggled them. The paint had all chipped away there as well. When would I find myself in a salon of any kind? My life had gone sideways. When I finished showering, I wiped away the steam from the mirror and studied myself.

Did I look different? I definitely felt different, but could they see those changes or was it just in my head? When my gaze dipped to the little trail of kiss-marked bruises on my neck, I blinked. He'd formed a heart out of hickeys.

I didn't know whether to be delighted at the creativity or smack him in the head. Maybe both. I took the time to towel off and to squeeze the excess water from my hair. Bless Rachel, she even had lotions in here and moisturizer. It just felt nice to pamper myself a little.

Once I was dressed in yoga pants, a tank top, and thick socks, I shrugged on a hoodie. Another question for the guys, how did they keep restocking me on clothes. We lost clothes, we found clothes, but they always seemed to have new ones. Clean underwear too. The panties were plain cotton and so was the bra, which was just fine.

The sky had lightened while I lingered in the shower. The scent of coffee hit me as soon as I opened the bedroom door. I followed the siren scent straight toward the kitchen. Two of the other bedroom doors were closed. I really wasn't sure how many bedrooms she had.

One of the rooms had been set up as a dark room and another as an office. It really was quite the lush space here. Just as I got to the swinging door to the kitchen voices drifted out.

"She's not ready..."

I froze. Those words came through clearly.

"Get her out."

Their voices. Low. Serious. Like they were planning a war. Like I was the prize they had to carry out. Hadn't we already discussed this?

"She just has to live through it."

Bones' flat delivery made me ache. I thought we'd moved past this. I thought...

She just has to live through it.

Curling my fingers into my palm, I closed my eyes. It hurt. There was no escaping that fact. Them having this discussion about me, without me, and making decisions like shuttling me off—*hurt.*

Blowing up wasn't going to win me any battles. While Bones didn't always explain, they often had plans and "reasons" for the choices they made. Hadn't I already learned that?

Still pain washed through me, because trust had to go both ways. Sending me away—to where? With who? Shouldn't that be my call?

My pulse climbed, growing louder as it thudded in my ears. Breathing was harder and my hands shook. Backing up, I kept my eyes closed as I forced myself to breathe.

C'mon—you have to breathe. If we don't breathe, we won't get answers. They'll have some rational explanation. Just have to go in and get it.

Bit by bit, I regained some semblance of control.

They don't want to hurt me. They don't want me to hurt at all. This isn't about keeping me. They care. Maybe too damn much.

Maybe that was what hurt the most. We had a deal.

I thought we had one.

"She'll forgive us."

I almost snorted. Bones sounded absolutely certain.

"You think so?" At least Legend hadn't gone totally over to their side on this.

"No." At Bones' admission, I put my hand on the door. "But I'll take that hit if it keeps her breathing."

I pushed it inwards. They both turned to look at me. Legend's expression gentled, but I held up a hand as he started toward me. Honestly, if he touched me right now, I might go up in flames.

We needed to discuss this and I had to keep my emotions in check as much as possible. So I studied Bones.

His cool gray eyes were marred by dark shadows under them. Had he slept? The stubble on his face was practically a beard now. His hair was disheveled.

He looked like hell.

But I'll take the hit if it keeps her breathing.

As much as I studied him, he returned the favor. *What does he see when he looks at me like that?*

"You're making a call." That was what he'd said.

He didn't flinch. Nor did he look away. "We did."

From the corner of my eye, I caught Legend's faint jerk. Still not onboard with him, but not denying it either.

"So you *all* made it without me." All seemed to be missing two people.

Now Bones leaned back. Face grim. Solid. "We're trying to keep you alive."

"And I love you for it."

I laid it out there, for what it was, a fact.

He blinked. Once. Shock disturbed the unreadable mask he wore.

"But if you think that means you get to decide my story without me..." I shook my head slowly. "I'm not going back in a box."

"We're not putting you in a box." He rose, his expression still cool but his eyes were fierce.

"No?" I didn't bother to disguise my own doubt. "Then let me in the room where the decisions are made."

When his eyes flicked to Legend, I glanced at him as well. He stood, arms folded and chin down. It was like he was physically restraining himself. Not threatening, just not interfering. He and Bones just stared at each other. Having some silent conversation I couldn't understand?

Fine.

"You want to shield me. I get that. Lunchbox wants to

hold me. Alphabet wants to fix me. Voodoo wants to steady me." To heal me. They *all* wanted me *safe.*

"But *none* of you get to *own* me."

That snared Bones' attention and he focused on me again. "You think I don't know that?"

"I think you forgot it this morning." I blew out a breath, the wild tremor of my heart slowed from a run to a jog. "I'm not walking away from a plan. I'm not discounting that we need to make one—that you need to make one." I moved over to the table until I stood just a foot from him. "Note, I am being reasonable..."

A flash of humor sparked in his eyes like dry heat lightning. There and then gone again.

"I'm not throwing a fit—or the coffee cup. Or the cutting board and the knives over there."

Legend snorted a laugh behind me.

"What I am doing is what you *asked* me to do. I'm choosing to trust you." Now I took a risk and I put my hand on his arm. "So trust me, too."

For a moment, quiet invaded the kitchen so intensely that a distant car horn outside seemed loud. Bones stared into my eyes. Searching. Measuring.

God what does he see?

The brief glimpses of personality he let me have left me craving more.

Finally, he nodded and the sinking sensation fled.

"We're going to stay dark here for at least another forty-eight hours. Rest. Everyone needs it and we need to refuel, rearm, and surveil." He flicked a look past me. "Alphabet needs time with the intel."

"Once we have it?" I included myself in that.

"Then we identify the soft entry points, break the chain,

locate Reznik—cut that one off. Then eliminate the rest." Eliminate. Kill.

I nodded slowly.

"Grace..." He sighed. "You don't have to do this. We will make it happen. You can sit it out, stay—"

"Safe while you guys risk everything?"

"You're not going to go for it." The muscles in his arm bunched but he put his hand over mine and held it there. "If you stay, you will follow the plan to the letter. That means there will be times you stay in the car or stay behind. Times where you have to move when we say move."

"No questions asked." I remembered. "But I'll at least be a part of the plan and I won't let you down."

He squeezed my hand once, then shifted his attention to Legend. "Let him feed you. I probably need to eat. I'm going to roust Voodoo and Alphabet. We'll handle the first round of planning over breakfast."

When he released my hand, I let it fall away and he brushed my shoulder lightly before he strode out of the room. All at once, I sagged as the breath fled my body.

"Hey," Legend was just there, arms sliding around me and I didn't even try to pretend I didn't need the support. "You did good."

I huffed out a laugh that ventured dangerously close to being a sob. "I was really pissed."

"Was?" He seemed almost hopeful.

I twisted to look at him and he just picked me up and put me on a counter so our heads were closer to level. It was irritating and adorable all at once.

"Might still be," I said, testing the emotion. "I don't like hearing you guys discussing getting rid of me."

"You made that clear." He brushed his knuckles down

my cheek. "For what it's worth, I don't want to send you away and I'm almost certain Bones doesn't either."

"He just wants to protect me. You all do."

"Guilty," Legend said with a shrug. "Not going to apologize for it."

"Not asking for one." I cupped his face in my hands. "I get that I am a liability. That I don't have your training. That there are things you can do that I can't. I understand all of that. Just don't decide for me. Don't box me up for my own good without consulting me. A cage is a cage, Legend, no matter how pretty you decorate it."

"Did you mean what you said to Bones?"

"That I love you for it?" The question was the right one. I hadn't meant to confess something like that but it wasn't just words. "I do."

He leaned into me and I spread my legs so I could brace my knees against his hips. Pressing his forehead to mine, he seemed to be breathing me in. Or maybe that was me soaking in his nearness. The pounding of my heart had steadied and the panic in my soul eased.

"Say it again," he ordered in a soft voice.

"I love you," I whispered and his smile was sudden and fierce. Then my stomach growled and it was not remotely subtle. Laughter spilled out of him.

"I can make omelets if you like and I have potatoes for fried potatoes. What can I get you Gracie?"

The last time I'd said I was hungry flashed through my mind and he winked.

"You can have me anytime you want, but you do need to eat."

Now I giggled and his expression brightened further. Love threaded through bruises and fire. That was what brought me here. Brought *us* here.

"You know... I'd kill for french toast right now."

TWENTY-TWO

VOODOO

Breakfast proved illuminating. Fortunately, I wasn't the only one who noticed the shifting dynamic in play. Her night with Lunchbox just clarified that he was as committed as we were. Though, he wasn't getting her tonight. Hours of listening to her had been a delightful torture and it had given me ideas.

Alphabet wasn't focused on them so much as he was Bones. As aware of Grace as I was, I was with Alphabet on this. Something had happened with Bones and more than him just wrapping around her and getting her to sleep when her dreams woke her.

Nightmares. She wasn't always aware of them. At least as far as I could tell. Sometimes, the nightmares would rip her out of sleep shrieking. Those, at least, released her. The other nightmares were more insidious. She would whimper, a lost sound that broke my heart.

It had happened in the van. Another reason to wrap her up tight. It was also why Goblin wouldn't leave her. I spared a glance at Lunchbox and he raised his eyebrows. What did I need?

I lifted my chin in Grace's direction. He held up two fingers and followed with a flattening of his hand. Two moments. She'd had two dreams, but he'd chased them away. Nodding, I leaned back in the chair.

Grace had eaten her french toast with gusto. Was her eating so enthusiastically what put the smile on Lunchbox's face or was it all the sex?

Probably both. If it wasn't both, I'd be more worried about him. Amusement trickled through me when Grace glanced at me. There was a sparkle in her eyes, even with all the quiet intensity marking her movements.

Uncertainty flickered in her eyes and I smiled. She had nothing to worry about. Sharing her with these guys was not a problem. I'd only object if some dick tried to cut any of us out. Biting her lower lip, Grace sent me a smile and I winked.

"If you two are quite done," Bones stated cooly. "We need to get back to the briefing."

"Oh," I said easily. "I'm never going to be done." The last I sent right to Grace. The pink that stained her porcelain cheeks satisfied me. But, I shifted my gaze to Bones anyway. "But don't let that stop you. What's the call?"

His stare was all steel and restraint, void of even a shadow of amusement. If ever a man needed to get laid, it was Bones. I kept that comment to myself, because as long as he waged a war against what he was feeling, we were going to have to deal with him.

Maybe we could find somewhere to spar. Or we could do a raid, nothing like beating the shit out of the bad guys to ease some tension.

"The call," Bones said, tapping two fingers against the table, "is we're remaining in this apartment for the next forty-eight hours." He spared a glance at Alphabet. "Do you have an updated ETA on decryption?"

"It's running," Alphabet said. "Biggest problem is the processor on the laptop. Doesn't have the power I need to speed the process up. If we picked up some more equipment, I could try to build something that would help. Even if Voodoo magicked it up for me this morning and I got it running by tonight, we'd still be looking at thirtyish hours. Go faster if we were at base. Travel time robs that advantage."

He gave Goblin a slice of his bacon and the dog thumped his tail happily as he took it.

"We need to take him for a walk," Grace said, twisting down to shower the very happy canine with some affection. I knew exactly how he felt.

"After the briefing," Bones told her in a far gentler tone without an ounce of reprimand for going off topic.

He had it so bad.

I swallowed my amusement with coffee.

"Let's see what we can do with equipment here," Bones said after a beat and *after* Grace sent him a small smile.

Yep, he had it *so* bad.

"Make a list for Voodoo to source," Bones continued. "We need a full resupply anyway. Weapons, ammo, body armor. Include Grace in the last." A frown tightened his brow. "You have someone here who can do custom sizing?"

Yeah, we'd need it. Grace was tiny. "I know a couple. I'll put some feelers out. Big trick will be how effective it will be if we have to speed the process up."

"Won't they need to do fittings?" Lunchbox folded his arms, expression sober.

"Nope, I have her measurements." A grin curved my lips when Grace shot me a look. "Don't worry, Firecracker. I know every divot, curve, and line." Tapped the side of my head. "All memorized. But I'll definitely refresh before I head out."

Laughter bubbled out of her and Alphabet snorted, amusement tinging the respect in his expression. "Smooth."

I just spread my hands and inclined my head. "I try."

"You succeed, smart ass." Lunchbox gave my shoulder a friendly bump. I was still grinning when we all returned our attention to Bones.

He just shook his head. "Check on the body armor for her. We need options. We need to vet the intel we have, Lunchbox and I will take care of that. Particularly with regard to Reznik and O'Rourke."

Some of the humor in the room dried up.

"Since rumors of their deaths have been greatly exaggerated, I want the military records." That might be reaching. "Intelligence had to have some idea and if they didn't —then I want to know why." He focused on Lunchbox. "Can you tap your guy?"

"I can, whether or not he answers, that's debatable." He tilted his head to the side. "Might ask Spook Lite if I can find him."

"Spook Lite?" Grace turned wide eyes up toward Lunchbox. "Do you guys know anyone who doesn't have a nickname?"

"We know you," I said, and she snorted even as she grinned, which had been the goal.

"You call me Firecracker." She made a face.

"You like it," I countered and she stuck her tongue out at me. "Promises, promises."

Bones cleared his throat. Killjoy. "Back to the subject. Spook Lite?"

"Yeah," Lunchbox grunted. "I don't think he is active anymore, at least not on their books. Under the table? Who knows, but I can touch base. See what we can see."

"Still on the subject," Grace said with a wrinkled nose at Bones before she looked at Lunchbox. "If Spook Lite isn't the main person you can reach out to, who is the main one? Spook Senior?"

It was my turn to snort a laugh and even Alphabet grinned. Lunchbox met her gaze easily, but it was Bones rolling his eyes that damn near did me in.

"Actually, he goes by Redacted." Not even an ounce of humor in Lunchbox's deadpan response. Which was fair, cause that was what the guy went by. Fuck I couldn't even remember what his actual name was.

"Redacted?" Grace gaped at him. "Seriously?"

"Yes, seriously. He used to run in military intelligence. Ran more than a few ops with us and used us for others. Smart, sneaky, and just paranoid enough to be fucking brilliant at his job. He was there one day and then gone the next. Pretty sure one of the alphabets scooped him up."

"Intelligence agencies," Alphabet said to Grace with a faint smile. "Not me."

"CIA, FBI, NSA—one of them." Lunchbox shrugged. "He's probably in some basement somewhere arguing with satellites. But Redacted always kept his fingers in, multiple strings running. Not a lot slipped by him. He liked to know things."

"Kind of like Tyrion from Game of Thrones, with less bloodshed." Maybe. Eh, probably not. But we didn't need to go there.

"Regardless," Bones said, pulling us back to the topic at hand. "Let's see what strings we can pull and what noise it makes. Chances are, they won't confirm or deny a damn thing, but..."

"Intel is never a bad thing." The fact Grace finished his sentence was amusing.

"Miss Black," he said almost primly. "You and I should have another discussion before we leave."

"Whatever you say." She spread her hands. "I'm here all day, clearly."

"Hmm." He spared her another long look before shifting his attention back to us. "Alphabet needs to stay focused on decryption. I want to know everything about their operations, vulnerable points, operators, contacts, what kind of network they are running. Those twelve names are an excellent start. But I want to gut it as well as take off the head. I really don't care who gets the credit. When we're finished, they won't be an issue again."

He didn't have to look at Grace to underscore the why of any of that or the bottom-line. They weren't going to be an issue for her.

"Forty-eight hours gentlemen, lady," Bones said as he stood. "Operational readiness briefing at thirty-six. Until then, hit your tasks and rest—"

"Wait," Grace said abruptly. "You didn't give me a job."

"You secured shelter," Bones said. "You'll be assisting Alphabet and Goblin. I also expect you to rest and be available for other tasks as they come up. For now, you're support."

I braced, half-waiting for the explosion, but it didn't come. My firecracker studied Bones for a long moment. Probably wondering if he was just giving her a shit job to keep her busy or if he actually meant it.

"I can help with translations too," she said. "But okay."

"Understood and accepted," Bones told her. "Grace,

give me ten and we can take Goblin. Everyone else get to work."

Everyone else...

He strode out of the room and I wasn't the only one who turned to follow his progress or stare at the swinging door as he left the kitchen.

"Did he just..." Alphabet asked.

"He did," Lunchbox confirmed.

"Did what?" Grace wanted to know and I swung back around to grin.

"Just sidestepped all of us to be the one who took you out for a walk."

"Oh." The pink flushed her cheeks again. "That's... not a problem right?"

"Of course not," I said because jealousy was not going to be an issue. At least not that way. "Except I've got dibs for the next walk."

"Hey," Alphabet straightened. "Get your own dog. I also need the walks, you know."

"Yeah, but he isn't going to let you get away from those machines until the decryption is done." Lunchbox patted him on the shoulder.

"How about," Grace said, reaching over to put her hand on Alphabet's. "I come hang out with you for part of the day. That way I can make sure you have drinks and that you get up and walk around. I can do that thigh massage again too."

I slapped some duct tape over my inner twelve-year-old's mouth and downed the rest of my coffee. Lunchbox just grinned.

"I can make that work," Alphabet said after a beat as if he had to really think about it. "We can see what else we can do to speed up the process."

"I'll do my best," she promised. "Just tell me what you need." It was her turn to huff out a breath as she stood. There was no missing how gingerly she moved. "I need to go find shoes and a jacket."

"If you need any other clothes, Firecracker, just give me a short list. I'll take care of it."

"More underwear would be nice." She paused next to Alphabet and pressed a kiss to his forehead. "I'll come grab Goblin in a minute."

"Take your time." He slid an arm around her hip and gave her a light squeeze. "You doing okay after last night?"

"Walking a little funny." She flashed a grin at Lunchbox. "But I'm fine. I think this walk will help me too."

"Good." He patted her ass once, then held up his hands when she gave him a look. "Just wanted to test the waters. I've resisted patting that exceptional ass but..."

"You can pat my ass whenever you like," she offered, then paused to glance at me and Lunchbox before she focused on Alphabet again. "Tell you what, since you are going to be chained to the computer and they can go for walks with me, you're the only one who can pat my ass right now."

"Hell yes," Alphabet said with a fist pump. "Thank you."

"You're welcome." She grinned then circled the table, she paused to rise up on her tip toes as Lunchbox bent his head and brushed her lips with his own. It was a quick there and gone again kiss.

When she reached me and put her hand on my shoulder, I covered hers with mine. "How soon will you be leaving?"

"I'll wait until you two get back, so you can give me a list too." I needed to do inventory anyway. When she dipped her head, I moved my hand to her nape and held her there for a longer, deeper kiss. I savored the hint of maple still lingering on her lips and the richness of the coffee.

Woman was a drug and I was addicted.

Happily so.

She sighed against my mouth and seemed to soften as she leaned against me and the chair. With some reluctance, I let her go and she was flushed a gorgeous pink as she straightened.

"I love you guys," she said softly. "All of you." The words took me out at the knees. The emotion sucker punched me and, for a moment, I thought she broke my damn jaw with it. She swept her gaze over the guys before she retreated for the door. "I just wanted you to know that..."

Then she was out and the door swung closed behind her.

"Did she just..." Alphabet found his voice first.

"Yep," Lunchbox said and there was definitely a smug air about him. "She admitted it this morning."

"Holy shit," Alphabet muttered.

Yeah.

Holy shit.

CHAPTER

TWENTY-THREE

GRACE

I knew something was up the second he told me, *"Shoes. Don't ask questions."*

No gun. No emergency. Just that familiar curve at the corner of his mouth that wasn't quite a smile—but in Voodoo-speak, might as well have been a damn neon sign.

He led me downstairs without a word, stopping in front of one of the empty units—one of the ones Rachel said sat vacant while the university was on break. When he pushed the door open and stepped aside like some kind of dark fairytale prince, I arched a brow.

"Am I walking into a trap?"

"If it is," he said, voice low and lazy, "it comes with wine, real food, and if you want to be tied to a chair—well, I'm not here to kink shame."

Laughter burst out of me before I could stop it. "Good to know."

I stepped inside.

The air was warm, laced with garlic, oregano, and something sweet beneath the spice. The apartment was stripped down to nothing—except for a small table in the center of the room. Two chairs, one already pulled out. Plates. Actual silverware. A candle that looked like it had been stolen from a stash someone actually cared about.

There were takeout containers from a little Italian place around the corner.

"Takeout?" I asked, voice catching halfway through.

He leaned against the doorframe, arms crossed, expression unguarded in that way he only ever got when it was just the two of us.

"It's dinner," he said simply. "With me. You're allowed to have that."

"Oh, am I?" I tilted my head, playing along because he'd opened the door—and because I couldn't help myself. "Hence the takeout? Even with Lunchbox upstairs just begging to cook for someone?"

"Only tonight," he said, closing the door with a soft *click*. "And if it's my date, I'm the one taking you to dinner. Staying in just happens to be safer than going out."

He circled the table and pulled out the chair for me like he did it all the time, like it wasn't wildly intimate.

"I'm so underdressed for this," I muttered, gesturing to my hoodie, yoga pants, and the loose topknot barely holding my hair together. No makeup. Chipped nail polish. And yet—my heart thudded hard enough I swore he could hear it.

"You're perfect," he said, and it wasn't a throwaway line. It landed low in my chest—slow, solid, and startling. Not playful. Not casual. Just...true.

Something in him eased when he said it, like a blade finally sliding back into its sheath.

He moved to the other side of the table and sank into

the chair across from me, gaze locked on mine, steady and quiet and sure.

It was ridiculous. It was dangerous.

And it made my heart ache in a way bullets never could.

After he poured the wine, he raised a glass to me. "What should we drink to?"

I pretended to think, swirling the deep red in my glass.

"To not being kidnapped tonight feels a little on the nose."

He raised an eyebrow, waiting.

A grin tugged at my mouth before I gave in. "All right. How about... *to surprisingly thoughtful date nights in abandoned apartments with devastatingly charming lieutenants?*"

His brow lifted a fraction higher.

"Devastatingly charming?"

"I said what I said." I shrugged, taking a small sip of wine like I hadn't just handed him a loaded compliment.

"Hmm. Then only one lieutenant, singular, not plural. There's only one of me."

My heart hitched. Just for a second. "There is definitely only one of you." I clinked my glass against his, letting the electricity of the moment hum between us.

He leaned back slightly, eyes still on mine, that faint not-smile tugging at his mouth.

"You keep saying things that make me want to kiss you."

I arched a brow. "And yet, here we are. Drinking wine. Fully clothed. Civilized."

"For now," he said, and took a long sip. "But you did start it."

I laughed, a low, surprised sound I barely recognized as mine.

"*Did I?* I think you're the one who lured me into your evil lair with pasta and mood lighting."

He tilted his glass toward me. "It worked, didn't it?"

I matched his gaze, unblinking. "It did."

And it hit me right then—not just the warmth in my chest or the buzz of the wine, but *him*. The quiet way he watched me. The careful distance that suddenly didn't feel like distance at all.

He dished out the pasta from one of the boxes then added the garlic bread to the side. "Eat up. You need energy for tonight."

I took the bite, eyes narrowing playfully. "I see and what menace do you have planned for me?"

"Careful. Compliments like that might get you tied to a chair."

"Oh, is that your kind of magic trick?"

He smirked. "Maybe. But I have better ones."

He reached into his pocket and pulled out a small, worn deck of cards. "Pick one. Any one."

I rolled my eyes, but played along, pulling a card and holding it tight.

He fanned the cards like a pro, then with a quick flick, flipped mine face up on the table. "The Queen of Hearts," he said with mock solemnity. "Fitting."

I blinked, amused. "Are you trying to flatter me or just scare me?"

"Both," he said with a grin. Then, for good measure, he snapped his fingers and made a napkin vanish in a puff of smoke.

I clapped softly, eyes shining with delight. "Okay, I admit it. That was impressive."

He leaned forward, voice dropping just a notch. "Wait till you see the grand finale."

My breath caught as he brushed a stray lock of hair behind my ear, fingers lingering a moment too long.

The room seemed to shrink, the candle flickering shadows dancing over his face.

"Grace," he murmured, eyes dark and serious now, "I'm not just playing games."

I swallowed hard, heart hammering as the space between us closed.

And then—just as I thought the moment would shatter—he smiled softly.

"Relax. I'm not rushing anything."

My lips twitched into a grin. "Not sure if I should be happy about that or not." Because he'd barely touched me and yet I was so wildly aware of him.

He laughed quietly, that rare genuine sound, before finally lowering his hand to rest over mine.

The next hour drifted by in a pleasant haze. We talked about everything and nothing. Voodoo liked old-school blues and modern synth. The playlist on his phone swung from Muddy Waters to Glass Animals.

I would have called it chaotic, but he had music for mission prep to winding down to another really moody acoustic one that was just downright relaxing. Apparently, he preferred vinyl to MP3s, but the playlists were easier for travel. I could respect that.

"So, you're a nature nerd *and* a coffee snob," I said, testing how that sounded after his last story.

"These are not mutually exclusive, in fact, I'd argue that because I know edible plants, how to track, and have even been known to beat GPS before—that I have every skill I need to recognize *good* coffee."

Grinning at the very idea, I raised my wine glass.

"That's—you know, I'm surprised you don't just roast your own coffee beans."

"Who says I don't?" The dare was right there in his voice. No way was I going to take that bet.

"Pictures," I said, toasting him with the wine glass before I took another drink, "or it didn't happen."

The spaghetti was absurdly good, the red sauce rich and just the right side of spicy, and the garlic bread? Downright sinful. I was so full I'd resorted to nibbling like a raccoon hoarding scraps. But still—I didn't want the night to end. Not yet.

I leaned back, glass in hand, watching him from across the candlelit table. "If you weren't doing this—you know, the chaos, the missions, the world-saving—what would you be doing instead?"

He didn't even pause.

"Small café. Vinyl playing. No Wi-Fi. Just good coffee, better music, and real conversations."

The answer hit me sideways—simple, specific, honest. Like he'd carried it with him for years.

I blinked, then smiled, slow and wide. "That's... unexpectedly wholesome." It also sounded dangerously perfect.

He tilted his head, that rare grin tugging at his mouth. "Scary, huh?"

"Absolutely terrifying." I set my wine down. "You might have to let me hang around. Supervise the pastries. Guard the espresso machine."

"I'd even let you sit in my lap," he said, with a gallant little bow of his head that would've seemed ridiculous—if it weren't for the heat behind his eyes.

I laughed, heart thudding a little too hard. "What a generous proprietor."

"Only for my favorite customer."

And just like that, the air between us shifted—lighter, sweeter, but laced with something deeper. After downing the last of the wine in my glass, I rose and circled the table. He tracked me as I closed the distance and pulled the napkin from his lap as I took a seat.

"You are out of wine," he murmured as I hooked my arm around his neck.

"I am," I admitted, but set the glass on the table. "But I didn't come over here to get more wine."

"No?" He dropped the napkin onto the table next to his empty plate. Then he drew a light finger down the curve of my cheek to my jaw. "What did you need then, Firecracker?"

"You."

"Is that so?" His voice dipped like he'd rolled it in thick chocolate and added a decadent richness to it. He was… comfort wrapped in passion and safety made heady with desire. The competing feelings were hard to put into words.

"Absolutely so…" Then because I wanted no misunderstandings, I added, "I was with Lunchbox last night…"

He pressed a finger to my lips. "I know. We all know." Heat scalded my face and he grinned. A genuine, brilliant, grin. "You with my brothers is never going to be a problem for me."

My heart did this little rebound from my ribs. Need and relief twisted me up. "You're sure?" I didn't need to test him, but I wanted to reassure myself.

"Always," he murmured then pressed his lips lightly to mine.

"If that changes," I said, tasting the wine and the sauce on his lips. More, I tasted *him* and the flash fire of hunger that went through me had nothing to do with food. "Tell me?"

"You'll be the first to know," he promised, peeling the hoodie off me so smoothly, I marveled at the fact he'd unzipped it without me noticing.

"Thank you," I whispered the words, savoring his nearness. "As for dates, ten out of ten, I'd totally recommend."

He chuckled, running his hands up and down my arms. "Planning to give me a five star rating?"

"Maybe." I made a show of thinking about it. "Wine? Excellent selection. Meal? Hot and tasty. Ambience? Delightful."

"But?" Amusement had him smiling as he slid his fingers under my shirt, I didn't even protest as he tugged it upward.

"*But*," I added some extra emphasis to the word just for him and because it just seemed to make him happier. "What about dessert? Do I have options?"

"Now I'm intrigued, what options are you looking for, Firecracker?" He tugged my shirt upward and I raised my arms to let it go up and off. The bra I wore was demi cup and I'd mostly put it on to keep my nipples from poking through the shirt.

Course, nothing could save them from the heat stroking over me from his eyes. He ran his nose against my throat, a caress from just behind my ear to where my breasts pushed up from the bra.

Shivers raced over my skin. "Hmm... dark chocolate fondant, especially the one that comes with the raspberry coulis."

He nuzzled a kiss to the top of one breast and his beard tickled me. "Hmm-hmm."

"Vanilla bean crème brûlée," I gasped out the words as he sucked my nipple right through the cup of the bra and his fingers slid beneath the waist of my yoga pants. "Panna cotta maybe... oh fuck."

He lifted his head and my bra whisked away leaving cool air to tease me. "Is that all?"

Temptation, if it were a person, was Voodoo. I licked my lips as I went to work unbuttoning his shirt. If we were getting naked, it was important that both of us were. "Sometimes there's a fruit tart..." I watched him from beneath my lashes. "And I can be tart."

The corners of his mouth twitched into a slow, knowing smile. "Then I know exactly what I'm having."

In one swift motion, he rose and swept me up, carrying me away from the table and across the room. The bedroom awaited, bathed in the soft glow of candlelight. Dozens of flames flickered—just enough to spark romance, not risk a fire—casting golden shadows that danced along the walls.

Rose petals were scattered across the bed—lush, red, impossibly perfect. When had he even found the time to get roses?

"Voodoo..." I breathed his name, my voice barely more than a whisper as I took in the room, awash in warmth and flickering candlelight.

"You like?" His voice held a note of hesitation, just enough to pull my gaze from the surroundings and back to him. Was he... nervous?

The thought only made my heart ache sweeter. I cupped his face gently, fingers brushing over the strong lines of his jaw.

"I love it," I murmured. "I love you."

His eyes darkened, heat flaring in their depths. "We'll talk about your dessert after I've had mine..."

A slow, wicked smile curved his lips.

"I promise—you're going to love it."

Not a doubt existed within me. He stripped me out of the rest of my clothes so efficiently, he left me breathless. The rose petals were like silk against my skin after he set me in place then rose.

I tugged my hair loose and shook it out as he stripped off the rest of his clothes with the same kind of efficiency as he had mine. He was a beautiful man. They all were, each in their own way and I wanted to memorize every inch of them.

"What are you thinking?" He was already crawling onto the bed, his heavy erection dragging along my thigh and leaving a little path of pre-cum.

"That I want you." I managed to push the words out before he stole my soul with a kiss.

"You're going to have me," he promised. "Everything, Firecracker. You're going to have everything."

He didn't need words after that. He told me he cared with every stroke of his finger. Made promises with his tongue as he ripped orgasm after orgasm. When he raised his soaked face to grin at me, there was such a wild energy in the air.

"I was right," he murmured and I blinked.

"About?"

He slid up along me, settling into the cradle of my thighs and with his hand around his cock, he thrust into me in this slow, perfect slide. I arched to meet him, but I couldn't take my eyes off him.

"I love my dessert," he whispered. "And I want more."

His next thrust pushed all the air out of me. The one after that began to rock the bed. When it knocked against the wall, I laughed. Humor filled his eyes as he wrapped his hands against the top of my head, shielding it. Then he really pounded me, the bed, my thoughts, and pretty much everything else right into that wall.

I might have screamed. I might have just shouted out his name. Honestly, I lost track of how many times he made me come. When I roused enough to catch my breath, he offered me water and then my options for dessert.

Hopefully, we'd survive round two.

CHAPTER

TWENTY-FOUR

GRACE

We left Rachel's Paris apartment seventy-seven hours after we arrived. It was a little longer than Bones wanted, but no longer than necessary. At least, that was how it came across. Alphabet hadn't slept much. He'd either been building a new machine while babysitting his laptop or he'd been chaining them together.

It was fascinating to listen to him describe what he was doing and why he was doing it. I could *almost* follow the steps, even if I could never replicate the instructions. I split my time between all of them. Lunchbox and Bones were out of the apartment more than in.

Meetings.

Supplies.

Other stuff.

It was the other stuff that made me curious, but they weren't always specific on what they were doing. Voodoo had to leave for twenty-four hours to collect "weapons." Considering we were in France, that made sense. They didn't have access here to what they had at home.

Not that it seemed to slow them down. They focused on what they needed, they made a list and it just happened. Like the rest of the chaos we'd been embroiled in. Like surviving. Like breathing.

We needed it. They would get it.

Simple as that.

From Paris, we headed to Lyon. We cleared out the apartment, including packing up extra food to take with us to our new safe house. I left a physical note at the apartment to thank our hostess and sent Rachel a message thanking her as well.

Her response just made me laugh.

Rachel: *Just remember you owe me a photo shoot at some point. I will collect.*

It was so utterly normal. As long as I was still breathing when this was over, I planned to deliver. Unlike our first trip out of Paris, we didn't split up completely. We did take two vehicles—and neither was one we'd been using.

"What are you laughing about?" Lunchbox asked as I climbed into the backseat with Goblin.

"Just—you guys change vehicles more often than some people do their underwear."

"This is why I skip underwear," Alphabet said over his shoulder. "Everyone's a critic."

Giggling, I shook my head and then twisted to look back at the other vehicle. We were in a pair of SUVs now. Both muscular, heavy duty cars. Plenty of room for our supplies, including a whole new damn wardrobe for me apparently, body armor, weapons, and computer equipment.

At least from what I'd seen while they packed. I knew they had to have more in those cases and boxes or arranged for more to be waiting for us somewhere. Their minds were playgrounds of possibility; clever, unpredictable, and always two moves ahead.

It took a few hours to get to Lyon, but the drive was far more relaxed than our in the dark of the night rush to Paris or our escape from the raid. The guys played music, laughed, teased, and it was—fun. We stopped once for bathroom breaks, to stretch legs and let Goblin out.

Maybe it was the calm before the storm or all the emotion swirling around me. Maybe it was because I'd staked my claim in all of this. I wasn't just along for the ride. Or maybe it was because I was no longer the damsel in distress. I was a key player and they acknowledged it.

I was part of the team. It gave me purpose and a place. What we were doing mattered. Stopping these sick bastards *mattered*. But *they* mattered too. These men—brilliant, unpredictable, and gloriously outside the lines—had let me in. And that meant something. It wasn't just their brains or their bravado—it was their belief in me. In this fight. And suddenly, I wasn't just surviving. I was *belonging*.

The new safe house, as it were, was... a house. They definitely had a way of getting what we needed. I wasn't even going to ask this time.

It was late afternoon when we got in.

"Eat. Shower. Sleep." Bones ticked those items off. "Or sleep then shower. Everyone up and ready by four hundred. Grace, you're with me."

"I already called dibs for tonight," Lunchbox argued even as Alphabet snorted.

"Grace?" Bones held out his hand and I shouldered the one bag I'd been allowed to carry before sliding my hand into his. "She's with me because she needs sleep and so do you. Let's go."

The muttering behind me almost made me laugh. As it

was, I was biting the inside of my lip as he guided me down the hall, up the stairs and to a bedroom. It was a little frilly for my tastes, but it looked comfortable.

Once in the room, he set his bag down and lifted mine from my shoulder. "Bathroom is yours first."

"Don't we need to eat?" I was pretty sure that was the first order of business.

"Yes, I'm going to get our food then come back. You stay in here."

Hands on my hips, I raised my eyebrows. "Bones."

Teeth gritted, he gave me a long look. "Please stay up here. I meant what I said downstairs, you will all distract each other and play. That will likely lead to some very noisy, if athletic sex that will cost you in sleep and flexibility tomorrow. I need you sharp, I need them focused. If we—you and I—eat up here, then fewer distractions and you get the rest you need."

"So, no orgasms for me tonight?" Was I baiting the bear?

Absolutely.

"I didn't say that."

Heat swept through at a fiery rate and I swore steam had to be rising from my head. I could *feel* the roots of my hair as he held my gaze for an endless moment, then nodded once before slipping out of the room.

Wow.

I had no idea who was winning in this tug of war between us, but I couldn't say I was unhappy with the current results. Putting a hand to my stomach, I took a deeper, steadying breath. Then I headed for the shower.

While I didn't waste time, I did linger under the pulsating heat of the hot water long enough to relax the tension in my back. I also took the time to put on lotion and slip into a clean pair of panties and a sleep shirt.

The scent of food hit me as soon as I opened the door. Bones stood with his back to the room, the soft cotton of his boxers clinging low on his hips, revealing the carved architecture of his body, a frame forged through years of brutal discipline.

The warm pools of yellow light from the twin lamps spilled across the floor and over him in fractured streaks, casting shadows that rippled across the dense muscle of his shoulders and spine. Each contour, from the hard angles of his trapezius down to the taut lines of his lower back, was defined in stark contrast, like a sculpture half-snatched from darkness.

His legs, powerful and lean, were braced apart with a casual menace, the cords of muscle tight under skin bronzed and dusted with faint scars, more reminders of the violence he'd lived through, and carried with him. There was no softness to him, no spare weight, just efficient strength, honed and ready. Even in stillness, he radiated that quiet, dangerous energy, the kind that turned a room electric without a word.

Behind him, the room breathed with shadow and heat, the lamps casting golden halos on the walls. It seemed the space itself, like me, was holding its breath.

When he did turn, it was slow, deliberate, like a man used to controlling more dangerous urges than desire. His weathered face, all brutal angles and healed fractures, came into view beneath short dark hair, still damp from a recent shower. Instead of rushing me along, he'd showered elsewhere. A muscle flickered along his jaw.

His gray eyes, pale and unreadable, met mine. That was where it lived, the heat. Not in the flex of his chest or the subtle roll of his hips as he faced me, but in the way his gaze swept over me, slow and unflinching, as if he could see through the fabric I wore and into the thoughts I hadn't dared speak aloud.

Admittedly, there weren't many of those. Something about Bones made me happy to tell him off. I certainly seemed to throw things at him a lot.

Yet, there was restraint in the set of his mouth, in the way his arms remained at his sides, but in his eyes, that cold steel turned smoldering, and seemed to house a promise of everything he wasn't saying.

As much as I might want to hear all the things he didn't vocalize, I wasn't going to force it. Not when we had so much to do. What had he said earlier? We couldn't afford to be distracted. He didn't step forward. He didn't have to. The room pulsed with it anyway.

All the moisture in my mouth had dried up but I forced myself to wet my lips as I yanked my gaze off of him. "Something smells good." At least that came out relatively normal without a squeak to betray me. I carried my clothes over to the bag and stuffed them into the side pocket.

"It's soup, mostly," Bones said. "A couple of sand-wiches. Light but hearty."

"Sounds good," I said over my shoulder. "Smells good too. Just getting my things out for tomorrow." Voodoo had brought me gear. There was a vest for me too, but they hadn't put it in my bag, it was in Bones'. As if reading my thoughts, he set the vest down on the dresser next to my stack of clothes.

His nearness was so close, the heat of him brushed against me. "Come eat," he said, running his fingers down my arm. Goosebumps raced over my skin at the contact. The food was on a tray at the foot of the bed. He'd moved over and pulled back the covers on the side of the bed farthest from the door. "This is you."

"Okay." The jittering of my nerves left me unsettled, but I tried not to focus on that. Instead, I climbed into the bed and he tugged the covers over my legs even as I pulled them up to sit cross-legged. Then he moved the tray between us as he took a seat on my side of the bed facing me.

As promised, there was soup and sandwiches under the domes. There were also two bottles of water. He loosened the first top then tightened it again before setting it on my side, then opened his own.

Beef barley soup, I hadn't had this in forever, and grilled cheese sandwiches. The bread was thick and fluffy. I spread a napkin over my lap for crumbs, but still leaned forward to eat over the tray.

"Do you want to talk to me about anything before tomorrow?" Honestly, that wasn't the question I intended to ask when I glanced up to find him studying me. Still, it was the question that slipped out.

"I should be asking you that," he said.

Shrugging, I downed the last of the soup before reaching for my water bottle. I'd been a lot hungrier than I realized. "But I asked first, ergo, you get to answer first."

His lips twitched, a vague suggestion of movement. "Has anyone ever mentioned to you whether or not stubbornness is an attractive quality?"

"No," I said, recapping the water. "Are you trying to tell me something?"

His chuckle was so soft and unexpected, it floored me. Was I supposed to have seen this side of him? Was it an accident? Or had he really just let me in behind the walls he kept up? The chuckle itself was so low it seemed almost barely there but there was a warmth to it that wrapped me up in a hug.

The way it lingered in the air, Bones appeared almost surprised by it except... Except his eyes were more molten steel than cold. The chuckle itself was full of layers and I wanted desperately to have recorded it so I could keep it forever. Yet, I wasn't likely to forget this moment. Fleeting as it might have been, it was going to stay with me.

As long as this moment lasted, holding us utterly suspended, he didn't respond. So, I gave him an out after I wiped my mouth from eating the last bite of the sandwich. "Don't think I didn't notice your lack of an answer, there. But I'm going to do you a favor."

"Are you?" He rose, removing the tray from the bed and carrying it over to the dresser. With his back to me, I could enjoy watching him move. There was nothing spare about him at all. Everything was just corded muscle and sinew.

"Yes," I said, scooting down under the covers to hide the fact I'd been ogling. He shut off the lights, robbing me of the view. I would have complained except he was just there and sliding under with me. Man moved like a ghost.

"What favor is that?" He curled an arm around me and dragged me back against him until my back was snug to his chest and his hand spread against my abdomen. A full body shudder rippled over me as he slipped a finger beneath the waistband of my panties.

The fact he punctuated the question with his teeth scraping over my earlobe threatened to short-circuit my response. When he bit down on my earlobe, I ground my ass back against him. Need unspooled so violently, I thought I was going to come just from his fingers sliding down to stroke my clit.

"Fuck..." The word left me on a groan.

"You wanted an orgasm for sleeping," he murmured in that decadently deep tone that seemed a caress all its own. "So let me do this for you."

"I want to touch you." It came out a protest with a hint of whining, but he just continued to stroke his mouth from my ear to my throat. The pressure of his bite had my pussy clenching.

"Not yet," he said. "Give me this, darling, open your legs and let me have this."

"You can have anything you want," I gasped out each word as he increased the pressure of his fingers. There was no reticence in him, no teasing, he was sending me down an ever tightening spiral of pleasure.

"Good girl," he practically hummed the words. "Give me your cries. Come for me."

The man and his orders, but fuck if I didn't ride a burst of pleasure that soaked his hand and my panties. That soft, decadent chuckle erupted out of him again and he cupped one of my breasts, tweaking the nipple almost painfully through the fabric.

The scrape of his teeth and the vise of his fingers added an edge that burst that first bubble, but he was already stroking me back up higher. Bones was relentless, every twist of his fingers against my body wrenched more feeling from it. When I came again, I floated on a drunken, sensual haze.

"What favor were you going to do for me?" Elements of laughter punched up his voice even if he was whispering against my ear. I wanted to hold onto the moment, memorize it, but I was already drifting back under.

"Something," I promised and his body vibrated where he wrapped around me. Laughter, I hoped, but his fingers started to move once more. "I can't come again..."

"You can," he said, that snap of command back in his voice. "You will."

Bossy.

So bossy.

But I let go of everything, because he wouldn't let me drown. He told me to come and my body damn well did as he said before I slipped beneath the pleasure-drenched tide entirely.

TWENTY-FIVE

GRACE

The sun wasn't even a promise on the horizon when Bones woke me with a gentle hand to my cheek and a cup of coffee in his free hand. Despite releasing a groaning yawn, I wasn't remotely upset by the wake-up call. I'd slept like the dead and my body still hummed from the multiple orgasms he'd pulled out of me.

I'd finished most of that first cup of coffee by the time I got dressed and braided my hair back. The unrelieved black made me seem a little too pale, and added hollows to my cheeks. This wasn't for a shoot though, so I didn't have to worry about reducing the glare or the shine. It helped that the collar hid the presence of the fresh hickey that Bones had left on my neck.

Tingles raced through me when my gaze lingered on it. Still, probably not the time to get turned on. I'd just tied my boots and studied the bulletproof vest he'd put on the table for me when Bones slipped back in.

"Put that on last," he said, scooping it up. Like me, he was also dressed in all black. He looked like some dark angel come to life. "Breakfast is ready and we need to brief."

Downstairs, the kitchen doubled as a war room. The table had laptops open, maps spread, weapons lay spread out, where Voodoo was going over each one. The scent of black coffee was so strong, I could take hits off of it.

Lunchbox handed me another big mug of coffee and a pocket pastry with eggs and sausage inside of it. It was like a hot pocket but home made. "Pay the toll," he teased and I pushed up on my toes to meet his kiss.

Alphabet patted the chair next to him and I slid onto it and got another kiss from him as Voodoo grinned at me from across the table. Goblin let out a yawn from beneath the table and then set his head on one of my feet. It didn't take him long to start snoring all over again.

I was with him on that. I didn't even want to know what time it was, but since it was hardly my first early call, I didn't complain. The only difference was I might be doing some of the shooting on this one and it had nothing to do with pictures.

Putting a pin in my own internal joke, I focused on Bones who took position front and center.

"We strike the compound from the east entrance.

Alpha team, made up of Lunchbox and Voodoo, hits the control room. Bravo team is Grace and me. We'll move through the VIP hall, clear room by room. Alphabet runs overwatch and external feeds. Goblin stays with the vehicle."

Surprise flared through me. I half-expected to be the one in the vehicle or in the vehicle with Alphabet. I studied the floor plan of Reznik's estate. It looked like it had been designed for opulence but resorted to ugly. Squared off corners, a bad mix of architecture, what looked more like a Norman fortress than anything gothic, and overloaded with cameras just stripped it of any kind of soul.

"Entry's quiet," Bones continued. "We go in masked, we get out clean. No collateral. Priority is the drives in the vault. Secondary is confirmation of the buyer list. According to the decryption, he's their security specialist." Something cruel moved through his smile. "He keeps all the records including their background checks and likely blackmail material."

It was hard to work up any sympathy for people being blackmailed over their propensity to *buy* other people. Boo. Hoo.

"If Reznik's on-site," Bones stated. "He's mine."

No one challenged that. Frankly, they all had the right to tear him apart.

"We extract in two teams as soon as we're done. North stairwell for Alpha, west service for Bravo. Fourteen minutes, in and out."

It sounded so clear, so straightforward. We'd get in, get it done, and get out. My pulse thudded a little too fast and heat seemed to burn beneath the chill as I stared at the floor plan.

"You good for this?"

I glanced up to find Bones assessing me. A flicker of the night before seemed to be present in his eyes, but it vanished before I could focus on it.

Straightening, I held his stare and lifted my coffee mug in quiet salute. "You made me a part of the plan, Captain. I'll handle it."

At my use of his rank, the hint of a smile kissed his lips again. I wanted to make him truly smile, unguarded and without any need to shield me or anyone else from what might make him really happy.

For now, though, I had to settle for his nod. "Fair."

Lunchbox grunted as he slapped a magazine into one of

the guns Voodoo had been going over. "Fourteen minutes," he muttered the complaint. "That's not even enough time for me to get dramatic."

"That's why we love you," Alphabet said dryly. "Short fuse, high yield."

Another smile tried to escape out of the locked barricade of Bones' expression but he just shook his head. Voodoo shot me a wink. The guys were winding themselves up. Goblin huffed from under the table. I bent and scratched behind his ear—gentle, a grounding motion.

As I straightened, Alphabet leaned in close even as the other guys were already moving to load the equipment in the vehicles.

"You need anything?" His eyes were warm. Steady.

"Just you in my ear when it counts."

"Always."

"What about you, AB? Do you need anything?"

"For all of you to come back in one piece." He held my gaze for a long beat then nodded once.

"I'll keep that in mind."

"Don't make me come in there after you..."

"Yeah," I said slowly, recognizing the invitation to play in his blue eyes. "Bones might get upset with us."

Alphabet smirked. "That's one way of putting it."

Bones was back before Alphabet finished closing his laptop. He lifted the tactical vest and held it up for me. At my nod, he slipped it over my head then secured the velcro straps. When he finished, he dropped to one knee then slid a holster around my hips, buckled it before he tied it to my thigh.

He added another one to the opposite thigh, though one got a gun and the other a knife. When he stood, he checked the fit of the vest then added a secondary holster to the first belt and that had my taser in it.

Another pat down, then he flipped open a case and held out the comm unit. "This goes in your ear. It will lock over the shell and tucks right into the canal. It will hold in place even if you have tiny ears—which you do, since you have a tiny everything."

I wrinkled my nose, but took the comm unit. Our fingers brushed, but he didn't pull back. Instead, he watched me set it in place, then brushed my fingers aside to check the fit himself. The contact just threw me back to when it was his teeth and not his fingers.

"If things go sideways..." he began, dropping his hands to rest on my shoulders.

"We adapt," I finished. "Wing it, but—I follow your lead. Follow your orders. No questions, just move when you say move."

"You've never done this." Who was he reminding? Me? Him?

"That's why I'm with you," I said.

"Yeah." He blew out a breath. "You stay with me, too. Like we're sharing one skin. Got it?"

I saluted. "Got it."

His eyes gentled, the crinkles at the corners deepening. "You really like giving me shit."

"Just a perk. I promise." But he'd almost smiled and that was worth it.

"Let's go." He jerked his head toward the door and I followed him out.

Everyone was at the pair of SUVs and they loaded up in silence. The kind that wasn't awkward—just full. Bones and I took one vehicle. The guys were in the other with Goblin.

Not a word was exchanged as they finished. But the looks I exchanged with each of them before I climbed into the second SUV felt like everything.

The darkness seemed almost thick with few if any lights on the roads as we headed for Reznik's compound. If I hadn't looked at the map, I wouldn't even know what direction we were headed. Clouds obscured the skies leaving no stars or even moon to navigate by.

"Bravo team," Alphabet said via the comms, his voice the first I'd heard since we left the safe house an hour earlier. "You're clear to separate. Twenty minutes to target. You have thirty to get into position."

"Copy," Bones answered, his voice clear as steel. We took a right off the road we were on as the SUV the guys were in continued ahead. We were following a different path that would take us around to the other side of the compound.

Time seemed to slow to a crawl. If this were a movie, we'd see some kind of weird montage scene in slow motion while Time in a Bottle played or something. A nervous giggle tried to escape, but I managed to swallow it down.

The wild pound of my pulse threatened to make me hyperventilate. Bones set his hand on my thigh, and he began to tap two fingers in a slow, rhythmic pattern. "Tell me five things about where we are."

"What?" I cut a look toward Bones.

"Five things about where we are right now. Go." He punctuated the order with a squeeze to my leg.

"We're in SUV, in France, ninety minutes away from Lyon, on a road, in the dark, and we're together." That was six things and with each item I listed, I had to suck in a gasp of air.

"Now four things you hear."

What? I frowned. Why did he—"The SUV engine, you talking, um..." What else did I hear? "Me mouth breathing way too loud." That almost made me smile. "The road? I think I hear the tires on the road."

"Good." He patted my leg. "Three things you feel."

My breath wasn't coming in such hard pants now, but I stared at him. "Your hand on my leg. My heart was beating a little too fast, it was a lot too fast but it's better now." A third thing that I felt? "The air is kind of chilly in here. Or maybe I'm just a little too warm."

His smile flashed in the dark. It was there and gone again too fast. "Two things you smell."

"If you fart, I will hurt you." The words just fell out of me and he laughed. A real laugh came up from his belly. "But fine, I smell you. Your soap I think. It smells like the soap from the safe house. It's very clean, and neutral. And leather. I smell leather." Maybe that was the belts?

He pulled the SUV in and stopped. Killing the headlights, he shifted in the seat and it wasn't hard to imagine him looking at me. "Better?"

It took me another moment to just process the question and how my heart had slowed from a gallop and my breathing deepened. "Yes." I exhaled slowly. "Thank you."

"You're welcome." He touched a hand to his ear. "Bravo team in place."

We were? I glanced out the window. The ugly ass compound rose in the distance, but only visible through the faint light creeping up from the fog.

"Bravo," Alphabet acknowledged with a crackle of the comms. "You're green."

"Mask on," Bones ordered, pressing a knit mask into my hand, before he opened the driver's side door. No interior lights came on. I opened the passenger side door to follow him out.

I tugged it over my head once I was outside. It had two small cutouts for my eyes and one for my mouth. The one over my mouth was even smaller than my eyes, but it let me breathe.

The longer we stood in the dark, the more my eyes adjusted.

"Alpha team," Alphabet said. "You're a go."

"Copy," Voodoo said, the soft acknowledgement all to let us know they were on the move.

"Bravo, start the count," Alphabet said. "Going dark."

The count.

"Thirty seconds," Bones said in a low voice before he clasped my right hand in his left. "Stay with me."

CHAPTER

TWENTY-SIX

GRACE

Somewhere between leaving the SUV and shimmying over the wall with Bones, I had a moment of *what the fuck am I doing?* He didn't use rope to go up, instead, he did this running leap that had him at the top in nothing.

After a sweep of the area, he reached out a hand. "Jump," he said almost too softly to hear. I probably wouldn't have heard it if not for the comms.

Right. This was the part of the roller coaster ride ticking its way to the top before the sickening drop happened. The moment when all your life choices flashed before your eyes and you wondered, why the hell did you eat those nachos before you got in line.

Swallowing my objections, I dashed forward and put a foot on the wall as I jumped. My palm slapped against his and he hauled me up like I weighed nothing. At the top of the wall, he dropped to the other side. I rolled right after him and he caught me before he set me on my feet.

The whole thing took less than a minute. Bones led the way between the lights casting their eerie spots up on the compound's perimeter as well as the walls of what looked more and more like an actual fortress the closer we came to it. He moved like a shadow, only taking my hand twice.

The first time was when we had to press against a jut in the wall to let a sweep of light pass by. The second time when he opened a door that I couldn't even *see* and let us into a pitch black—somewhere.

The door clicked shut behind us. The sound seemed incredibly loud in the silence swallowing us. He moved my hand to his belt, then curled my fingers over it. Hold onto him there. Understood. I tugged once in acknowledgement.

No guards. No footsteps. Nothing. Our boots didn't scuff or squeak as he walked forward. My eyes had to have adjusted because ahead, I could just make out a faint grayish seam in the darkness. It grew brighter as we got closer, then Bones eased us around the corner into a hall illuminated with ancient fluorescents that had not quite burnt out.

"Bravo team inside," Bones said softly. "Moving to north wing." He glanced back at me once and I nodded. He hadn't said let go of his belt, so I kept my hand locked on.

We were close. Too close. Not close enough. Still, when he moved, I moved. When he stopped, so did I.

"Copy that." Alphabet's calm voice in my ears helped to soothe my jangling nerves. Like Bones, he projected nothing but confidence. "I've got eyes on thermals. Two guards in the next hall, staggered pace. You've got a twenty-second window before shift change."

We moved.

The hall grew progressively brighter until we reached a new door.

"Door locks cycling," Alphabet warned. "You're clear to enter in five, four, three, two..." On the one he didn't say,

Bones opened the door. We were in a proper hallway for a home. Thick rugs muffled our passage and the lights were still on low here. The pools of golden light were ideal to let you see where you were going without keeping anyone awake.

Bones tapped my hand on his belt and I unpeeled my grip. He pointed to my taser, then held up two fingers and pointed behind him.

Stay close, no more than two steps behind him and get out the taser. At least, that was my rough translation. Once I had the taser in hand, Bones took the lead again. He made his way through the hall like he'd been here before, slipping into another alcove and up stairs that were hidden by a wall.

I'd reviewed the plans too, so some of this was familiar, but I didn't have it memorized. At the top of the stairs, he slid out, doing a full sweep before beckoning me out. He moved like a wraith, fluid, efficient, and deadly.

"Alpha team to vault hallway," Lunchbox's damn near gleeful tone gave me a jolt. It was only loud in my ear because of the comms. "There's a pressure trigger on the panel and Voodoo's throwing glares. It's hot."

"Because you're humming while disarming explosives." Voodoo's irritation didn't sound *deep* but it was real.

"I'm humming because I love my job."

It was impossible to not smile at how irreverent and upbeat Lunchbox sounded. Yes, this was serious and we all had very specific jobs to do, but the borderline giddiness threw me back to him and Alphabet debating throwing a molotov cocktail out the window at the car pursuing us.

They were just—cheerful.

Movement ahead of us wiped away my smile. A guard stepped around the corner. Bones raised his gun and fired, two rounds. The suppressor didn't rob the weapon of all sound, but it didn't blow out my ears.

I fired the taser at the second guard who had a hand up toward his comm. The dual wires snapped out as the prongs attached and the charge took the man down. As soon as he was down, Bones pointed to the door ahead of us on the left. After loading a new cartridge in the taser so it would be ready to fire again, I hurried to open the door.

The room itself seemed mostly empty. There were some boxes, and tables stacked up, but that was it. Storage maybe.

Bones dragged the guy he shot in by the collar. He retrieved the second, then slit his throat once they were in the room. Quick. Brutal.

My hands were shaking but I flexed my fingers and my grip to fight the reaction. My pulse was steadier than it had been outside, but it was still accelerating. Bones patted the men down while I kept watch from the door.

"You okay?" He added some items to one of his many pouches.

"I'm not fragile," I whispered back. I wasn't going to fall apart. At least, not while we were in here. Maybe I would when this was over, but I was allowed to freak out then.

It had to be in the rules somewhere.

"I know," he said, his mouth barely moving as he shaped the words. "That's why I'm checking."

We left the dead men behind us and continued down the hall. The surroundings grew more lush, the decorations more fine, and the furnishings promised opulence and comfort. The man didn't go for antiques, despite the staging.

He did go for expensive damn artwork though. There was a Degas on the wall, one of his black ink on brown paper pieces. Pretty sure it was the *Jockey à cheval*—or Three Mounted Jockeys, a work that was stolen decades earlier.

"Heat sigs moving below you. Might be a patrol. Four minutes until the next security sweep. Reznik's office is two halls over. Go left."

We slipped through an open archway and through a gallery. There was more art in here, some of those paintings had to be worth millions.

There was a marble figure of a woman, with bronze added to the parts of her clothing. Her bare breasts were small but clearly a woman's and her direct stare faced any possible challenge. She was familiar, but I couldn't place her offhand right now and it wasn't important.

On the far side of the gallery, we reached a hall that divided, Bones followed it unerringly and I was right behind him.

We reached the door. Locked. Biometric.

"Vault is cracked." Lunchbox let out a low whistle over the comms. "We're in. Holy shit, this server array's alive. Pulling the whole damn skeleton closet."

"Focus," Voodoo cautioned. "We've got five minutes max."

"Bravo—two guards outside the office." Alphabet hummed. "If he's inside, you're going to have to do a soft approach."

Bones frowned then glanced at me.

"Soft approach?" I mouthed the words. I would rather go through this locked door, but that wasn't an option right now.

"It means distract them," he answered, his gray eyes intent on me. "You saunter out there and get their attention, non-aggressive, not a threat."

Oh. "Kind of like when I played bait."

He grimaced. "Yes."

"Okay." I tucked the taser back under the vest then glanced down at myself. "Not really that sexy at the moment. But I can make it work."

I started toward the hallway but got hauled back when he wrapped his hand around my biceps. "Distraction, only. I will be right there. You think they aren't going for it, duck, cover, shoot, or stab. Got it?"

"Well," I murmured. "That's a bit intense even for me." I pushed up on my toes and pressed a kiss to his jaw. "I can do it."

Comms had gone almost dead silent. When he finally nodded and released me, I flashed a smile at him.

Deep breath. Second deep breath, and I shook out my hands before I headed around the corner and down the hall. There was no mistaking the two guards standing there, chatting with their weapons holstered or slung by a strap over a shoulder.

Nope, they weren't expecting anyone.

I grinned as their surprised gazes lifted toward me.

"Hey, boys," I purred the words, mimicking one of my favorite actresses. "I'm lost." I kept my hips fluid, the slow, swaying walk that accented the flow of whatever clothing I was wearing. In this case, I just wanted to keep their attention up and not on the holster I had on.

Spreading my hands out, I added, "Could one of you point me toward the tasting room?"

Incredulity took root on one guard's face as he reached for me while suspicion marked the other man's as he went for his weapon. Neither fully completed the move. I stumbled forward even as Bones just raced past me.

He caught the second guard in the jaw with a pair of hard hits, then a third one dropped him. The first guard gaped even as I caught his arm for balance and then slammed my knee into his crotch.

Bones had him in a headlock not even a full second after. He locked gazes with me as he lowered the guard to the ground as the other man's eyes rolled up in his head. He pulled a card from the man's pocket and didn't bother to clean up either man, though he did strip down their weapons.

One swipe and we were in Reznik's office. A massive desk occupied the center with a fireplace on one wall. Velvet drapes framed the huge windows and sheers kept anything from being visible from the outside.

It was also empty.

"Alphabet, we're going to need an extraction route. Any surprises?" He pulled a thumb drive out of one of his many pockets and pointed to the computer before he headed for the file cabinets.

The thumb drive sparked a memory, but I shoved it away for now. I had another one but it was in my stuff back at the house. I pushed the drive into one of the USB slots, then hit the spacebar.

"Motion sensors just tripped near the east stairwell," Alphabet warned. "You have about a minute. Package up what you need and get out."

The drive did its job, the screen's password lock cleared, then a couple of other windows opened and code flowed as the hard drive began to hum.

Bones pulled out burner phones, passports, and what looked like small books from one drawer. He stuffed them into his backpack. I opened the desk drawer and searched it. It seemed pretty normal.

Bottom drawer was locked. Bones moved to me and wedged his knife in and then popped the drawer open.

"That's a lot of cash," I murmured. Stacks of bills in different denominations.

"Take it." Bones began loading his bag as I did mine.

"Eureka," Lunchbox said, satisfaction filling his voice. "Files transferred. We've got the blackmail, auction records, buyer IDs. Numbered accounts. Pretty sure we have their bankers too."

I zipped up the bag with the cash in it and slid it back on. The machine was almost done, the windows flickering until the last one closed.

A sharp crackle over comms made me flinch. I jerked the thumb drive out.

"Bravo, company coming your way. Not guards. *Tactical.*" The urgency underlying Alphabet's message didn't make him louder. If anything, he was softer and he sounded even more dangerous.

Bones grabbed my hand. "Move."

We left the office the way we came in, stepping over the bodies on the floor before racing back toward the gallery.

"Halt!" A shout echoed toward us and a bullet pinged off the stone wall. We didn't slow down, if anything, Bones went faster. He pulled me around the corner, then another, then he pushed open a door I hadn't even seen and into a narrow stairwell.

He retreated into an alcove almost tucked behind the door, arm around my middle. His breathing was a bit ragged, fast, and real. The door moved and he raised his gun, it was pointed at the door itself even as the door pushed back toward us.

I held my breath.

"Clear," a man grunted, then withdrew and the door closed again, before a bolt slid home. They'd locked it. "Spread out. Find them. *Now.*"

We didn't move, and I only took in a little breath, sure that even a single gasp would give us away. The thud of footsteps beyond the door moved away.

Bones pressed his lips to my ear. "Right behind me."

"Yes, sir," I answered, and he paused to shoot me a what might have been a smirk. Maybe.

What? He wanted obedience, he was getting obedience, even my heart had started to gallop again. I stuffed the thumb drive into a pocket under my vest, just in case.

"Bravo team heading to ground floor," Bones said quietly. "Give me eyes and ears."

CHAPTER

TWENTY-SEVEN

GRACE

"Bravo, east exit compromised. You're rerouted. Kitchen access stairwell leads to the wine cellar." Alphabet's voice was low, intense and deadly serious. "Cuts under the south wall."

We were out of the stairwell and into another back hall. We were down an extra floor from where we'd come in. Boots hammered against the marble floors. A sound on the steps behind us warned that pursuit was closing in.

"Coordinates," Bones snapped.

"Sending," Alphabet assured us. "Thirty seconds. Go now."

Bones moved with ruthless precision, a storm bottled in flesh and bone. One moment he was beside me, the next he surged ahead, a blur of motion slicing down the corridor. The man in our path barely had time to register the threat —two strikes landed so fast, so clean, it was as if time had stuttered. By the time I blinked, their obstacle was crumpling soundlessly to the floor, and Bones was already moving on, as if nothing had happened.

Gunfire cracked behind us, sharp, brutal punctuation in

the narrow hall. A bullet slammed into the stone just inches from my head, coughing up dust and rock in a violent spray. I flinched, heart hammering, but Bones was already moving, jerking me forward, spinning me behind him with a force that brooked no argument, even as he returned fire.

More shots tore through the air, lighting the corridor with bursts of muzzle flash, each one a strobe of chaos. The walls pulsed with noise and heat, their footfalls pounding over broken bodies and spent casings. It was no longer about the mission. It was breath and bone, instinct and survival, the raw electricity of the moment thrumming through every nerve as we ran.

We pressed on down the corridor, the air thick with smoke that burned like acid in my lungs. The taste of blood, sulfur, and something charred clung to my tongue, turning every breath into a choke. I wanted to run, to scream, to drop and curl into the floor, but there was no time. My eyes stung, vision blurring as I blinked against the haze.

Every footstep felt loud, exposed. We darted from recess to recess, shadows barely deep enough to hide in, with Bones behind me—always behind me—keeping death at our backs with bursts of gunfire that cracked through the hall like thunder. When we reached the door, I hesitated, just for a second—and he shoved me through with enough force to steal the breath from my chest. I stumbled forward, terrified of what waited ahead but more afraid of what was closing in behind.

It was another stairwell. This one was narrow, dim, and reeking of mold and gunpowder. I took the steps two at a time, heart hammering against my ribs like it was trying to escape. Bones was right behind me, a shadow breathing fire. I didn't know how much time we had. Seconds, maybe less. The walls felt like they were closing in.

Two men waited at the bottom. Not guards. These were professionals. Tactical gear. Masks. Silent and ready.

I barely had time to register them before Bones barked, "Down!"

I dropped, heart slamming into my throat, and gunfire split the air above me. Two sharp reports. The bodies hit the ground almost in unison, crumpling like puppets with cut strings.

The bile clawing at the back of my throat finally won, souring the burn already sitting there. I gagged it down. No time. I vaulted over the bodies, legs shaking, and Bones was already behind me, hand at my back, pushing me forward.

We burst into a wine cellar, massive, cold, and sprawling. Floor-to-ceiling racks lined with dust-coated bottles loomed like silent witnesses. The air here was cooler, but it didn't matter. Death could still bleed through the walls.

"This place has a million ways to die," I muttered as we sprinted between the racks, the thought of bullets punching through the bottles and our bodies just one heartbeat away.

"And one way out," Bones growled beside me, voice low and hard. "Don't slow down, Dollface."

I ignored the stitch in my side and ran faster.

"We've got smoke in the main corridor," Lunchbox's voice crackled over the comm, labored and strained. He was running too, probably as close to the edge as we were. "Pinned near the fountain. Vault route's dead. Taking the east stairs. Voodoo's covering."

"This is me covering," Voodoo's voice was flat, the distant crack of gunfire punctuating his deadpan tone.

"Rendezvous moved to the garden-side greenhouse. Bravo's almost there. Locking exterior gates now—force them into the kill zone." The calmness in Alphabet's delivery was chilling, like he was narrating an execution, not coordinating an escape. Every word precise, every moment under control. It was terrifying. Awe-inspiring. None of them ever cracked.

Ever.

"Remind me never to piss off Alphabet." The words slipped out before I could catch them, and it took more breath to gasp than I'd thought. The stitch in my side flared, a fresh wave of pain shooting up my ribs.

"Nah, I got you, Gracie," Alphabet's voice came through, low and reassuring. The promise was grim, but it made me believe it.

We reached the end of the wine cellar, and Bones surged ahead like a predator scenting its prey. The door was locked from the inside, no surprise, but he wasted no time, ripping the bolt free with one savage yank. In one smooth, practiced motion, he shoved the service hatch open, spilling us into the cool, open air of the back gardens. The first light of dawn bled across the sky, soft and silvery, but it didn't soothe me. Not with the sound of distant chaos still ringing in my ears.

Trees whispered above us, leaves rustling like they were hiding secrets, but before I could even feel the relief of the fresh air, an explosion tore through the cellar behind us, rattling the ground beneath our feet.

"Bravo team approaching," Bones muttered, his grip tightening on my biceps as he yanked me closer, pulling me toward the cover of the garden.

"You bring us any wine?" Lunchbox's voice crackled through, rough and strained but still trying to crack a joke.

"Sorry," I wheezed, struggling to catch my breath. "Didn't really have time to stop for a bottle. But we've got blood and adrenaline for you."

"We'll take it," Voodoo's voice was dry, but there was a hint of something else in it as he appeared from the edge of the hedge maze. Smoke-streaked, bruised, sweat glistening, he hauled an unconscious man over his shoulder like it was nothing. He lifted his chin at the sight of us, his eyes already scanning for threats.

Voodoo didn't hesitate and shifted into position, guiding us with sharp, silent gestures while Lunchbox and Bones covered our backs. There was a distant crack of gunfire, then two heavy thunks. They were a *lot* closer than before.

One of our pursuers let out a grunt, a sound that made me freeze. I didn't want to look.

"You're clear, Bravo. Alpha, keep moving," Alphabet's voice was ice-cold, the faint sound of gunfire in the background like a promise.

I kept moving with the others, pushing through the pain in my side, though it screamed for me to stop. I tried to suck in air, tried to ignore the stitch that felt like a blade in my ribs. Every step was a fight against the burn, but there was no stopping. Not yet. Not until we were out.

"Split here," Voodoo said. "Lunchbox get back to Alphabet, you guys keep them scrambled while we grab the other vehicle."

I wasn't sure where here was but Lunchbox jogged up and brushed his fingers down my cheek before he disappeared into the gray light. Here turned out to be a little ravine, or culvert. A divot in the land.

There was water at the bottom and we splashed through it. Their longer strides meant I had to take two for each of theirs. Of course, Voodoo was carrying someone. The last thing I planned to do was bitch.

Finally, we made it around the far side of the building,

through the trees, and into the clearing where the SUV waited like salvation on wheels. I skidded to a halt as Bones' hand caught my shoulder. At his signal, I dropped beside Voodoo, chest heaving, while Bones swept the vehicle for threats.

Stopping might've been a mistake. My lungs were on fire, each breath razored and raw, and the stitch in my side had turned into a white-hot blade twisting deeper with every second. When Bones waved us forward, I shoved to my feet, but my legs betrayed me—I pitched sideways. Voodoo caught my arm, steady and silent, anchoring me before I could hit the ground.

He didn't let go. He kept his grip tight as we pounded down the steep hill toward the SUV. At the bottom, he tossed his prisoner into the back like deadweight, checked the bindings with the same brutal efficiency he used in a firefight, then slammed the door shut.

"I'll ride in the backseat," he said, nudging me toward the passenger side. "In you go, Firecracker."

"Should I take off the—" Talking hurt. My throat felt like ground glass. I was never calling myself *in shape* again. The guys might be winded, but at least they could still speak in full sentences.

"Not yet," Bones said, voice clipped. "We're moving first."

I all but collapsed into the seat and fumbled with the belt, finally snapping it into place. The SUV roared to life beneath us, and just like that, we were peeling out through the early dawn haze, shadows sliding past the windows as Bones took us toward the road.

"On the road," Alphabet's voice crackled through comms. "Left them a little present in their system. First time they access the cams, it's gonna crash everything. Hard."

"How sad for them," Lunchbox replied, his grin practically audible. "Anyway. ETA, Bravo?"

"Two hours. Long way around. Dumping ours, grabbing the new ride, then we'll come get you."

I let my head fall back against the seat. Every cell in my body was wrung out, nerves frayed to threads, exhaustion bleeding from every pore.

"Copy that," Lunchbox said. "Call in two hours. Syncing now."

The comms went silent. Bones reached up and ripped his mask off, then pulled out his earpiece. He glanced over at me, and I blinked at him, dazed.

"Mask, Dollface?" he said.

Mask?

Oh—right. I still had it on. I peeled it off, and instantly it felt like I could breathe again. The vehicle reeked of smoke, sulfur, and sweat—but somehow, that last one was almost comforting. Maybe because it meant we were still here. Still breathing.

"Water," Voodoo said, shoving two bottles through the gap in the seats. My hand trembled as I took one. Bones glanced sideways at the shake, but I didn't hide it. What was the point?

I drank deep. The water was lukewarm and tasted faintly plastic, but it was everything. As I stared out the window at the quiet roadside—little houses, gardens, fences—I couldn't help the disconnect. People out there were waking up to coffee and morning news. They had no idea what we'd just crawled out of.

Or what still lay ahead.

"You did good," Bones said, finishing his water and

flinging the empty into the back like it was just another spent round. He set his hand on my thigh—solid, warm, steady. It shouldn't have been comforting. But it was.

It didn't stop the tremble still running through me. But it helped slow my pulse from full-on panic to something survivable.

"Well, gee, Cap," Voodoo drawled from the back. "Don't hurt yourself with all that praise. How'd I do?"

Bones didn't miss a beat. "You've got room for improvement."

That dry, brutally neutral tone was the last straw.

A laugh escaped me, sharp and startled. Then another. Then I was giggling, full-on, uncontrollably. Tears streamed from the corners of my eyes. I wasn't even sure what was funny. Nothing. Everything.

Bones didn't say anything. Just kept his hand steady on my leg.

And that, somehow, was enough.

TWENTY-EIGHT

GRACE

It was mid-afternoon when we arrived back at the new safe house. We'd picked up a larger vehicle, rolled our passenger over into it and then picked up Lunchbox, Alphabet, and Goblin from the outdoor cafe where they'd stopped for lunch.

They both looked showered and fresh, somehow. Considering my own bedraggled and somewhat offensive to myself state, I eyed them with more than a little envy. They brought bags of croissant sandwiches that were to die for.

Arriving at the safe house, Alphabet and I waited with Goblin and our guest in the car while the guys cleared the house. I sat sideways in the front seat, studying the building. What did they see when they looked at it? The house? The safety? The weaknesses?

Maybe all of the above.

"Gracie..."

Twisting around, I met Alphabet's gaze. His stubble was rough, his eyes sharp despite the bruised shadows beneath them. His hair had dried in a mess of half-curls and cowlicks, giving him that charmingly disheveled look.

God help me, I loved it.

"Yes, AB?"

"You really doing okay? After everything?"

Voodoo stepped out front, waved us in, then veered off toward the back of the SUV.

"I think so," I said as the rear hatch lifted with a mechanical sigh. "I'm wiped, and yeah, it was a lot. Hopefully, I pulled my weight. Bones pretty much had to drag me through the last half."

"He said you did good, Firecracker," Voodoo called from the back. "And he doesn't hand out compliments unless he means 'em."

"Facts," Alphabet added, both of us reaching for our doors. I eased out with a groan, legs protesting every inch. Goblin hopped down beside me, stretching like a pissed-off cat. None of us were moving fast. My whole body felt like one big bruise, and I hadn't even done the bulk of the fighting.

Voodoo hoisted our prisoner out like a sack of grain, slinging him over his shoulder with casual effort. As I stretched, a warm hand pressed gently against my lower back. I glanced toward the house, watching Voodoo disappear inside with his unwilling cargo.

"Problem?" Alphabet asked, nudging me lightly.

"Just thinking..." I gestured toward the door. "When did bringing prisoners back from field ops become normal? He was already lugging that guy when we regrouped in the garden—after we *raided* a warlord's compound."

I paused, brow furrowing.

"Is Reznik even a warlord? Is that the right word?"

Alphabet snorted, grabbing his gear. "He's a jackass.

Criminal. Traitor. Backstabber. Petty motherfucker fits too. Warlord feels like we're giving him too much credit."

I took one of the bags and slung it over my shoulder, walking beside him toward the house.

"Petty jackass it is, then."

The safe house hummed with activity. Lunchbox was scrubbing his hands in the sink as we came in. "Go shower, Gracie. I'm going to get food started." He held up a wet finger when I opened my mouth to say "thank you," and I snapped it closed again. "You might not be hungry now. You might not be hungry later, but you still need fuel for recovery. I'll make sure you have light options."

When I drifted closer and pushed up on my toes, he dipped his head. "Thank you," I whispered, then pressed a light kiss to his lips. "For the food," I continued, then gave him another kiss. "For remembering that you're all giants and I am short."

His eyes softened and lit up with his quick grin. "Anytime, Gracie."

"I'm gonna start sorting the files," Alphabet said.

I snapped my fingers. "Wait." Memory hit like a sudden jolt. "I've got something for you."

I didn't wait for a response, already hurrying through the living room, heart pounding as I reached the bedroom I'd shared with Bones. My bag was in the corner, barely holding together after everything. I unzipped it, rummaging past shirts and scattered gear until my fingers brushed the little toiletries case I never let go of.

There. Nestled inside, safe somehow through all the chaos.

I rushed back out, adrenaline kicking up even though it wasn't life or death, just something that *mattered.*

Alphabet and Lunchbox were still in the kitchen when I skidded in, slightly breathless.

"This," I said, holding out the flash drive. "I found it the day we left. It was in Goblin's harness. Totally forgot in the middle of everything—sorry. But... here."

Alphabet's eyes lit up. His grin broke wide like sunrise after a blackout.

"You *found* it."

"I had to clean him up," I muttered, jaw tightening at the memory. "He was covered in blood."

"Wasn't his," Alphabet said, hand on heart. "Wasn't mine either."

"Good to know."

He dropped his bag and closed the distance between us with a few quick strides, then gently cupped my face like I was something fragile and worth holding.

"Thank you, Gracie."

"You're welcome," I breathed. "Sorry, I forgot I had it."

His kiss was soft, barely there, more a whisper than a press. But it sent a shiver rippling all the way through me.

"You kept yourself and Goblin alive. That's all I care about." Another kiss, just as light but deeper somehow. "Now, go shower."

I smirked. "Are you saying I stink?"

"Never," he said, tone wicked. "Though I wish I had time to wash your back."

The flush hit me hard, sharp and low. "Raincheck?"

He winked. "Definitely." Then made a lazy shooing motion. "Go. Before I decide to make time anyway."

Still tingling, I turned back toward the bedroom, already tugging my shirt loose. I pushed the door closed behind me with a soft click—only to find Bones standing with his back to me, wrapped in a towel, steam curling off his skin. His hair was slicked back, droplets still clinging to his shoulders.

Already showered. Already hurting.

The bruise on his side stole my breath. Dark and brutal, it bloomed across his ribs like something rotten trying to surface. Pain radiated from the sight alone.

He turned slightly, typing something on his phone, and I saw the bruise stretched further, sprawling across his chest like a shadow trying to consume him.

"You're bleeding," I said, moving before I even thought.

"Not the worst I've had," he replied without looking up.

"That doesn't mean it doesn't *hurt*." My voice cracked sharper than I meant it to. "Did anyone even patch you up?"

He looked at me then, and what hit me wasn't defiance or pride or even irritation. It was... weariness. A kind of soul-deep fatigue that went beyond physical pain. His face, usually locked down, was just *tired*. Tired of hurting. Tired of pretending not to.

Then I saw them. The bruises. Dozens of them. Fist-sized, angry, purple-black marks stamped across his skin like someone had tried to break him apart piece by piece.

"Oh my god," I whispered. "You got those... covering me." Back there. When they opened fire. I hadn't seen anything hit him, but then it had all happened so fast, so loud.

"I got them doing my job," he said stiffly.

"Your job?" I echoed, voice rising.

"Keeping you alive," he replied. His eyes shuttered again. "I agreed to you being there. So it was on me to make sure you came out."

The guilt in his tone made it feel like we didn't.

"We *both* came out."

"This time." His fingers clenched around his phone.

"But I keep thinking... if that guard had fired a second earlier. If Alphabet missed a camera feed. If you had flinched..."

His voice trailed off, and the look in his eyes hollowed out into something raw and terrifying.

"I know what it would've done to them," he said. "And what it would've done to me."

My throat closed. I crossed the space between us in a heartbeat, close enough to feel the heat radiating off his skin, the coiled tension beneath it.

"And what about what it would've done to *me* if you didn't come back?" My voice was low, but it hit like a slap. "If you died? If any of you had?"

He didn't hesitate. "I don't care about me."

I nearly slapped him right then, not out of anger, but from sheer helplessness. "Well, I *do*."

The fight bled out of his shoulders all at once, and the air around us shifted. The tension softened, but not gone. Just... waiting.

"I've led men into hell and pulled them out," he said quietly. "Lost some. Nearly lost others." His eyes found mine, stormy and sharp and bleeding. "But I've never had to protect someone I... someone I couldn't afford to lose."

I placed my palm carefully over one of the bruises on his chest. My hand looked small against the damage.

"You didn't lose me," I said softly. "I'm still right here."

His voice cracked on a whisper. "But it's coming, isn't it? The part where I do."

My breath left in a rush. I leaned forward, pressing my forehead to his chest, right above the bruises. I didn't care if I was sweaty or dirty or shaking. He needed me. *Here.*

"You don't get to push me away to protect me. That's not how this works anymore."

He exhaled slowly. "You're still the mission."

There was something uncertain in the way he said it now. Less a statement, more a question. As if he didn't quite believe it.

"Not anymore," I whispered, insisting. My fingers splayed wider, feeling the thrum of his heart beneath the damage. "Maybe I was in the beginning. But not now."

"Dollface," he murmured, pained and exasperated.

"Bones," I echoed, matching his tone.

He made a sound—frustrated, maybe amused. His hand slid into my hair and he dipped his head to press a kiss to the crown of mine.

"Grace," he whispered. "Tell me what you need."

"To be here. For *you*." It wasn't hard to say. It was the most honest thing I'd ever felt. "You all think you're still fighting for me. Maybe you are. But you're the reason I'm still fighting, too. All of you."

He fisted his hand in my hair and just held on. Like if he let go, something in him would come apart.

Eventually, he lifted his head and looked down at me. His hand slipped from my hair to my jaw, tilting my face up.

"You need a shower."

I smirked. "Still bossy."

"Is that so?" That glint in his eyes was back, sharp and dark and full of promise.

"Don't play coy. You *love* trying to boss me around."

"Trying?" His voice dropped, low and dangerous. A growl on the edge.

"You heard me."

His thumb traced my lower lip, slow and deliberate.

"You know what happens to people who play with fire," he murmured, voice velvet-wrapped steel. "They get burned."

"Not me," I said, catching his thumb between my teeth, biting just hard enough to make his breath catch. "You're watching my back. No one's burning me."

The last bit of tension bled out of him. His smile curled slow and dangerous.

"Oh, I definitely enjoy your attitude," I said, stepping back and peeling off my shirt deliberately. My muscles ached, but I moved like I didn't care. Like I *wanted* him to look.

"Going to shower now," I added over my shoulder. "Feel free to keep watching my six."

As I caught his gaze in the mirror, dark, heated, and *hungry*. I smiled to myself.

Yeah. I liked playing with fire. And this one? What was a little scorch between friends?

TWENTY-NINE

ALPHABET

It was early, not as early as the day before, but early enough for the sun to paint through the dust-coated windows in streaks of smudged sunshine.

The files spread out like wreckage.

Flash drives. Printouts. Screens glowing with decrypted data pulled straight from Reznik's servers. Names. Transactions. Travel records. Coordinates. Bidders. Victims.

Not one of them Amorette.

It was in the first search string of every single program I ran. They'd started the night with me, but one by one, the team had dropped off. Sleep wasn't an option for me. Not right now, not while I dug through what we'd found, what it meant, and started putting together what came next.

The deeper we dug, the more complicated it became. It wasn't just one organization, it was several. It wasn't just one crew handling transport, it was dozens. It wasn't one geographic location at the epicenter, it was quite literally the world.

Layer after layer peeled back to unveil tangled knot over tangled knot. Decryption revealed the involvement of more than just criminals, oligarchs, aristocrats, and executives. It was probably the ugliest who's who list of entitled scum.

The one thing that frustrated me each time I managed to drill down past a new web of concealment: Amorette. Amorette Monet Black wasn't even a blip on the radar. Nor any *subject* that matched Grace's physical description and measurements.

They had reams of data on Grace, a mountain of it. I tracked every single place they'd pulled the info.

Social media

Agency websites.

Photographer's files—watermarked and not so much.

Reddit threads.

Substacks for fashion.

Gossip sites.

What proved even more frustrating was the *lack* of current information. She'd been missing for months and not even a whiff of her flirted with the headlines. Nothing popped up in front line searches. In fact, someone had done a damn good job of muddying the waters with search-engine poisoning.

If you looked for Grace Black or Amorette Black, there weren't stories about them being missing. Hell, you could barely get a photo to even pop. It was all spam and scammer sites. Instead it was a lot of noise.

A lot of it.

Search for her dead manager. Same thing.

The photographers? A blip. Their website had even been *erased*. Time Machine didn't turn up even a memory of it. The manager's agency had "closed" and currently turned up... nothing. The effort poured into the distraction campaign had to be ongoing or you'd think we might pop a mention on a gossip site.

But nope, even Grace's social media profiles were no longer available. At all. Not the legitimate ones, but the fake ass posers and scammers?

They were everywhere.

Goblin ran races in his sleep, little yips escaping him as his claws scraped at the floor. I nudged him gently with a toe. He let out a grunt, then a sneeze as he sat up abruptly and looked around.

"Sorry bud," I told him and rose myself. My back cracked along with my shoulders as I stretched. Too many hours hunched over the laptop and my ass was also numb. I carried my empty mugs—both of them—back to the counter and rinsed them out.

The coffee pot was empty, and thankfully had turned itself off. If not, I probably would have scalded the damn thing. That would have triggered a shitstorm when the others started to wake up. After washing it out, I started another pot brewing then pulled on my gun holster and a jacket over it before heading for the door.

I swore more of my joints creaked with every step. Goblin dragged himself up. Once on his feet, he took his time stretching before he followed me over to where I waited by the door. "Shall we?"

When I opened the door, he trotted out and gave a little shake. The sunrise was just at the edge of the trees, all pinks and reds and hints of purples where it slammed up against the dark gray clouds. Rain today would help. Even if Reznik's guys managed to track even *one* of the SUVs, they'd find picking up the rest of our trail next to impossible.

Smothering another yawn, I limped my way out to the garden behind the safe house. It wasn't kept in the neatest rows, but it was definitely lush enough. The path was visible enough to let me stretch my legs as I moved.

I rubbed the back of my neck as I ran the last set of decryptions through my head. We had more than enough to bury the political careers of at least a dozen different buyers. We had five different hedge fund investors that also sat on multiple boards, three CEOs, more members of the aristocracy than I wanted to count, a fuckton of so-called NGOs including some that were "founded" by so-called influencers.

That was just what I'd confirmed so far. The lists of movers, shakers, journalists, legislative, congressional, executive, and even judicial clients continued to grow. No wonder they'd been able to hide so much of this. They had people everywhere and in every government.

The bureaucrats. They were the ones who could bury just about anything. Repackage it, rename it, and then even sell it as something else altogether. Crowdfunding based on a network of half-truths and false identities. The crowdfunding proved to just be another way to make bids. Some of the anonymous bidders dropped huge chunks of change, while smaller bidders just added to the coffers.

So not only did they make money selling people, they hid it and washed their funds using the same types of services that also provided them with funds from people looking to help or to hurt. It was downright nauseating.

Though, currently, I wasn't sure what was worse in all of this... Was it the funds dedicated to raising money for the most reprehensible of people? The kind you wouldn't expect to generate sympathy of any kind. Or was it the false, misleading tales designed to shred the heartstrings so you donated immediately? Only, if you took the time to dig, you found the lie. It wasn't even that well hidden.

Goblin raced ahead then back to check with me before he took off again. My dude was restless and I didn't blame him. I was feeling it too. We had apocalyptic levels of information that could absolutely destroy careers and end reputations. Beyond selling people, and laundering the money —because sure that was more than enough—they feathered their nests with blackmail. Their leverage could be paid out in cash, materials, or favors.

Insidious, disgusting, and bafflingly clever. They increased their profits and avoided taxes all at the same time, while adding multiple shields between their activities and law enforcement. I'd actually dug into the terms and services for one of the crowdfunding sites. Sure enough, buried practically six feet deep, was a provision shielding them from having to reveal certain key identifying bits of data.

You couldn't indemnify someone from revealing blackmail or illegal activities. Non-disclosure agreements regarding illegal activities were non-enforceable. Didn't stop people from agreeing or fearing the repercussions.

Travel agencies, online as well as brick and mortar establishments along with retail warehouses based in foreign locations, offered other inventive ways to make sales and transactions. Spread it out enough and it turned into a near impossible set of needles hidden amongst an infinite number of haystacks.

Thirty minutes later and with my head clearer after the walk, I returned with a more relaxed Goblin too. Despite having left a mostly slumbering house, Lunchbox was at the stove working on breakfast, while Voodoo, Bones, and —there she was, I sighed as she cast me a swift smile— Gracie studied everything I had laid out.

The smell from the coffee pot said they'd made more. Excellent. I got Goblin his breakfast before I poured coffee of my own. "That's about a third of what I managed to decrypt so far. There's going to be a hell of a lot more."

"There's enough here to bury at least a half-dozen buyers I recognize just from their names," Voodoo said, his icier tone suggesting he had no problem with it at all.

"We could ruin lives with all of this," Lunchbox commented over his shoulder, but I didn't miss the way his gaze went to Grace.

"We *should*," Bones said flatly.

"Do we know that everyone on those lists is actually guilty of something? Or were they just put under the thumb of this particular organization?" The almost too damn reasonable question from Grace made me study her.

"That's a lot of evidence to manufacture based on the hope that someone will do what you want to keep a blatant lie out of the press." Or so I believed.

"Is it?" She tapped one of the lists that was attached to a series of payments. "Do you know how swiftly people fall for gossip? Especially salacious gossip? Maybe it all turns out to be bullshit, but the stories debunking the bullshit never have the traction of the ones who wreck reputations and end careers."

"That's unsettling," I admitted and I wasn't alone scowling at the information I'd scattered.

"Maybe they are all guilty. Maybe some are only guilty by association. Maybe some are just—covering their own ass." She sighed and picked up another photo. It was of a woman, she was a student from Bulgaria supposedly studying in the UK. She'd been missing for more than eighteen months and there was barely even a blip for her via law enforcement.

Unscrewing a water bottle, I downed about half of it

before I carried my mug back to the table. "According to the dates, every few weeks, they host another 'gathering.' Another sale. They rotate countries, cities, and 'hosts.' Our twelve big buyers all serve as traveling hosts or have, but they aren't the only ones."

"So Monte Carlo wasn't a chokepoint." All emotion drained out of Bones' voice.

"It was," I assured him. "The hit they took there, at the secondary event with O'Rourke, and even with what we took here, they are going to feel it."

"But they aren't going to just curl up and die." Lunchbox flipped pancakes as he stared at the stove. "Even if we shove a bomb up their asses and blow it."

"No," I said with a sigh. "We kill this arm, another will pop up. Probably two based on what I've pulled apart so far. There are other 'organizations' involved. One in Eastern Europe, Russian, another in Singapore, probably something for Australia and we know the U.S. is in there."

"Central and South America," Bones added both items like ticking a box.

"Definitely, but that gets us into cartel land and there are some we don't want to start a fight with," Voodoo murmured.

"Not right now," I agreed with him. "We've already got a lot on the board."

Grace hadn't said a word since she asked if there was a way to be certain if the blackmail list clients were guilty or not.

"I've run every tag and ID through facial recognition. No hits on Amorette," I said softly. "I have another program running descriptions, keywords that could apply to either of you and some that would only apply to her."

Grace didn't react. Not visibly.

"She's not in this cluster," I continued "I don't think this was her pipeline." I hated telling her that. Hated telling her that while this had been her destination, it wasn't her sister's.

"So we keep looking. Right?" Lunchbox had the pan off the stove and he flicked a look at each of us.

"It's not our only option," Voodoo said slowly, but I could hear the dislike he chewed over with each word.

Grace turned to face him. For his part, he focused on her and not us.

"We could turn this over," Voodoo continued. "Interpol, a contact in MI6 I trust, maybe even leak it. It'd go wide fast. Public. Big splash, lot of heat." It was what she'd wanted to do for herself, only then it was FBI or Homeland.

"But no control." Bones shook his head, despite his neutral tone. Again, facts, but even he seemed to find impartiality a challenge. "Once it's out, we don't get to decide how or when it ends."

"We *might* get Amorette's name in the noise," I added, because we couldn't afford to *not* take all the acts into account. "But she'll be just that. Noise."

The room fell still. Lunchbox shut off the stove and joined us in studying Grace. The food smelled good but none of us were going to eat with this hanging out there.

"Your sister's not in there. But you are." Bones braced his knuckles on the table, his gaze fixed on her. "Every risk we take now—it circles back to you. So... it's your call."

"We keep hunting," Lunchbox added his vote "Or we light this fuse and walk away." He clearly had no interest in walking away, but I was with him on lighting the fuse. We might not ever burn it all down, but it had to go.

"Any way you want to do it," Voodoo summed up. "We back your play."

Bones folded his arms. "You're not the mission anymore. You're the center of it."

I damn near wanted to cheer. Never thought I'd see the day Cap took the stick out, but he cared and it *showed*.

She didn't answer us, not immediately. Instead, she studied the files, the papers, the notes I'd cobbled together.

"Then we go after the rest," she murmured, touching another picture, one of a girl who couldn't have been fourteen when it was taken. She'd vanished into that system four or five years earlier.

"Even if Amorette's not part of this?" Bones met her gaze. He wasn't doubting or testing her, he was verifying.

"*Especially* if she isn't," Grace said. "Because that means the system is bigger. And I want it to choke on everything it tried to take from me. From her."

"Then we burn the rest down," Bones stated and he flicked a look at us. "One name at a time. Some of it we handle personally..."

"Some of it, I can take out from a distance." Yeah, I knew exactly where he was going with this. Some would need a bullet for real, and others? Well, with what I had here, I could drop them with the metaphorical shot.

Either way, they would bleed.

"We still need to eat," Lunchbox stated and I didn't have to glance at him to know that by "we" he meant Gracie. "Then we have to clean up the debris from the last mission. Alphabet is gonna need time to finish breaking down the master list."

"Oh," Grace blinked. "I almost forgot. What did you do with him?"

Voodoo grinned and Lunchbox chuckled. Only Bones maintained his guarded expression. He lifted his chin when our gazes met. He wanted a word, in private.

I nodded.

We'd make it happen.

THIRTY

LUNCHBOX

"The root cellar?" Grace glanced at each of us with a mixture of surprise and puzzlement. "We have a root cellar?"

I hid a smile while I washed down the last of the pancakes and bacon with coffee. There was a faint smear of syrup on her lower lip. She'd eaten a pancake and one egg, poached, not fried, but then she had two pieces of bacon. Calorie deficits were a thing, but she was making an effort to eat. I'd leave it alone.

"Yes," Voodoo said, before he caught her hand and tugged her a little closer. Dammit, he kissed her and cleaned that lip right up. "Tasty, could definitely go for more."

Grace laughed. "I have some left if you…"

He shot her an exasperated look and nudged her plate back to her. "You have two more bites and it's not worth my life to try and take 'em even if I wanted them."

With a slow blink, she looked from Voodoo to the rest of us, then back before she snapped her gaze to Bones. "You know, if you keep scowling, your face is gonna get stuck like that." Her lips pursed. "Or maybe it already has."

He spared a single look. "Hilarious."

Amusingly enough, he wasn't glaring anymore. Grace appeared more than a little pleased with herself. I could put up with just about anything to keep that look on her face. "Last call," I informed the guys as I stood. "Want anything more?"

"All good," Alphabet said, though he cracked a yawn right in the middle of the second word. "Let me get the next round of files running and I'll be ready."

I swapped out his coffee for water and he gave me a gimlet-eyed stare that I ignored. Keep downing the gallons of coffee that he had been and even we risked disintegrating our stomach lining. Grace collected the other plates and empty mugs and ferried them to the sink.

Voodoo was a half-step behind her and he took over washing up. I'd already cleaned most of the pans I'd used, but I went over the stove area and packed away any supplies that had remained out.

"We have enough supplies for a midday meal and a decent dinner." I caught Bones' eye and nodded to Grace. We had more than enough to feed her. *We* might be stuck with rations. "So if we're planning to be here longer, we'll need another supply run."

"We may need a supply run anyway," Voodoo said, drying his hands off after stacking the last of the now clean dishes in the rack. "Once we decide the next part of the plan, we go from there."

"For now," Bones straightened and swept a look over all of us before he focused on Grace. "We have an interrogation to get to. You do not have to be involved. Particularly because we will need to be aggressive in our tactics."

Torture was on the table. There was no other way to ensure that our guest cooperated. Extracting a pound of flesh that was dearly owed?

That was just a perk.

Grace didn't immediately launch into an argument over his cautious warning. Instead, she folded her arms and chewed her lower lip. Between the sweatshirt—it had to be one of Bones'—and her leggings, she looked almost painfully young.

But then, all I had to do was gaze into those brilliant blue eyes to see the scars life had already left on her.

"Will it create an issue if I am present?" Not an unfair question. I had my opinions. Clearly, we all did. Voodoo and Alphabet, like me, also waited for Bones' verdict.

"An issue for us?" Bones restated the question, clarifying it before he shook his head. "No. We can handle it. Nothing he says or does can actually hurt you and any threats he makes won't go far."

Because the man would be dead when we were done. I didn't fully agree that he couldn't hurt her with words though. She was tough as hell, but she wasn't *us*. Her skin hadn't been turned to rawhide by training, war, and loss.

I never wanted her to experience that or to have to feel those things. Ever.

"You," Bones continued after letting his response settle for a beat. "It might create more bad memories for you. More fuel for your nightmares."

Dropping my chin, I let my gaze pass back and forth between them. Bones couched his own objection in a kind observation. Just telling her no wasn't going to fly, she had to choose whether she went down there or not. Choose whether to stay or not.

If we could have brought the guy in and dealt with it

without her ever seeing a thing? Yeah, I probably would have let her continue in ignorance. Some things she didn't have to experience and more she didn't *need* to, particularly when she had nothing to prove.

"Because you're going to beat the shit out of him." She wasn't asking, more testing herself maybe with the statement. "How bad?"

Bones shrugged. "As badly as he requires to answer our questions. We need to be efficient, which means a certain level of brutality. Enhanced interrogation is not for everyone, Grace. You don't *have* to do anything. We will get the answers we need and any that you need whether you are in the room or not."

A faint smile touched her lips. Go Bones, I thought with no small amount of admiration. He'd laid it out with facts, not feelings.

"Can he hurt any of you with me in the room?" Also not a bad question. Her compassion really was a strength, even if it also opened her up to pain.

"He can try," Voodoo answered with a nonchalant shrug. "Bones is right, we're going to hurt him, Firecracker. He can make it worse for himself by being a dick to you. But it won't get him out of this life any faster than necessary unless he just decides to cooperate from the word go."

Alphabet snorted. My thoughts exactly.

"Then I'd like to be present, if for no other reason than to support you all." She pursed her lips. "That said, if it becomes too much I'll just storm out—maybe slap him and storm out."

"You won't slap him." Bones didn't even let her finish her statement. "You won't be anywhere near him."

She wrinkled her nose but this was not a battle she'd win and she seemed to recognize it. "Acceptable." Huffing out a breath, she scanned us again. "Do you want to have a code phrase to tell me to go if you need me to leave?"

Damn if she didn't have Bones' number. There was no mistaking the genuine smile that appeared and disappeared like the sun behind fast moving clouds. Yes, she had his number and let him know it.

"We'll ask you to take Goblin for a walk." Straightforward enough code phrase. "If any one of us asks, you go. No hesitation. No arguments."

"Agreed," she said with a nod. "Do any of you need key phrases to get out of there?"

The silence that hit the room after that question was almost like a blanket bomb hitting.

"Coffee," Alphabet said. "If I need to get out of there, I'm going to say something about coffee. You can tell me to go make it."

"Magic trick," Voodoo said after a long moment. "If I mention a magic show or trick, that'll be my cue. You can ask me to walk you out or whatever."

When she glanced at me, I blew out a breath. "Food." Easiest answer for me. "If I say something about needing to start on dinner. Then damn straight it's time for me to go." I'd never needed an out before.

None of us had, but Grace offered us a way to get her out of the room, she wanted to give us the same chances.

That just left Bones. He didn't say anything for a long moment. Almost too long. "Stick," he said finally. "If I mention I need a stick. That'll be my cue."

"As in the stick that used to be up your ass?" The level of skepticism and amusement tangling in her voice made me laugh. I wasn't alone. Everyone cracked up. Everyone except Bones.

"Maybe," was all he said. "You'll have to wait and see, won't you?"

"What a way to dare me with a good time." So very dry and deadpan, she could have given him a run for his money. "I guess that means we're ready."

"I guess so," was his response.

Watching them flirt was wild *and* entertaining.

"Oh, Gracie," I said as we all straightened. "Boots on."

She glanced down at her bare feet, then up again before she nodded. "I'll go get them."

As soon as she was out of the room, Alphabet glanced at Bones. "You sure about this?"

"No," he said. "But it has to be her call. She'll leave if she can't handle it." At least he sounded certain on that subject. "If any of us see it going sideways for her, then call it for her."

Worked for me.

"Shall we?" I asked, offering her an arm when she came back. Curiosity filtered through the worry in her expression, but she settled her hand on the crook of my arm. "Down we go."

A light swung from the ceiling in the root cellar. It was a muddy light, enough to let you see but hardly bright enough for reading.

Our guest, Reznik, bled from the temple. A vicious bruise around his right eye stretched down to the second bruise on his jaw. He could look worse. His chair creaked as he leaned forward, partially rocking against his restraints.

We'd shackled him in place, then left him for the night. The insulation down here kept the sound from traveling. I'd also done a full scan for any trackers. Cocky bastard didn't bother with one for himself.

Oh well. Too bad for him.

"Well, well, welll," Reznik said slowly as we filed into the room. There were crates in the back. Shelving. In addition to the environment providing cooling, there was actually a freezer down here. It was far enough back from the bastard, that he wouldn't even be able to spit on her.

I hoisted her up to sit on it, that way she could also see past all of us. The faintly incredulous look she gave me had me winking.

"You want to start with your partners?" Bones asked in an icy tone.

"My partners?" Reznik made a face. "I'd rather start this with a lawyer."

"All out of those right now," Alphabet said in an almost too happy singsong. "If you want to skip your partners, we can go with fourteen girls. Fourteen, all under twenty, three dead before they made it to the first auction. Four more dead during the auction. Seven left, three returned for another auction—the other four? Presumed deceased?"

"Law. Yer." Reznik elongated the word, heavily playing up each syllable.

"Azwai City?" Voodoo suggested, Reznik didn't even glance at him though a smirk touched his mouth.

"Attorney."

"Basra?" Voodoo added.

"Yes, you probably still struggle with English, don't you?" Almost dismissively, Reznik said, "Abogado." He played up each syllable. Racist prick.

"Five women, all between the ages of eighteen and twenty-one, acquired from a *school trip*, all auctioned eighteen months ago. Then vanished." Alphabet had a digital tablet with him and he made a point of tapping it like he made notations.

"Le-gal. Coun-sel." The exaggeration of each word didn't do him any favors.

Bones struck him. The swift jab with his right fist made Reznik jerk. Blood and spit flew from his mouth as his head snapped to the side. The chair went down with him chained to it. He hit the floor with a bang and another flinch.

With a sigh, I pushed away from the wall next to Gracie and converged on Reznik with Voodoo. We picked the whole chair up and set him upright.

"Ten minutes," I told him, keeping it laid back and conversational. "Then I get my meat tenderizer and I break every bone you have from the waist down." I glanced at my watch, set the timer then resumed my post near Gracie.

Instead of a snide remark, Reznik adjusted his head and his attention. He focused on each of us. His smirk flickered back to life when he eyed Alphabet. Then he settled his attention on Gracie.

"Are you the attorney or the model?"

I would have said that I was by far the most reasonable one coming into this room. As much as I wanted to take our pound of flesh, it was all about justice. Justice for Alphabet. Justice for Doc. Hell, it was even justice for Bones, because Reznik tried to make everything Bones' fault. Frankly, I would have placed a solid bet on him not being able to say a damn thing that would have me ready to castrate him now and to hell with whatever else he might know.

I was wrong.

The way he stared at Grace made my blood boil. That he raked his eyes over her and shot her a bloody-toothed smile? Nope. I had good knives upstairs. I also had some really shitty rusty ones.

They would take a while and hurt a hell of a lot more.

"This only ends two ways for you," Bones informed him in the precise tones. "You answer the questions, get a bullet in the head. Quick. Done."

"Or you don't," Voodoo said with a smile that actually made the hair stand up on the back of my neck. "You don't get a bullet in the head and you sure don't get quick. You're dying Reznik, that's nonnegotiable. How you die? Well, keep fucking around."

"You think I'm afraid of some pain? That you worry me?" Reznik's derisive laughter earned him another punch. This time, the blow caught him on the side of the head. The ear.

Fuck those hurt. Not enough for him, but they hurt.

With a sigh, I walked back over and hauled Reznik up with Voodoo.

"You have her yet?" Reznik asked me. "I didn't get the pleasure. Saw the videos though. She was a wild—"

I snapped every finger on his left hand. Then his ulna. Sweat beaded his face as he paled, then he laughed.

"You think I'm afraid of any of you?" Reznik coughed, then spat out more blood. "You the jolly happy chef, who just wants to feed everyone. Should have opened a fucking diner. Voodoo, the man whore who was too pretty for hard work. But why work for something when you can steal it?"

Voodoo had a hand on my shoulder. It was a light touch. A reminder. Grounding me in the present so I didn't just rip this asshole's head off.

"Or maybe it's Alphabet, the man who was too stupid to read the trap for what it was, so sure he knew everything. Couldn't even wait five minutes, cause he had to be right." His gruesome expression just grew more foreboding. "You seem to have lost your medic, but then Bones isn't that good about bringing all his people back."

Finally, that wild-eyed gaze fixed on Grace again. "You think you know them?"

Grace merely blinked at him, not saying a word. I was so fucking proud of her.

"Whatever, suck their cocks. Spread your legs for them. Hopefully you're charging them millions, cause that's what you cost me and I didn't even get to touch that ass." Then he took his life in his hands. "Course, there's always tomorrow. They'll get bored eventually—then I'll be there."

The timer on my watch went off. I pivoted and went up the stairs. When I returned, I had the meat tenderizer, and a couple of rusty knives.

"Lunchbox," Bones said as I set my tools down.

"Cap?" I met Gracie's gaze as she flicked a worried look from me to Reznik and then back.

"Break both of his knees." That was one order I would happily follow. I kept my gaze on Gracie however.

"Do you want me to go?" She asked so softly, I damn near missed it.

Yes. I did. This wasn't a memory of me I wanted her to have. But...

"It's going to be messy," I warned her.

"I can handle it." Of that I really had no doubt. "But would you rather I didn't?"

I rolled my head from side to side. "Stay, Gracie." I picked up the meat tenderizer. "At least for this part. Since he brought up your sister..."

After I closed the distance, I didn't offer him another warning or way out. I struck his right knee with the meat tenderizer. One blow wouldn't do it.

It took three for the patella to crack. He was screaming before then.

It took longer to break the other.

While he pissed himself, he was still conscious.

"Let's try this again," Alphabet said easily. "Fourteen girls..."

CHAPTER

THIRTY-ONE

GRACE

I didn't think we'd been down there longer than a few hours, yet it felt like an eternity passed. I stayed for all of it. From Legend breaking the man's kneecaps to the shattering of each of his feet to when they began to carve pieces off of him.

The horror of it all seemed permanently etched into my brain. Not because of what they did to him—frankly, Reznik was trash. He traded in people. He made his money off the suffering of others. He'd also betrayed the guys. He'd betrayed them and cost them.

No, I was fine with them taking him apart. What I couldn't quite shake was how long he held out. How much pain he endured before he finally started answering questions. Even though it had been cool in the root cellar, I was sweaty and gross.

Once back up in my room, I stripped and climbed in the shower. I scrubbed every inch of me, then washed my hair. By the time I rinsed off, I'd rediscovered some measure of peace. How much hate and spite did you need to harbor toward people to endure that much pain?

I wrapped up in a towel after I squeezed all the excess water out of my hair. Imagining it was the stress, the memories, and the pain I squeezed out also helped. Sighing, I let myself out into the bedroom.

"Don't be too surprised."

The voice came from across the room, calm and gentle.

Alphabet was there, seated in a battered armchair near the window, a tablet in hand, boots unlaced, sleeves rolled. He hadn't looked up yet. The tablet he'd had earlier was in his lap. Goblin lay sprawled on the floor, snoring. He thumped his tail once then closed his eyes again.

"Hey," I murmured, moving to the bag to fold up the clothes I'd changed out of. The sweatshirt was huge and I loved it, so it was going in my bag.

"Hey," he answered, closing the tablet he held and setting it aside.

"How are you doing, AB?" I pulled out clean panties and a sports tank with a built in bra. I had one pair of clean jeans left and another pair of yoga pants. I tugged the latter out.

"Pretty sure I should be asking you that," he murmured, studying me.

"Well, you can, but since I asked first." Since I was still in a towel, I had a few of choices. Go back into the bathroom to get dressed, wiggle into panties one-handed, just drop the towel here and dress, or set the clothes aside for now and stay in my towel. "Will you tell me if something else is wrong?"

Huffing out a half-laugh, he shook his head. "You already learned how to ask questions carefully. Not asking 'if something is wrong,' but 'if something else is wrong.'"

"I like to think of myself as a fast learner." I set the clothes aside and crossed the room to him. With care, I eased onto the arm of the chair. This angle put me closer to eye level with him. I braced one hand on the back of the chair and trusted the towel knot to do its job. "I know there's lots of stuff wrong. There's a few things that are right too, but... today was a lot."

He dismissed that with a shrug. "Weirdly, not as much as you might think it was, Gracie."

"Okay."

As he stroked his hand along my thigh, he studied me. I'd seen the same look in Lunchbox's eyes earlier. When he told me I could stay but it wouldn't be pretty.

"Just okay?" A boundless kind of curiosity reflected in his blue eyes.

"Yes, you know what is a lot or not for you. I accept that. Just like I accept that something else is wrong or maybe it's just more of the same. You really haven't been sleeping."

That last part worried me most at the moment. I stroked my fingers through his hair. It was even more disheveled than usual, yet, that chaos just suited him. His eyes drifted half-closed as I massaged his scalp.

"No," he half-mumbled the words. "I've got too much to do. I'll be fine with naps. Promised you I would find your sister. I'm going to find her, dammit."

"AB," I whispered the letters of his name, trying to sum up all the emotions swarming me. "You *need* real sleep. You can set up one of those decryptions and tell me what would be a problem. I can wake you up if it happens." Was I offering to babysit his computer program? *Absolutely.*

A long sigh escaped him as he leaned into the contact. "I'll be okay, Gracie."

"Will you?" Worry crept through me. Because he seemed to grow wearier and wearier each day we'd been here. The attack at the house hadn't helped nor the separation from Goblin. Since we reunited, the stress seemed ever present. "This isn't what you signed up for, you know?"

That made him tip his head back, eyes narrowing as he really looked at me. The sleepiness vanished, chased off by something sharper, something awake. "Gracie... *you* are the reason I signed up for this. Exactly you."

I swear the air snagged in my lungs like it forgot how to move. His fingers brushed my jaw, light and deliberate, like he was mapping something he didn't want to forget.

"We promised each other honesty, remember?"

The reminder caught what little breath I had left and tangled it in my throat.

"We did," I murmured, tipping my head into his touch as his hand slid higher.

One second, I was perched on the arm of the chair. The next, I was in his lap with my damp hair clinging to his skin, towel somehow still in place.

The sudden shift made me laugh under my breath. I glanced down, then met his eyes again. "Very smooth."

He didn't even blink. "I liked it."

"Me too." The words barely made it past my lips, more breath than sound, as he pressed his forehead to mine.

Then his mouth found mine—soft at first. A promise more than a kiss. A tease.

The second was bolder. Deeper. Heat curled low in my belly as he gathered me closer, arms tightening, his body folding around mine like he needed me under his skin.

I let him. Leaned in until there was no space left between us. My fingers dove into that riotous mass of wild hair, twisting tight, anchoring me to the moment.

His tongue swept against mine—slow, deliberate— igniting a fire that roared through my system and burned the weariness to ash.

Then came the scrape of his teeth over my lower lip, just enough to sting, just enough to make me gasp. The rasp of his stubble across my skin dragged me back to the edge even as the passion beneath my skin spiraled higher.

"I don't know how to be soft with you," he murmured, lips brushing mine, his breath a furnace of want.

Then he kissed me—deep, possessive, devastating.

My thoughts scattered like embers in a storm.

When I moved to shift, he caught me—hands locking around my waist—and lifted me without hesitation. Like he couldn't stand the space, not even an inch. I found myself straddling him, chest to chest, heat to heat.

"You don't have to be soft," I assured him in between gasps of air "You just have to be here with me."

"Nowhere else I'd rather be," he promised, kissing me again before finding the knot where I'd tucked the towel ends between my breasts. "Are you cold?" The heated question against my lips made me laugh.

"Actually," I admitted. "Quite the opposite. I'm suddenly very warm."

"Let's see about helping you out with that."

He tugged the towel wide, not that it did more than fall to my waist since I was currently straddling him. He settled his hands just above the towel.

"You're so damn tiny."

The way he exhaled the words had goosebumps racing over my skin. His grin grew a tad more wicked as he lifted me again. It let the towel slip further, so I tugged it out from between us and let it fall.

"So tiny," he repeated, gaze stroking over me until even my nipples went taut just from the heat in them. "You don't ever seem so tiny until I'm touching you."

"I like it when you touch me." Probably didn't need

saying but I wanted him to know regardless. "I like touching you even more."

"Well, that makes one of us," he said before he tugged me forward and locked his lips around one nipple. The man was determined to send me up in flames. The contact between his mouth and my skin sizzled. In my mind, it was a brand but instead of pain, he seared me with pleasure.

He took his time, laving one nipple then moving to the other. Each slow pass of his cheek dragged that deliciously rough stubble over my skin, the rasp sending tiny shocks through me—just enough sting to sharpen the haze, a bite to anchor the melt.

Cradling his head, I raked my nails through his hair, drawing out a low sound from deep in his chest. I guided that sinful mouth to keep exploring, feeding the slow burn between us as his hands slipped lower.

Every brush of his fingers sent jolts of heat racing under my skin, tingles sparking into something darker, needier— until I was burning everywhere, thighs trembling, breath catching, desperate for his hands to keep going. When he cupped my ass, squeezing and pulling me in tighter, I vibrated with the moan that escaped.

With a wet pop, he pulled his head back to stare up at me. Rousing from the cocoon of pleasure, I drank in the expressions chasing across his face like a fast-moving storm —anger, hunger, frustration, joy, a fierce, almost primal intensity. Each one flared and faded until only one remained: the look he wore when *everything* in him was locked on me. As if the world had narrowed to this moment, to *us*, and nothing beyond existed.

I had never felt so bare—stripped open, seen down to the marrow—yet somehow powerful, untouchable.

Exposed and vulnerable, yes... but wrapped in the kind of protection that didn't cage, only worshipped.

"AB," I pushed his name past the choking emotion wrapped around me. He turned his head and pressed a kiss to the faint scar left from where O'Rourke had torn the skin. Then he moved up to kiss a bruise I hadn't noticed. There were a few of them over my arms and then down my torso.

One by one, he mouthed kisses to each and every mark until I trembled from the affection he showered on me. The singular caress of his lips on my skin turned me inside out. I wanted him and wanted to wrap around him until the rest of the world faded to just us.

There was a half-formed growl followed by a yip then a noise I could only describe as a "woop-woop-woop" like he was Curly or Shemp from the Three Stooges. The unexpected noises had me twisting a little and even Alphabet leaned forward. Goblin raced in his sleep.

Adoration swarmed me. He was such a good boy. Also, I loved that dogs could dream. He definitely sounded happy.

"Gracie," Alphabet summoned my attention back to him even as he surged upward. He stood, balancing me easily, and I looped my arms around his neck. Nose to nose, I smiled at the ease around his eyes.

Passion crackled in the air and need simmered around us, but Alphabet was just there. Solid. Strong. Warm. He kissed me again. This one wasn't urgent or fiery, yet it could so easily transform and burn us both up.

But this kiss was different. It was a promise. It said, *I see you, and I'm not going anywhere.*

I answered the pledge in his kiss with one of my own. I saw all of them. Loved them...

"AB..." His name was a prayer on my lips as he took a single step. Then the door opened without a knock. It cut off Goblin's sleep romp. He thumped his tail twice, but didn't leap up.

So, unsurprisingly, the person at the door was a friendly.

"Well, damn," Legend drawled, stretching the words, thick with surprise and something else simmering beneath. "Should I come back later—with flowers and a formal apology?"

Alphabet smirked, the expression softening his sharp features in a way that was almost criminal. "Serve you right if I told you to get lost."

I shifted just enough to glance back. Alphabet moved with me, instinctively—just a small step so I could stay close, still pressed to his warmth, but now able to meet Legend's gaze.

He lounged in the doorway like he owned the moment, arms crossed, a slow burn of curiosity and hunger flickering in his eyes. He wasn't just watching—he was *drinking us in.*

"Or," I said slowly, flicking a look to Alphabet as I spoke. "You could stay and make it interesting."

Alphabet's smirk deepened, turning sly—dangerously close to a dare. His gaze flicked to Legend, then back to me, like he knew exactly the effect we were having and was perfectly content to let it simmer.

Legend arched a brow, amused and undeniably interested. "Alright," he said, voice lower now, velvet and heat. "How *interesting* are we going to make it?"

"As interesting as Gracie wants," Alphabet murmured, still watching him. "But you're going to have to figure out what she likes..."

That landed like a spark in dry grass.

"You sure about this?" Legend asked, eyes fixed on where I leaned into Alphabet. "Both of you?" He cleared his throat and his gaze came up to my face though it definitely seemed to take some effort. "I can fuck off."

I almost laughed. It was exactly what he'd said to whomever had knocked on the door at Rachel's apartment. "I am," I said, testing the words. "I don't mind if you stay as long as AB is okay with it."

Switching my attention to Alphabet, I frowned. We hadn't really talked about this. I was basically intimately involved with all of them, even Bones. Though I hadn't gotten to so much as kiss him yet.

"Tell me to fuck off, brother, if you just want the time with our girl."

Three things hit me all at once.

First—Alphabet's expression softened at Legend's offer, the edges of his usual guarded confidence rounding into something almost tender. There was a quiet exchange in that look, unspoken but unmistakable. The connection between them wasn't just history—it was *depth*: loyalty, affection, a hard-earned trust that ran bone-deep.

Second—being called *theirs* shouldn't have felt sexy. I wasn't a prize, or a toy, or some fragile thing to be claimed. After years of being reduced to looks and curves, that kind of language usually set my teeth on edge. But somehow, when Legend said *"our girl"*, it didn't land like ownership.

It landed like *home*.

The third surprise—though maybe it shouldn't have surprised me at all—was Alphabet turning his full focus on me. The weight of it nearly stole my breath.

"Whatever you want, Gracie," he said, steady and certain. "We'll make it work." Then the corner of his mouth quirked into that crooked, dangerous smile. "We'll just make *him* figure out the complicated positions."

The air shimmered, thick with possibility. The kind that curled around your spine and dared you to say *yes*.

My heart swelled, too full to hold the moment—and then the laughter burst out of me, bright and breathless. Because this wasn't just intriguing. It was *everything*. I clenched around the idea of *both* of them, already hungry for it.

"Only one caveat," I said, and instantly their attention sharpened, twin spotlights pinning me in place. "I've never done this before. So if we're doing this... I'm gonna need a little guidance."

Alphabet's arms tightened around me in silent reassurance. "We can handle that. Right, brother?"

"Oh," Legend said, his voice slow, smooth, and simmering. He pushed off the door frame with lazy confidence and reached back to shut the door behind him. The quiet *click* of the lock was louder than any promise.

"Yeah," he said. "We've got you."

THIRTY-TWO

GRACE

Legend walked right up behind me, and slid his hands over my shoulders then down my bare back. The desire to cuddle Alphabet closer while simultaneously leaning back against Legend held me fast. He pressed a kiss to my bare shoulder, and the tension binding me up for the last several hours just eased.

Sighing, I closed my eyes and let my head drift back and Legend rewarded me with a kiss to my jaw then another to my ear. "Any preferences?" The gentle question sparked a thrill that danced down my spine.

"I have a few," Alphabet admitted, a sly edge in his voice. "No way we get to all of them tonight."

The words hit like a spark to dry kindling. A shiver of anticipation ran through me—not just from the promise in their tone, but from the electric fact that they were talking about me. To each other. Like I was the subject of some delicious, shared secret.

I barely had time to register his words before his mouth was on mine—slow, scorching, and all-consuming. The kiss stole the breath from my lungs, burning everything else away until only need remained. Then Alphabet deepened it, his body closing in, pressing me flush against Legend like he was the only thing holding me up—a solid wall of heat and muscle that made my head spin.

Legend ran his hands from my hips to my chest then down again. He feathered kisses against my shoulder, teasing little bites alternated with firm, bruising sucks. Hickeys. He was leaving another trail of hickeys.

Raw delight surged through me—laughter echoed inside me, even as I groaned and then released a longer, softer sigh when Alphabet lifted his head. Every moment of our connection blended playfulness with raw intensity, making each touch feel electric, each kiss a spark of something deeper. Lovemaking became a dance, a perfect balance of fun and passion that left me in awe.

"I love you." I whispered the words, because they were important words. Even more important right now, sandwiched between the two of them with all that wild energy wholly focused on me.

Alphabet's expression grew impossibly gentle and he traced his fingers down my cheek. "Can you hold our girl for a minute?"

"I can do just about anything for her," Legend said, the handoff so smooth between them, I barely registered Alphabet's hands leaving me or how Legend cradled me closer. "Naked and warm, this is how I'd like you to be on a regular basis."

"I might have to bump up the heating bill in Montana," I joked, "because without clothes, it'll be *way* too damn cold."

The words tumbled out before I could stop them, and as Alphabet's laugh filled the room a fresh bolt of delight struck me. It was like the world had tipped on its axis, and suddenly, everything felt light—*too* light, like I was floating. I couldn't tell if it was the air, them, or just the sheer rush of being alive right there. They were everything.

His eyes softened, that knowing smile curling at the corners of his lips. "Don't worry," he said, his voice low and warm, "we'll make sure you're never cold."

The promise hung in the air between us, and in that moment, I didn't just believe it—I *felt* it. Not that I was remotely cold at the moment.

"Gracie." Legend snared my attention, and then his mouth was on mine. Time stopped as I opened to the demand in his lips. The kiss held longing, but also offered so much more. My pulse quickened as I twisted to wrap my arms around his neck. Once I hitched my thighs to his hips, he cupped my ass. Those strong hands massaged and stroked, petting me everywhere.

The roughness of his clothes grounded me back into the moment as a drunken haze of sensuality threatened to overwhelm me. Every movement seemed to take on a life of its own.

"Share her." The command sent a new riot through my senses as Legend moved closer to the bed. After one more breath-stealing kiss, he lifted his head and lowered me.

"Go kiss, Alphabet now." The slow, burning hum of passion deepened Legend's voice, making it darker, richer, and impossibly more seductive.

"I can do that." I was more than happy to do just that. I turned to crawl up the length of the bed, well-aware of the image I gave Legend. Based on his hard groan, it was one he definitely enjoyed.

Alphabet was already sprawled on the bed. Naked, his red, heavy cock in one hand as he stroked it. He was totally naked, and I had my first real look at the whole of him, right prosthesis in place and all.

The weight of that trust threatened to shatter me. With one hand on either side of his legs, I met and held his gaze. The intensity in his blue eyes held me hostage. I pressed a kiss to his left leg, just above the ankle. Then did the same to his prosthesis on the right. Not once did I look away.

He needed to know that when I said I loved him, I meant all of him. I accepted every part, and wanted every part. Awareness seemed to flood his gaze and it shimmered until he blinked. Kiss by kiss, I made my way up to his knees, and I made sure to kiss both the flesh of his right thigh where it slid into the joint sock securing the prosthesis in place and the prosthesis itself.

"Gracie," he exhaled my name like a prayer.

"She's a keeper," Legend said from behind me. I'd just made it to where Alphabet stroked himself and I covered his hand with my own so I could caress and pet him. The droplet of pre-cum beading at the slit in the swollen head drew me like a magnet.

"Fuck," Alphabet swore as I lapped up that drop and tortured him with the same soft, kittenish licks that had driven Legend crazy. Getting to touch them was becoming my new favorite thing.

"Her mouth," Legend said as he nuzzled a kiss against the curve of my ass, "is the perfect shape for sin."

Alphabet fisted my damp hair, but he didn't pull even as he thrust upward. I was ready though, swallowing around him as he bumped against the back of my throat. "God, she's going to make me come right now."

The hand skimming over my ass paused, then delivered a light, if stinging slap. I pulled off Alphabet's dick long enough to twist and *stare* at Legend. His absolutely unrepentant grin turned me inside out.

"So, you're not quite into the pain thing unless you're already on the edge." He nodded once. "Good to know. Alphabet would like to play more before you make him blow his load."

For some reason, the absolute absurdity hit me in that moment. "AB can talk for himself, Legend."

"Legend..." Alphabet groaned. "Fuck me, you told her your name?"

As Legend's grin grew, more of his tension just seemed to wash off of him. All the earlier worry in his eyes was gone. On impulse, I cupped his face in my hands and dragged him in for a kiss.

He didn't make me wait nor did he remotely complain about it. Understanding struck like lightning—sudden, blinding, and irreversible. And in its wake, a storm of want surged through me. I needed them both, wildly, unbearably. "How do we do this?" I asked on a gasp as I pulled back and looked at Alphabet.

"Yes, I told her my name." Legend's smile echoed in his words. "Worth it. Tell her yours... I bet it turns her on even more."

"Tell me, don't tell me," I said, waving that aside. "Right now, I want to feel you both. I want—I *want* to come and I want to come with both of you."

It might have come out a plea, but I was serious. Why had I never paid attention to all the sexcapades the other models sometimes got into? I'd never done a threesome. The shakiness in my limbs came from wanting to touch them and be touched and it was a little harder to do when I was focused on one or the other.

How was I supposed to do both?

"C'mere, Gracie," Alphabet spoke in a low, molten voice, each word dripping with intent as he curled his fingers with slow, deliberate grace—like a promise wrapped in silk. "Come kiss me, we need to make sure you're wet and figure out if you want anal or to do this another way."

The offer spun me out—heat rising, balance gone. I couldn't tell how my arms and legs kept moving when everything else had gone slack. Then I was over Alphabet and he claimed my mouth as he pulled me down flush against him.

His kiss turned slow and almost sweet, small biting nips interspersed with longer, deeper invasions of his tongue. It was hard to hold onto anything as they seemed intent on taking me apart.

What a way to go.

Legend's fingers trailed along the back of my thigh, a reminder that he was there. Then those magical fingers teased along my slit and I was pushing back at the first push of two fingers into my cunt.

Moaning into Alphabet's mouth, I tried to rock back on Legend's fingers, but he was already pulling away. Alphabet's arms tightened around me, not letting me go.

Their hands were everywhere and they were hot, demanding. One moment I would be grinding against Alphabet and then Legend would stroke me and I would arch, trying to press back to him.

Dark laughter, deep and hypnotic shook me between them. When Alphabet finally released my mouth, he didn't let me go far. Instead, he pulled me up a little higher so he could tease and torment my nipples.

"One sec," Legend murmured, but the words only half-registered as I arched against Alphabet's wicked mouth. He pushed us up, until he was sitting and half bent as I arched backwards. Yoga practice suddenly seemed like a good thing.

This position also let me see Legend coming back out of the bathroom with a smirk on his face. He paused to tilt his head to the side as he watched us.

"Does his mouth feel good on you, Gracie?"

"Yes," I exhaled the word because even with me trying to stroke Alphabet's shoulders and his head, I couldn't reach everywhere. At the same time, his cock was pressed right up against my cunt. Each time I started to glide, one or both of them would lock my hips into place. "Mean."

The complaint slipped out on a bit of a whine. Alphabet gave the nipple he wasn't sucking a firm twist. The pain lanced right through the pleasure, twisting me up like a live wire and sending fresh shocks with every new caress.

"Keep her busy," Legend ordered.

"With pleasure," Alphabet responded, with a fist in my hair, he pulled my mouth back to his as he stretched out flat. Legend stroked his hands up and down my back, roaming from my nape to where my ass curved against my leg.

Thoughts scattered under Alphabet's full sensual assault, then Legend lifted my hips. Cool air flowed between my legs, but Alphabet kissed a path to my ear and it gave me a moment to press biting kisses of my own to his neck and then to his pec.

"A hickey for a hickey," I informed him and his laughter just added another drug to our kiss when he hauled me back to him. Fingers teased along my slit, then began to lightly massage my clit as another pair of fingers pressed into me. I swore, but the word was utterly muffled by his gagging kiss. The caresses from both hands sent me skyrocketing.

Then something warm dribbled along my crack and I tensed, but the pressure from the hand on my clit burst through the dam and Legend sank a finger into my anus. That—was weird. But not at all unpleasant, particularly while I shook with the aftershocks of orgasm.

"Again," Alphabet ordered and he delved his fingers against me as Legend eased another finger into my ass. The burn lit me up, even as Alphabet stroked me toward another swift orgasm. These men seemed to figure me out so quickly. I wanted to learn their bodies the same way, but they had me writhing as Legend scissored his fingers in my ass.

"She's loosening right up," Legend said with a hum. "I can't wait to slide into this ass and you're going to take me, aren't you? You're going to take both of us."

I wanted to beg or to plead, anything that would let me come, because Alphabet would take me right up to the edge then Legend added another finger. I was pretty sure he had four of them inside of me.

"Too much," I complained on a whine, but when he would have pulled away, I pushed back against him. "No, stay."

"It's all right," Alphabet crooned, easing his fingers from between my thighs. He let me lift my head, but only so he could suck his fingers clean and I shuddered. "You still ready for this, Gracie-girl?"

"Yes!" I burst out, the word barely containing itself. "God, yes. Please—right now. I need you. I need both of you. Don't make me wait. Please!"

"Do you have any idea how gorgeous you are with your skin flushed, your lips swollen, and your ass in the air taking my hand like you were made for me?"

"Made for us," Alphabet corrected. "He's right, Gracie,

you're so fucking beautiful. I can't wait to feel you around my cock."

I wanted them so badly, I was clenching around Legend's fingers and around emptiness. A shudder worked its way up my spine and sent out happy little jolts like I'd gotten hit with my own taser.

"Please…" I was begging now, twisted up between them as they passed me back and forth for kisses. Then Legend's hand left me and I wanted to cry, but Alphabet was already pulling me up to straddle him. I covered his hand with mine and we positioned his cock so I could sink down.

Oh, there it was. The sweat made him slippery, or maybe it was me, but I had my hands balanced on his shoulders as I rolled my hips. At least I could move now. Not far, but it was almost enough.

"Stay with us," Alphabet said, his voice choked as he spread his legs more and the weight on the bed shifted. When I dipped my head to kiss him, he met me as eagerly as I felt. He gripped my hips, forcing me to go still as another hand stroked down over my ass.

Legend. Then he was using his cock and not fingers as he pressed right up to the ring of muscle he said he'd already loosened. I'd felt him in my cunt, swallowed around him in my throat. What if… what if he didn't fit?

Panic slipped through me and I jerked my head up. But they were both stroking me, whispering words of encouragement. They wouldn't hurt me…

"You ready?" Alphabet verified and I nodded, holding his gaze as Legend began to press deeper. More lube dribbled on my ass. Some distant part of my brain figured out that was what he'd been pleased about earlier.

Lube was a good thing, because as Legend rocked his hips in shallow thrusts, he was sliding deeper and deeper into me. Alphabet gripped my ass, spreading my cheeks in a way that was almost too intimate and yet just right at the same time.

A glaze of lust covered everything and Alphabet's eyes were shining as he stared up at me. "Look at you, perfect girl. You're taking both of us just like you said you wanted to. Can you feel us?"

Legend sank in almost to the base and I swore my whole body was stretched to the point of bursting. Alphabet gave a little bump upwards with his hips and a jolt of pleasure raced through me. Then Legend eased back and thrust in again.

Each movement added another layer of sensory overload. A hand on my arm. Lips against my throat. Nipples to Alphabet's chest. The guys adjusted their grips as they rocked me between them.

It was like the most hedonistic see-saw of my life, only I was riding them and they moved me back and forth. They moved me between them, shuttling me forward and then back. Alphabet kissed me until Legend wrapped his hand in my hair, he pulled me up and I arched as I pumped my hips in time to theirs.

Then Legend kissed me as I fought to hold onto Alphabet's slick skin. I'd long since gone up in a carnal blaze. Someone teased my clit or maybe I bumped it against Alphabet but I keened into Legend's mouth as I came, clenching around both of them.

They swore. Or maybe that was in my head. I lost track of everything except the inferno that gobbled me up. It melted me between them and my mind just checked out. I never wanted to move again.

Right here, impaled on both of them, was where I wanted to stay.

THIRTY-THREE

BONES

Reznik broke. They all did, eventually. We told ourselves we wouldn't—that we were built differently. Trained in every technique imaginable to endure torture, to think clearly through the agony, to plan escape and evasion no matter the cost. And if all else failed, we were prepared to goad our captors into killing us before they could break us.

Reznik tried everything. Desperate to flip the script, to get under our skin so we'd end it for him. He taunted Alphabet. Took low blows at the rest of us. Then he went after Grace. That alone nearly earned him the quiet, swift death he craved.

But we'd trained for that too. And Grace?
Grace didn't flinch.

She met his venom with that same calm, unshakable presence. Eyes like frozen fire, so wide, sharp, and impossibly blue. She stood there, silent witness as we dismantled Reznik piece by piece. No pity. No triumph.

And when he finally cracked? She gave the faintest nod. No celebration. No gloating. Just cold acceptance.

Fierce. Unbreakable. Stronger than I ever could have imagined.

Pride burned in me—hot, steady. For her. For my boys. For this damn team that somehow held the line when everything else fell apart. I gave them the night to rest while I pored over the mess we'd just crawled out of. Though, judging by the sounds drifting down the hall, rest wasn't exactly the priority.

When Voodoo walked in and started brewing coffee before even sitting, I almost laughed.

He just shook his head with that half-exasperated, half-amused look he wore so well.

"I'm going to kidnap her at some point," he said. "Sharing's fine, as long as some of you remember how to share."

I didn't smile. Just gave him a long, pointed stare.

"I'll bring her back," he added, then smirked. "And yeah, I'll make sure you know exactly where I take her."

That was enough.

I nodded.

It took most of the night to sift through Reznik's confession—cross-checking, parsing, verifying every sick little detail. Around four a.m., Alphabet wandered in, yawning like a damn lion, shirtless, covered in hickeys and fresh scratch marks he clearly wasn't trying to hide.

One look at us, one grunt, and he disappeared with Goblin to give the dog a walk. No questions, no commentary.

When he came back, he fired up his laptop and dropped into the grind without a word.

Then Lunchbox strolled in, smug as sin, wearing the self-satisfied look of a man who'd just eaten well and slept better. No shame. No rush. Just sauntered in like he owned the place.

I didn't even hesitate—dumped the grunt work straight in his lap. Felt zero guilt.

Hell, I almost enjoyed it.

Grace came down nearly an hour later, moving slow and deliberate—like every step was a silent negotiation with sore muscles. I paused mid-scroll, watching her carefully measured movements. She didn't limp, but damn if it wasn't close.

Lunchbox was on his feet before she hit the bottom step, launching like he'd been shot out of a cannon. Off to make food—his version of penance—but not before handing her a mug of coffee and dropping a soft kiss to her lips.

She murmured something low and grateful, then made her rounds.

At Alphabet's chair, she pressed a kiss to the top of his head. He grinned like a kid at Christmas, leaning into it while she crouched beside him to greet Goblin. It wasn't the motion that gave her away—it was the care. The way her body moved like it remembered everything from the night before. She was sore, and not from combat.

Voodoo didn't even speak, just tilted his head back as she passed. She met him with an easy kiss, then stepped on.

When her eyes landed on me, I didn't move—just raised a brow.

She lifted her coffee in a lazy salute, smirk tugging at the corner of her mouth.

"You get nothing until I can walk straight again," she said, voice like smoke and steel.

I didn't miss a beat. "Then maybe you should stop trying to outpace four men like you're bulletproof."

She took a sip of coffee, slow and smug. "Where's the fun in that?"

I snorted, returning my focus to the screen. "Y'all are degenerates," I muttered. Then, louder, "Next time, give her a break before she starts limping like she took shrapnel."

Grace eased down into the chair opposite me and winked. "That's not limp—that's swagger."

Amused, despite myself, I waited for the plates to hit the table—eggs, toast, thick-cut ham, and hash browns. Lunchbox was burning through the last of our supplies like a man on death row.

"Eat and listen," I said as soon as he sat down. No preamble. No warm-up. "The plan's layered. It'll take coordination, patience, and most importantly—time." I aimed that last word straight at Grace.

She met my gaze, steady and sharp. "I get it. I'm listening."

Good girl.

"We've got names. Locations. Schedules. The gods of timing are finally on our side. We *could* hit multiple targets at once with one well-placed detonation. But that would throw every red flag up the chain. They'd lock things down tight. No—we go surgical. Clean. One by one."

I laid it out—how we'd move, who we'd hit, what methods gave us the best odds. The map lit up in my mind: multiple countries, multiple hits. Reznik was done, but O'Rourke was still breathing. And no illusion—we wouldn't catch them all.

Some would slip through.

We were ready for that.

"Alphabet, you, Grace, and Goblin head back to base."

Grace froze mid-bite, ham still speared on her fork. She looked at me, eyes sharp with protest, lips pressed in a hard line.

I didn't blink. Didn't soften. "You'll get to Paris. From

there, separate planes, separate paths. We'll split up to reach our target zones."

Her brow tightened into a stormcloud frown. She shoved the ham in her mouth and chewed slow—too slow. Deliberate. She was holding her tongue.

For now.

Fair enough.

"This is personal now. We divide the targets for three reasons. One—we're easier to track in a group. Two—we're all trained for solo infil, exfil, and wet work. And three—Alphabet needs time to keep breaking down Reznik's files. There are more names. More missing people."

What I didn't say: Grace had enough blood on her. More than most. She didn't need to carry more.

Alphabet didn't miss a beat. "If you send Grace to base with me, she'll make sure we eat. And sleep." He said it dry, like it was a complaint. It wasn't.

It was a cover—an assist. A way to make it look like logistics, not protection.

Sharp play.

I caught Grace's glance toward him. She'd understood. Of course she had.

"Will you wait for us to reach base before you strike?" she asked, voice calm, but eyes digging into mine like she already knew the answer.

Smart girl.

Good girl.

"No."

The next part would hit harder. I braced for it.

"Keeping our heads down—moving target to target with zero trace—means you don't call us. We'll call you."

Her jaw tightened. "I *hate* that." She didn't flinch from

saying it aloud, and that honesty—raw, unguarded— almost cracked my resolve.

Almost.

"We don't get the luxury of comfort," I said, voice low. "You'll survive."

"Yes," she said, lifting her chin, that familiar, firebrand spark flaring in her eyes. "If for no other reason than someone needs to be around to yell at you."

"Whatever helps you sleep at night."

She snorted, the smile that followed short but real.

Still has her bite and still in the fight.

Satisfied, I moved on. "Next…"

~

LUNCHBOX

VIENNA, AUSTRIA

Surveillance locked me in place for over half a day. Guard rotations, security sweeps, household staff—I tracked them all. Tagged, timed, cataloged. When the target finally arrived, his security did a full sweep, then got the hell out. He dismissed them like hired help overstaying their welcome.

He didn't like company. Valued his privacy.

Considering what he kept in the basement, that didn't surprise me.

Stupid move. But I love when their stupid worked for me.

I checked my watch. Thirty more minutes to sit and wait.

Albrecht Weiss. Biotech mogul. Private collector of the grotesque. Publicly, he was married with four children. Privately, he and his wife had a transactional arrangement —she showed up for events, played the doting spouse, and raised the kids. He bankrolled the whole façade while he fed his appetites elsewhere.

This house? It wasn't for family. It was for inventory.

At 1:40 a.m., I dropped a single word into a saved draft on the burner account we all monitored. Bones and Voodoo would know: I was in motion. The next draft they'd see would mean it was done.

Among the intel we'd pulled from Reznik's files were override codes for Weiss's security system. Gift-wrapped.

Lesson one: never make deals with devils.

They always come back to collect.

It might be a bit dramatic, but I'd planted explosives on the glass of most of the upstairs rooms including the very lovely solarium on the second floor.

I hadn't missed the stains on the floor below.

The sound of glass shattering room by room was almost symphonic—sharp, deliberate, controlled chaos. Inside, I followed the screaming like a bloodhound straight to the ground floor.

Weiss' office.

He was slamming his phone against the desk in a panic, shards glinting in his hair, scattered across the floor and furniture like ice. The lights were out. He was cursing in German, frantic and blind.

When he spun, gun in hand, I was already moving.

I kicked the weapon clean from his grip, then drove a fist straight into his chest. The impact lifted him off his feet —he hit the desk hard, glass biting into his skin. Blood bloomed in angry little flowers.

The second hit shut him down.

I slung him over my shoulder, deadweight and bleeding, and carried him down into the basement—to the secure room he thought made him untouchable. It required a fingerprint and a code.

He wouldn't be needing either again.

Inside, was a lab he used for his "screenings" and custom cages. They were empty. Relieved, I carried my prisoner over to the metal table and prepped him.

When he woke, he was strapped in place, naked and I had pulled on the hazmat suit I'd brought with me for just this occasion. It wasn't air sealed, but it would keep the blood off my clothes. I'd also gotten some tools from upstairs.

Weiss began to bellow in German.

"No sprechen zie deutsche," I informed him as I checked the meat cleaver from his kitchen. It was definitely sharp enough. Someone had taken care of his blades.

"Who are you?" Spittle flew out with his question.

"You bought people," I told him calmly. "You bought a lot of people. It's time to pay your debt."

"I have no debt—I paid for them."

"Just call me the repo man," I told him. Maybe he didn't get the joke. He would. It took a while, particularly while he squirmed and screamed. Butchering was gruesome work. His mind gave out long before his body did. Survival instincts and all that.

When I was done, there wasn't much of him left—just scraps, bone, and a red smear where a man used to be.

Cleanup took longer than I liked. Bastard had more servers than I expected. I pulled every drive, stuffed them into my bag.

"Went to Austria and all I brought back were these computer parts," I muttered.

Grace would want a souvenir. I glanced back at what remained of Weiss.

Yeah... definitely something nicer. She liked chocolate. Switzerland wasn't far.

I drenched the lab in chemicals—walls, floors, equipment. Nothing Weiss built, studied, or tortured into existence deserved to survive.

Back at the hotel, I dropped the full report into the draft folder.

Job complete.

~

VOODOO

SINGAPORE

Slipping into the penthouse like a shadow, I paused to listen and pressed a gloved hand to the wall. The guards maintained a strict patrol schedule. This time of night, only two were on duty. They traded off sweeping the place intermittently.

Right on cue, guard number one walked around the corner. I fired one shot, right between the eyes. The man still wore a puzzled expression as he stared at me. It took time for his body to catch up with reality. Then he dropped.

The silencer kept the sound from traveling too far. Cold certainty accompanied me as I stepped over the guard. The problem with "randomly" scheduling their patrols, nothing was truly random. Most people thrived on order, on precision, and they even "randomized" on schedule. Shifting five minutes forward, each day of the week until they started at the top of the hour again.

Not hard to figure out.

The second guard was in the kitchen, a television on low, with some show I couldn't make out. It wasn't important. The man had his back to the door, and he was drinking milk from a carton when I slipped the door inward, then fired.

This time, the shot went through the back of his head. It made a hell of a mess in the kitchen. Fortunately, it wasn't Lunchbox's kitchen, so I didn't have to worry about it. Verifying there were only two as per usual took all of five extra minutes.

Assured that we were alone, I headed up the stairs to Emil Zhang's bedroom. He was the spider behind the routes —a mover. He built invisible cages, and took care of transporting across the world. They had others, but Zhang was at the center.

The bedroom door was unlocked, the room was dark save for a light by the bed. A girl sat on the floor next to the bed, a shackle on her ankle and a miserable look on her face. She jerked her head up, eyes wide as I came in. I pressed a finger to my lips. She looked wildly toward the open bathroom door. Humming carried from inside.

With her delicate build and Asian features, the girl chained there gave my heart a vicious tug. I crossed to where she was, checked the shackle without laying a finger on her. I mimed "key" and hoped like hell that it translated.

Though I was dressed in black from head to foot, some of the terror drained from her expression. Course, when one lived with a monster, what was one more?

She looked at the bathroom, almost pointedly.

Got it.

I held up a finger for her to wait. Then I walked to the bathroom and cleared my throat. Zhang whirled around and I fired a single round into his knee. His scream was particularly pitiful.

Around his neck was a chain. I yanked it off and didn't care much if it tore skin with it. Then I seized him by the back of the neck and dragged him into the room. His prisoner flinched back, hugging herself. Then I held up the key and something painful crept into her empty eyes.

Hope.

I motioned to her hands and she held one out. I dropped the key in it. Probably better for her if I kept my distance. She fumbled with the lock, but the shackle came off and she shuddered. The poor thing was definitely shaky and the dark, raw circle around where the shackle had been told me everything about her treatment.

On shaky feet, she rose and then walked over to the dresser. Each step, she cast me a look, then took another. I hadn't missed the cutlery that was there on the tray with food. Zhang was begging, but I ignored him.

When she seized the knife I wasn't particularly surprised. I'd had a plan for Zhang, but she deserved to do it her way. She gripped the knife tightly then looked at me, wide-eyed and wary.

Fair enough, I holstered the gun, then wrenched Zhang's arms behind him.

"Go for it," I offered.

Whether she understood the words or the positioning. She didn't hesitate. She flew across the room and started stabbing him. She didn't have the strength to sink the knife in deep. But death from a thousand cuts worked for me...

I waited until she'd exhausted herself, then finished the

job. Zhang's funds would be drained, but I found the safe he kept and used the code for it. Inside was more than enough to fill a bag and give it to the girl he'd held. She stared at it and then at me.

When she kept repeating the same phrase over and over, I dug out my phone and the translation app.

"Thank you, dark angel. Thank you."

It took a little convincing, but she left with me. I found a shelter and drove her straight there. She burst into tears all over again but she took the bag and fled inside. I waited to yank off the mask until she was gone.

I sent a message to the draft folder.

Another one bites the dust.

BONES

OSAKA, JAPAN

I got into the underground club from the kitchen. No backup, no warning. The lights strobed inside and the dancers froze when they saw me. The guards really didn't have time to react. I already knew where they were. I didn't waste any ammo, each shot clean, efficient and unforgiving.

I found Renji Takeda, black market buyer and entertainer, in his private lounge, mid-toast.

"You," Takeda said, a rising shock reflected on his face. "You're real."

"I am," I said. "But you won't be for long." The two men with him were in the way. One shot. Then another. And we were alone.

I had a knife. I wouldn't need it.

Takeda had been the one who arranged Grace's initial kidnapping. He'd been the one who put her on the road to the hell she'd suffered. Didn't matter that he was fulfilling an order. Didn't matter that he hadn't actually targeted her personally.

No, he'd *hurt* her.

Now I was going to hurt him.

Takeda didn't scream. His broken jaw didn't let him. That was fine, I didn't need him to hear his suffering. There were two hundred and six bones in the human body.

I planned to break every single one of his.

THIRTY-FOUR

GRACE

SOMEWHERE OVER THE ATLANTIC

The cabin lights were dimmed to a dull amber, casting everyone in the same sleepy glow. The kind that made it feel like time has been suspended somewhere over the Atlantic. I'm not sure how long we've been flying. Hours, probably. Maybe more. Everyone else is asleep or pretending. I press my forehead to the window. It's cold against my skin. There's nothing outside—no stars, no clouds. Just black.

I'm not really awake, not really dreaming either. It's that in-between space, where everything loosens. Time, memory, control.

And then I feel her. Amorette.

She's not here—not really—but her voice comes so clearly in my head that I don't even question it.

"You always did get sentimental when you were tired," she says, teasing me like she always did.

I almost smile. "I'm not sentimental," I whisper. "I'm just trying not to forget how to talk to you."

"You're the one who left."

I don't bother arguing with that. I left everything. Her, home, the version of myself who grew up wanting big dreams, wanting fame, and maybe even fortune. I had those things now, but I didn't have *her*.

My hands were in my lap. Knuckles bruised, a thin line healing along the side of my thumb. The scar on my wrist seemed to be permanently etched there. My nails were still a disaster and I'd *forgotten* to fix them. Just like I'd not bothered with my hair, just braided it back and out of the way. Still, I stared at my hands for a while, trying to figure out when they started looking like someone else's.

"I think I hurt someone," I said, barely audible. Was I actually talking out loud? Or was I asleep? I really didn't know anymore. "Not out of panic. Not because I had no choice. I had the choice, and I still did it."

Her silence in my head is louder than the engine hum.

"I didn't feel sick afterward," I admitted. "No shaking. No hands clenching the sink. Just... quiet. Like it was over and that was enough."

"So you're getting good at it."

"I am," I said. "I've been watching the guys. I sat there while they interrogated someone. Seen just how violent they can get, actually did a raid. Me—on a raid." I closed my eyes. "I used to cry if I had to kill a spider, remember?"

No answer. Not really. Just the heaviness of her not being there.

"I don't flinch at blood anymore. Not mine, not theirs. It's just color. Noise. Sometimes I don't even see the person, just the angles."

That scared me more than the blood ever did.

"I keep thinking..." My throat tightened. "What if this is just who I am now? What if the part of me that remembered you in the middle of all that—the part that felt some-thing—what if that's gone?"

"Then why are you still talking to me?"

I swallowed. "Because I'm scared I'm getting numb to the separation. And if I stop feeling *you*... then I won't know who I am anymore."

Someone behind me coughed, stirred, and then quieted again. I stole a look at Alphabet, he was out, sprawled back in his seat, legs stretched out and Goblin slept on the floor between us.

"What if I never find you?" I glanced at the window, met my reflection's eyes. "What if I do but I'm no one you recognize anymore?" Am saved people. She was a crusader. I was so much not that at the moment. Would she be able to forgive me? "What if I've forgotten how to be me?"

I waited. Just the engines, the occasional beep of a seat-belt sign. The quiet stretched.

Then, softer: "Am, what if I was never who I was and now I'm this? What do I say then?" Did *I* even know what I was now?

That's the part I couldn't stop circling. If we found her, what happens then? What did I say?

Sorry I disappeared? Sorry I became someone you wouldn't recognize? Someone who doesn't recognize herself?

Would she look at me and see a sister, or just a stranger wearing her face?

I don't cry. I hadn't in weeks. I wasn't sure if I'd forgotten how, or if I'd just learned not to need it.

The window reflects just enough to show me my own eyes—strange, shadowed, unfamiliar. I don't look like me. I look like someone waiting for impact.

I pressed my fingers to the glass and whispered, "Please don't forget me. Even if I forget how to be me."

And just for a moment, I swear I feel something brush my hand. Maybe it's nothing. Maybe it's memory. Maybe it's her.

Or maybe I just really, really need it to be.

～

SOMEWHERE IN IDAHO

The road was long, flat, and soaked in gold. Sunset stretched everything out—shadows, silence, the distance ahead of us. Alphabet had one hand on the wheel, the other tapping out a rhythm on the console.

We'd indulged in a hotel after our flight landed. Showers. Food. And twenty-four hours of rest. It would be easier on his leg and Goblin definitely needed the break. AB was handling me and I let him.

As much as I'd tried, sleeping on the plane had proved impossible. It wasn't much better at the hotel. I kept going over everything in my head. I kept replaying the last several days on a loop that I couldn't turn off.

Bones explained we wouldn't hear from them until their missions were done. There were reasons for the choices they made. I *understood* that. I even respected it.

But it was so much harder in practice. If Alphabet wasn't right here, I might have lost my mind. We weren't talking, but it wasn't a foreboding silence. It was almost comfortable, or it would be if my thoughts weren't so jumbled.

"Gracie..."

"What if I approached Amorette's boss?" The idea just popped right out of me. The moment I said it, though, was the moment I realized how much I had been thinking about it.

"What?" He shot me a sideways look. "See her *boss?* The attorney dick who is pretending she quit?"

"Yes. Him. I go as Amorette, ambush him." The more I thought about this, the more I liked.

"I am so going to regret asking this," Alphabet said, his attention on the road ahead of us. "Why?"

"Well, I could say 'why not,' particularly when we know something is going on there. No one has reported us missing, no one is looking, and they are acting like she quit." Play devil's advocate, I told myself. Logic and reason over emotion. Except...

I twisted in the passenger seat, so I could face him. "I would like to preface everything with, I am going a little crazy right now because it's killing me that we found so much but nothing about Amorette. Does that make sense?"

His expression gentled as he slanted me a look, then he reached over to take my hand. "Yes, that makes sense and you don't have to explain wanting to find your sister."

Squeezing his fingers, I blew out a breath. "Thank you. Okay, so... I keep replaying everything that happened in France the past few weeks. Everything that happened before. The phone calls, the dismissals. What happened to Eleanor. But more than that—I called Rachel to ask her for a favor and she didn't even react like something had happened."

"Your friend the photographer."

"Yes, my friend with the apartment in Paris. I reached out, asked for that favor and she was all in. But not once did she ask me about Eleanor or being missing or anything. She didn't even seem to know there had been a problem."

"Which is a pretty key reason, I know there is some

conspiracy behind your disappearances. That we found so much about you in France and nothing about her makes it even more suspect." His tone had turned grim, but his grip remained comforting. A lifeline.

"Yes. That takes us back to Amorette's law firm. My manager was killed. Photographers I worked with have been killed. I haven't really dug in to see if any more people connected with me—people who would notice if I was missing and would say something—have been killed."

Eleanor would have. Without one iota of doubt, she'd have hunted me down herself if only to verify that I was the one who walked away. Not someone else.

Then she might have reamed me a new asshole.

God, I missed her.

I swallowed the lump of tears trying to form. "But you didn't turn up anyone missing at Amorette's firm. You didn't say a partner died or a secretary or a law clerk."

Alphabet frowned.

"When we were talking to Reznik, he mentioned Amorette. Not by name, but by profession."

"I remember," Alphabet said, stroking his thumb against the side of my hand. "In theory, researching *you* would have turned up information on her."

"Yes."

"So, just Reznik *knowing* about her doesn't mean he knew she was taken. It also doesn't let him off the hook." What Alphabet didn't add was Reznik admitting nothing about Amorette. Even when they broke him and he sobbed out answers in a wretched voice. She never came up. He *didn't* know. "That said, in their efforts to clean up your disappearance, they have eliminated people."

"So why haven't they eliminated her boss? Because you'd think by virtue of having to cover her cases, they'd be pissed that she just disappeared. Not to mention the story that she just randomly quit and left. That's *not* Am. You'd have to be a complete and utter moron with your head so far up your own ass you could tickle your own tonsils to miss how committed she is to her clients."

Is dammit. Is.

"Okay, that is a mental image I did not need to have, thank you."

Still, my lips twitched at his deadpan.

"But you have a point." One he didn't like. "Talk to me about ambushing him?"

"If you were responsible for someone vanishing, and it's been—" I faltered, time slipping through my fingers like water. "Months. What would you do if they just walked into your restaurant? Your office? Some fundraiser?"

"I punched Reznik in the face," he said flatly, sparing me a glance. "I thought he was dead. Now I *know* he is. We're not letting some asshole just punch you in the face."

"I appreciate that," I said. "But—"

"No *but*."

"Yes, *but*," I countered, popping the word like a balloon. "His reaction could tell us everything. If he's hiding something, we'll see it in that first moment. We only get one shot at shocking him. I can dress like her. Pretend to *be* her. Walk right up and watch him crack."

He said nothing as we chewed up the miles. I had no idea where in Montana this so-called base was, only that it wasn't close enough to fly. That meant road time—lots of it.

When his fingers started drumming faster on the steering wheel, I braced for the coming storm.

"I hate this idea," he muttered finally. No elaboration needed.

I licked my lips, waited a beat longer. "But?"

"But it could work," he admitted. "It could give us answers. And if he *does* know something... he's an attorney. Not a soldier. He won't last long once we start asking the right questions."

No, he wouldn't. A dark thread of satisfaction coiled in my chest. If he'd had a hand in what happened to her—if he'd hurt her—I might even enjoy watching him squirm.

"I need to know, AB." My voice was soft, almost swallowed by the engine. Grief painted every syllable.

"I know, Gracie." His sigh was heavier than his words. "We'll loop the others in. No way we're running off half-cocked while they're on mission. Bones would kill me."

"He wouldn't kill you."

"He'd make me *wish* I was dead—and he'd be right." Alphabet threw me a flat look. "That said, we can scout the perfect spot for the ambush, do more recon, and pull some data from his devices. I've been a little... distracted."

"You've been doing a hell of a lot," I reminded him. "This is just the next step."

"Gracie..." He sighed again, softer this time, covering my hand with his. "We'll figure it out."

His phone chimed. He picked it up, glancing at the screen. Several messages flickered by. Then he tapped a button and the car filled with the sterile tones of an automated voice.

"To check your messages: press one."

He hit the one without looking.

"Please enter your pin and box number followed by the pound sign."

His fingers danced over the keys. I chewed my bottom lip, nerves twisting. Was it the team? Had something gone wrong?

"You have one new message. Press one to—"

He didn't let it finish. Just pressed one again.

A man's voice filled the car—frayed, worn thin. *"I need help. Call me when you get this."* Then he rattled off a number. The message ended.

"Press one to replay the message, two to delete—"

He hit one again.

"I need help. Call me when you get this."

Then silence. He hung up.

"A friend?" I asked quietly.

"It's Doc," he said, voice gone grim. His expression darkened, and my heart clenched.

"He's in trouble." Not a question.

"Yeah. We need to get to base. I need to reach the guys, let them know—"

"I thought we couldn't contact them directly."

"Not *directly*," Alphabet said, a wry smile tugging at his mouth. "Did you really think they'd go so deep into the dark with no way to reach out?"

I made a face. "Another test?"

"Maybe." He reached over and brushed his fingers against my cheek. "But you're all A's in my book." Then he laced our fingers together.

"We'll help him," I promised.

"We don't even know what's wrong." That preyed on him.

Shrugging, I lifted his hand to my lips and kissed his fingers. "Doesn't matter. You'll figure it out. That's kind of your thing. We've been focused on my family for a while... I want to help with yours."

He let out a slow exhale, then pushed the accelerator. The engine responded with a growl.

One step forward, two steps back. But I knew what their team meant to them. To all of them.

Am would understand. I wasn't giving up. I was never going to give up.

"Gracie?"

"Yeah?"

"You are *ours*. Don't forget it."

To enjoy more obsession, vengeance, and surrender —
without having to explain your search history pick up
OATH, Book 4 of the Blood Brothers.

Be sure to grab this free alternate POV scene now and
slip deeper into the world of *Blood Brothers*.

AFTERWORD

Thank you so much for reading., we'll return to the chaos very soon. Don't worry about what the preorder date says, I will always shoot for an earlier release! If you enjoyed the read, be sure to leave a review and head over to the pack, we'd love to have you!

xoxo

Heather

Website:

heatherlong.net

Reader group:

facebook.com/groups/heatherspack

OATH

Blood. Fury. Desire. That's how our oath was made—and how it will be kept.

They say war changes people. I say it reveals them.

Over the past few months, I've watched the men I once called my captors become something else entirely—my fiercest allies, my deepest weakness, and the only ones I trust when everything goes to hell. They move like a unit, fight like wolves, and bleed like men who've been broken and rebuilt too many times.

And now they're fighting for me. For *us*.

The search for Amorette is no longer just mine—it's ours. We've cut off one head of the serpent, but the body still writhes, coiled tight around secrets none of us saw coming. When the call came for the fifth man in their fractured brotherhood, we didn't hesitate. They've helped me search for my blood. Now it's my turn to stand for theirs.

But with every answer, more questions rise. Loyalties shift. Lines blur. The deeper we dig, the more I realize this isn't just about my sister anymore. This is about something bigger, darker—something that won't let us go without a fight.

And still, they look at me like I'm theirs. Not a possession, not a hostage, but a woman who has carved her place beside them in fire and fury.

So when I set my plan into motion, they don't stop me —they stand beside me. Armed. Ready. Unshakable.

I won't lose my sister.

I won't lose them.

And if I have to burn everything to the ground to protect the people I love—

Then let it burn.

Grab Yours Now

About Heather Long

I *love* books. Not just a little bit, but a lot. Books were my best friends when I was growing up. Books didn't care if I was new to a town or to a class. They were always there, my trustiest of companions. Until they turned on me and said I had to write them.

I can tell you that my own personal happily ever after included writing books. I've always said that an HEA is a work in progress. It's true in my marriage, my friendships, and in my career. I am constantly nurturing my muse as we dive into new tales, new tropes, new characters and more.

After seventeen years in Texas, we relocated to the Pacific Northwest in search of seasons, new experiences, and new geography. I can't wait to discover what life (and my muse) have in store for me.

Maybe writing was always my destiny and romance my fate. After all, my grandmother wasn't a fan of picture books and used to read me her Harlequin Romance novels.

Follow Heather & Sign up for her newsletter:
www.heatherlong.net
TikTok

Also by Heather Long

82nd Street Vandals

Savage Vandal

Vicious Rebel

Ruthless Traitor

Dirty Devil

Shamelessly Loyal (Novella)

Brutal Fighter

Dangerous Renegade

Merciless Spy

Reckless Thief

Fierce Dancer

Dirty Dancer

Bay Ridge Royals

Shamelessly Loyal (Novella)

Battle Lines

Deceptive Truce

Wicked Surrender

Violent Chaos

Desperate Victory

BLOOD Brothers

Burn

Lure

Own

Blue Ivy Prep

Problem Child

Mad Boys

Party Crashers

Money Shot

Bravo Team Wolf

When Danger Bites

Bitten Under Fire

Cardinal Sins

Kill Song

First Chorus

High Note

Last Word

Chance Monroe

Earth Witches Aren't Easy

Plan Witch from Out of Town

Bad Witch Rising

Fevered Hearts

Marshal of Hel Dorado

Brave are the Lonely

Micah & Mrs. Miller

A Fistful of Dreams

Raising Kane

Wanted: Fevered or Alive

Wild and Fevered

The Quick & The Fevered

A Man Called Wyatt

Heart of the Nebula

Queenmaker

Deal Breaker

Throne Taker

Lone Star Leathernecks

Semper Fi Cowboy

As You Were, Cowboy

Shackled Souls

Succubus Chained

Succubus Unchained

Succubus Blessed

Shackled Souls (Omnibus)

STANDALONES

Kiss of Fate (w/Blake Blessing)

Taste of Karma (w/Blake Blessing)

I'll Be Home... (w/Tate James)

Overexposed (w/Tate James)

Switchboard Duet

Talk to Me

Don't Let Go

Untouchable

Rules and Roses

Changes and Chocolates

Keys and Kisses

Whispers and Wishes

Hangovers and Holidays

Brazen and Breathless

Trials and Tiaras

Graduation and Gifts

Defiance and Dedication

Songs and Sweethearts

Legacy and Lovers

Farewells and Forever

Hellos and Happily Ever Afters

Wolves of Willow Bend

Wolf at Law

Wolf Bite

Caged Wolf

Wolf Claim

Wolf Next Door

Rogue Wolf

Bayou Wolf

Untamed Wolf

Wolf with Benefits

River Wolf

Single Wicked Wolf

Desert Wolf

Snow Wolf

Wolf on Board

Holly Jolly Wolf

Shadow Wolf

His Moonstruck Wolf

Thunder Wolf

Ghost Wolf

Outlaw Wolves

Wolf Unleashed

www.ingramcontent.com/pod-product-compliance
Lightning Source LLC
Chambersburg PA
CBHW021726190726
48289CB00008B/2704